T0267486

ADVANCE PRAISE FOR *RABBIT & JULIET*

"I love it when I can root for morally questionable people doing morally questionable things. Prose and protagonists so sharp you could cut yourself—what's not to love?"

—CLAIRE ELIZA BARTLETT, author of *The Good Girls*

"Toothsome, smart, and darkly glittering, *Rabbit & Juliet* is a tour de force and one of my favorite reads of the year."

—BRITTANY CAVALLARO,
New York Times bestselling author of *A Study in Charlotte*

"Rebecca Stafford perfectly captures the obsession, passion, violence, and wry wit of teenage girlhood in her powerhouse YA debut. *Rabbit & Juliet* is a rare, dark gem."

—KIT FRICK, author of *I Killed Zoe Spanos*

"Powerful and provocative, Stafford explores toxic relationships in all their forms. A deep dive that asks what's right, what's wrong, and who is trustworthy."

—MINDY McGINNIS,
Edgar Award–winning author of *The Female of the Species*

RABBIT

&

JULIET

REBECCA STAFFORD

Quill Tree Books
An Imprint of HarperCollinsPublishers

Quill Tree Books is an imprint of HarperCollins Publishers.

Library of Congress Control Number: 2023948585
ISBN 978-0-06-335136-3

Typography by Kathy H. Lam
24 25 26 27 28 LBC 5 4 3 2 1

First Edition

FOR THE ANGRY ONES

RABBIT & JULIET

GIRL MEETS GIRL

Group was held every Friday evening in the basement of the Cross of Christ Fellowship. I wasn't Baptist and Group wasn't religious. But when you have the misfortune of growing up in a small town in north Georgia, there aren't a lot of community spaces or mental health professionals. Nobody even talked much about mental health except to call anyone who stepped out of line "crazy." That enlightened attitude is how you get a town where somebody like Sheila Bowers was running a group for "people coping with bereavement."

I was coping with bereavement, by the way.

Sheila was a florist who moonlighted as an expert in "empowering people to empower themselves" and "helping the grieving reach personal understanding." Those were the phrases that struck me as particularly ridiculous on the Group's xeroxed pamphlet. The Group was called Caring Hands, and sure enough, there was a drawing of a pair of hands holding a heart on the cover. Whoever drew the hands did not have a firm understanding of anatomy or metaphor.

Sending me to Group was one of the last parenting decisions my father made before he devoted himself entirely to testing the endurance of the human liver.

Group was dumb, Sheila was dumb, and I didn't think much of my fellow grievers because my capacity for empathy wasn't the highest. After sitting for an hour listening to sad stories, I usually found myself wishing I could be folded up inside a metal chair at the end of the meeting. But I went every Friday night. Sometimes it was enough to see just how truly bad Sheila was at her job. Excuse me. Her *passion*.

There was a kind of comfort in Group. Not that it really helped me feel better about my mom. It didn't help me *process*. But having somewhere to go that wasn't school, which I wouldn't have minded burning down, or my house, which I also wouldn't have minded burning down, was close to nice. There was a smell of wood and candles in the sanctuary that I would always catch just before I went down the basement stairs. Like I said, I wasn't religious, but when I glimpsed the sanctuary, and the stained-glass windows just barely illuminated by the streetlamps outside, I wished I was.

That night I'd arrived at Group ten minutes late. This was one of the things I liked to do to keep Sheila faintly irritated at a near-constant level. In my experience, when Sheila was unhappy, I felt a tiny bit better. Maybe *that's* why I went to Group, actually.

She looked up when I entered and gave me a curt nod and a strained smile. I took an empty seat in the circle of chairs and let her babble wash over me.

"So, ultimately, we can heal the holes these deaths have left in us by reaching out to others. By making that precious human connection once more. By realizing that the *cost* of love is the possibility of *loss*. And it's okay to take that risk," Sheila said. She made these kinds of speeches a lot, probably practiced them in the mirror the night before. There was something a little community theater about her delivery that suggested she'd once tried and failed for the lead in *Oklahoma!* Probably got cast as Cow #3.

There were only a few of us that night, but that's how it always was. Sometimes five, rarely six. It's not like we were a bustling metropolis with people dropping dead every day. But even in a small town, there are car accidents and lingering illnesses and farming disasters involving baling wire. I recognized everyone there, though I would struggle to name them if put to the test. I usually thought of them by their distinguishing features—if I thought of them at all.

But sitting between Wispy Voice (sister, blood disorder) and Topknot Karen (husband, cirrhosis of the liver) was someone new. She was my age, or maybe a little older. When she saw me, she smiled like we went way back, but I'd never seen her in my life. She had a delicately featured face lightly sprayed with freckles, and a generous, sullen mouth. She wore black cat-eye liner with perfect flicks, and her dark curls haloed her face like a personal storm cloud. I blinked in surprise. There were plenty of pretty girls where I lived, but they all came from the same starter pack: blond, tanned, and ready to pop out a family after high school. No one looked like this girl. She had the kind of beauty that didn't translate well in our town. If you couldn't put it in a sequined gown to win a sash and crown, it wasn't anything.

They'd already done introductions without me, so Sheila had me say hello and give a brief synopsis (mother, cancer, very sad) and just kept going. I could tell she'd been doing some reading over the weekend because she kept talking about "shadow work" and getting to know our darker selves. If that was nearly as witchy as it seemed, I would have been all in. But it was just more of her "know your wound" platitudes. Whenever Sheila talked about her own wound, it was all I could do not to snort. It *was* genuinely sad she lost her husband—even if he was the most boring man on earth—but "know your wound" just sounded so sexual.

"I totally agree," the new girl said. Her name was Juliet, according to her name tag. Sheila paused, thrown. She didn't really expect a response when she spoke, but smiled appreciatively and started up again, giving me a meaningful look as she did so. She was convinced I hated myself, and she loved to aim this stuff at me.

"By embracing your shadow self, your darker self, you're actually embracing all the parts of yourself that you don't like, you don't love, so—"

"Oh my gosh, I'm so sorry to interrupt, but where are the donuts?" said Juliet. She blinked innocently. This room was used as the church's preschool, so while there were plenty of badly colored pictures of Jesus and fat-legged plastic tables shoved up against the walls, there were no donuts. There was nary a hint of donuts. There wasn't even coffee.

"Excuse me?" Sheila looked puzzled, with a sprinkling of annoyance.

"Yeah," said Juliet, "like, usually there are donuts. There are always donuts at these things."

"Well, I'm afraid you'll have to do without here," said Sheila. "We've talked about taking up a collection for donuts, but it's never really stuck."

This was the first I'd ever heard about a collection for donuts, and I looked at the other group members for verification. I wouldn't put it past Sheila to fabricate a donut history. None of them looked back at me. I wasn't well liked.

"Really? I mean, how can you have an AA meeting without donuts? Isn't it required in the Big Book?"

I full-on stared at Juliet, trying to determine if she was a beautiful idiot.

Sheila had clearly landed on beautiful idiot. "My dear, this is a grief support group. I mentioned this at the beginning. You told us about your dad?"

"Ohhhhh, right. Yeah, I thought that was a really weird way to start the meeting. Usually, we talk about giving ourselves over to a higher power or the last time we drank."

Sheila just sat there, stunned. The rest of the group looked confused, and I didn't blame them. Juliet delivered these last statements with utter sincerity. One corner of her mouth twitched the tiniest bit, her only tell.

She was not a beautiful idiot. She was an asshole who just happened to be beautiful.

She looked back at Sheila. "So, no donuts?"

Sheila shook her head. There was a moment of silence. I felt a laugh deep within me struggling to find its way out. I couldn't think of the last time I laughed. It was a bubbly, foreign sensation.

Juliet's face was a study in sorrow. It was ludicrously effective. Even though at this point I knew she was completely full of it, I was almost moved by those gray eyes welling up with tears.

"God, I just . . . I just really wanted some donuts." She sniffled, and her shoulders started to shake. "I mean, I also wanted to find my way to sobriety and the Lord, but mostly I was here for the donuts!"

She put her head in her hands and began to sob. Sheila's face was frozen somewhere between concern and disbelief, while the rest of the group watched silently. Juliet hiccupped as she composed herself and wiped her cheeks with her sleeve, then dabbed at her eyes carefully. Her eyeliner remained intact and dry. Amazing.

"I'm sorry," she said. "You've all been fabulous and supportive, but I don't think I'm ready for this yet. I'm so sorry."

She stood up very suddenly and her metal chair fell backward behind her with an incredible racket. Sheila flinched.

Juliet picked up a saggy hobo purse from the ground and swept out of the room. But not before giving me a tiny flick of the head to indicate I should follow.

"That was really intense," said Wispy Voice wispily.

"Someone should go check on her," I said.

No one moved to do so.

So, I left.

COURAGE

Juliet was in the church parking lot, leaning against a black Camaro that had seen better days. Standing, she was not as delicate as she had seemed sitting in the church basement. She was tall and her shoulders were broad. As girlish as her face looked, her body was surprisingly boyish. Maybe it was just the way she was hooking her thumb in her belt buckle, like she was auditioning for Bad Boy Love Interest.

There was this one beat before she saw me where I seriously considered just walking away. I didn't know her. I might have imagined that gesture to follow her, and if the performance she gave in Group was any indication, she might be mildly unhinged. If I had only slipped away and biked home, a lot of things wouldn't have happened.

She saw me, though. She saw me, and her grin tugged my feet across the parking lot like she was pulling on a cord.

Now that I think about it, I don't know if walking away was ever even an option. There are some people who you're just supposed to meet. They come into your life and do all manner of damage or delight, but they were never *not* going to do those things. And you were always going to take part. It was inevitable.

Of course, that's how you justify any number of sins.

"Are the meetings always that fun?" she asked.

"I can honestly say they are *never* that fun."

"I can't imagine why. Courage?" she asked, offering me a stainless-steel flask she'd been palming in her free hand.

I took it reflexively, then stopped and smelled the metal tang of the flask, the wood smoke and vegetal matter. Whiskey. My dad drank gin and gin alone. I'd always thought it smelled beautiful, especially when he was still buying the good stuff. After a while, he moved down to cheap and watery with a blast of chemical juniper. What she had in that flask smelled leagues better than what was at my house.

I wanted to drain it to the dregs, to emulate her effortless cool. But more than that, the burn of the alcohol down my throat would feel daring. It would let me pretend I'd actually done something, or could, if I wanted to. I'd resemble a person who made real decisions, who took risks, someone a little dangerous and worthy of the breath in my lungs. And there would be a brief moment where I felt my mother's death lift off me. I'd be as light as air.

"I'm good," I said, and handed it back. "I don't drink." As soon as I said it, I regretted it. Either she was going to be sensitive and ask me why not, or she was going to dismiss me as a goody-two-shoes, a baby.

She was not sensitive. "Perfect," she said. "You can drive!" She took a jaunty swig.

"So, not so much the Alcoholics Anonymous."

"Not so much. But I really could go for a donut," she said. "And coffee."

I glanced at my watch. 8:30 p.m. I wasn't expected home for another thirty minutes, but my dad wouldn't notice I was late, or even if I was dead, for that matter. And it was a balmy night in early June, the first week of summer break.

"I can't promise donuts, but I can definitely find you something almost entirely unlike coffee," I said.

She shrugged. "My standards are flexible. Hot brown water, please." She handed me her keys. There was a car key, a house key, and a brass letter-*G* key fob. They were warm from her hands.

Decision made. I quick-released the front wheel off my bike and tossed it in the trunk, then I got into a car with a girl I'd never seen before and drove her to Hart's Run's only diner for bad coffee.

Would a depressed person do that?

COFFEE AND CHERRY PIE

The Double R Diner was small and narrow, unsurprising since it was two old-fashioned railway cars welded together, side to side. There was just enough room inside for a string of half booths lining the windows, and a counter running the diner's length, partitioning off the grill and prep stations. Most people preferred the counter, where they could talk to Jimmy working the grill while Dwayne took orders. They were the proprietors and hashslingers of the establishment, and it was well known that if you were on Jimmy's good side, he'd give you an extra slice of bacon. On the other hand, Dwayne resented every time Jimmy cut into their profit margins, and he was likely to give you a scant serving of grits or the smallest biscuit of the batch if he thought you'd taken advantage of his partner's generosity. Eating there was a delicate balancing act.

I chose a booth for us because I didn't want either man to notice me if I could help it. They meant well, but since my mother died they'd mostly given me sad looks, and I didn't think my arteries could handle the amount of bacon Jimmy tried to send my way. The booth was near the jukebox, an old one that still took coins although Dwayne eventually slapped a card reader on it. The catalog inside hadn't been updated since the 2000s, and the most current song was probably still "You're Beautiful" by James Blunt. My dad had liked to put in five dollars' worth to play it repeatedly while lip-synching it to my mother, just to annoy her. Of course, she secretly liked it, especially when Dwayne threatened to ban my father from the establishment. One time she'd consented to slow dance with my dad to it, and I was incredibly embarrassed because no one else's parents did that kind of thing.

They'd been cute like that.

"I'll have a cookies-and-cream donut, a slice of the cherry pie, and coffee," Juliet said, handing the laminated menu back to Pam, our waitress, with a smile. "Oh, and do you have real cream, or just those little plastic things?"

Pam, who had worked at the diner my entire life, let her eyes travel heavenward, then gave me a look as if to ask why I had brought this into her life. Pam did not suffer fools, but she did suffer. She looked at Juliet with weariness. "We have little plastic things with cream inside," she said. "Is that real enough for you?"

"Perfect," said Juliet. "I'll need six."

"And you, Rabbit Baby?" she said.

I winced. "Coffee and pie. The cherry, too."

As soon as Pam left, Juliet leaned forward to ask me the question I'd been dreading.

"'Rabbit Baby'?"

"Just Rabbit."

"Your parents named you after a small woodland creature?"

"It's just a nickname," I said. "What my mom called me. And she was kind of popular in town. Everybody knew her. She'd bring me around and call me 'little rabbit.' So, I ended up Rabbit."

My mom was the kind of mom who showed up everywhere for everything. There was no town happening too small to escape my mom's notice. She'd drag me to craft fairs and small business openings and yard sale after yard sale. She showed up for school board meetings to advocate for the books they wanted to ban because she loved books and hated bigots, but also just to irritate them.

Juliet leaned back. "I love it," she said. "I don't even want to know your real name."

"It's Sadie," I said, realizing now that I'd sat in a girl's car without even telling her who I was. Rectifying the situation didn't make it any less weird.

Pam came back with our sweets and coffee and the requested six creamers. I watched, fascinated and repulsed, as Juliet poured five of them into her coffee. The last one she opened and drank straight from the container.

I decided to let that pass without comment. People are complicated.

"So, do you just like to visit therapy sessions?" I asked. I traced my fork through the cherry pie syrup on my plate. When we'd first come into the diner, I was still giddy from the unlikelihood of what I'd just done, going off with someone I didn't know. I mean, I knew most everyone in town. It was hard to find a mysterious stranger to be impulsive with. Now I was starting to feel awkard.

"No," she said. "I just saw you go in and thought you looked pretty."

Here the record should state I did not drop my fork. But it was a near thing.

"You should see your face," she said. "I'm just messing with you. I was there before you, remember? I saw a flyer for the group and thought I'd drop in."

"Your dad, right?" I said lightly. There wasn't much I'd learned in Group, but I had picked up on the fact that people would talk about their pain in their own time. It made me nervous to ask.

She shook her head. "No, I made that up. He's alive, unfortunately. My mom, too, although she is mercifully out of the picture. Due to being an enormous slut."

I don't know if you have ever choked on the buttery crust of a cherry pie straight from the freezer section of the local Piggly Wiggly, but I don't recommend it. It took me a full minute to recover, during which Juliet watched me as though I were an interesting bug.

"I was bored," she said, and shrugged.

That answer should have made me angry. The very idea that you would be a tourist to other people's pain—to my pain—was disgusting. To go wading in sorrow, to listen to painful secrets, to violate that trust—because you were *bored*.

But I wasn't angry. I knew what I was supposed to feel, but I didn't feel it. Instead, I was weirdly relieved by her honesty. Here was someone who wasn't pretending pure motives, who wasn't lying to me about how everything would be all right eventually, who wasn't even pretending to understand what I was going through. It was the most sincere thing I'd heard in months.

I just nodded, accepting it. The sky is blue, plants are green, and visiting therapy groups is a valid response to tedium.

"Wow, so this is what passes for culture here," Juliet said. She cast her eyes around the diner, taking in the battered stainless-steel countertop, the mismatched stools, the dented paper napkin dispenser on our table with half its napkins vomited out. Her face wasn't entirely disdainful; her interest seemed anthropological.

Sure, I could have told her about the great Community Center, or the small art store downtown, or how the candy at the drugstore was still priced at seventy-five cents for a chocolate bar. I could have given a pitch for the lake our town was built around, largest in the region. Hart's Run wasn't total garbage. Some people would call it quaint.

But I desperately wanted her to see me as a fellow anthropologist, not a subject, and I instantly saw the diner through her eyes. The shabby blue waitress uniforms were from another era and not doing anybody any favors. The tile floor was clean but chipped. "Behold, the great works," I said, and then felt queasy, like Jimmy and Dwayne could hear my disloyalty.

"Well, I'm stuck here now, at least for the summer. Then I'll know if I can go back to New York, or if I'll have to start classes here."

If she'd told me she had already finished high school, I wouldn't have been surprised. I was envious. I had a baby face and got carded at the movies.

She sipped her coffee and grimaced. "Brown water indeed. What's the school like?"

"Like a high school imagined by TV executives."

"After-School Special?"

"No, just bizarrely traditional. There's only about thirty kids who matter, I guess, in terms of the school hierarchy. There's the Kellys, of course—"

"The Kellys?"

"Yeah. Kelly Xu, Kelly Proud, and Kelly Costa. Everyone calls them the Kellys. Kelly Xu and I used to hang out up until freshman year. Then Kelly got a chance to level up, I guess, so she took it."

"Got it. Kelly Xu is dead to us," Juliet said firmly.

I shrugged. "She's okay." I didn't really take Kelly Xu's departure that personally, although I know Sarah had. Sarah Taylor had been the third in our trio, and she was sensitive. But as I saw it, Kelly Xu recognized an opportunity to be a Kelly and grabbed it. She'd always wanted into that inner circle. I couldn't blame her for doing something I didn't have the bravery for.

"Anyway, then there's all the cheerleaders, except for Brittany Keener, because everyone knows she got pregnant last year and then she suddenly wasn't, and God forbid they cut her a break. Most of the first string of the football team. Plus a few smart kids who are also good-looking. Then everybody else is some kind of subgroup, like band kids or spooky kids. Like, have you seen *Heathers*?"

"It's a movie?"

"Yeah. It's old. From the eighties. Winona Ryder is in it? It's sort of a satire but it really gets at what high school's like. To me at least."

"What's it about?"

"Uh . . . well. It's about murdering the popular kids. And blowing up the school."

She nodded solemnly. "So, it's a documentary."

I grinned. I couldn't help it. It had been a long time since I'd had a conversation with someone who didn't have a paper-thin excuse to check on me. My mother had died over the winter holidays my sophomore year. So, for most of the preceding fall semester, everyone had known she was sick, and they gave me hand squeezes and Bible verses, all of which made me want to laugh maniacally until they slowly backed away. And spring semester had been worse—no one knew what to do once she died, so most of them just pretended it hadn't happened.

But even before I became That Girl Whose Mom Died,

people who would put up with me geeking out over movies were in short supply.

"Kinda. It *feels* real, even though it's not realistic."

"Is it streaming?"

"I've got a DVD."

She laughed. "Old school. We should watch it."

I wasn't about to try and respond to that. I'd only just met her, and the idea of sitting in a dark room with Juliet filled me with an unholy mix of excitement and anxiety.

"Anyway, the school's small. Like, nine hundred kids, I think?" That number sounded inflated.

"Nine hundred juniors?" said Juliet, appalled.

"No, nine hundred total."

"Oh." She paled.

"At least you haven't known them all since elementary. It's hard to respect someone when you used to watch them smear boogers on their jeans. Why are you stuck here, anyway?"

She sighed in response and took a dramatic pause with a long pull of coffee.

"I was kicked out of Miss Newsom's Home for Wayward Girls," she said. "For corrupting the youth." She speared a stray cherry off my plate with her fork and pursed her lips around it.

"Hey, that's my cherry!"

She widened her eyes and sucked it in, chewed it with great satisfaction. "That's *exactly* what Miss Newsom said!" She waggled her eyebrows.

I rolled my eyes.

"School is a waste of time," she declaimed. "The history is abridged to the point of lying, and none of the novels have sex in them. Worse, you're stuck with a bunch of dicks who think Ayn Rand is a complex thinker. Am I to subject myself to that?"

"That's actually a very Ayn Randian worldview," I said.

"Gross. I wasn't exactly kicked out. I was very nicely asked to never come back. So, I finished the semester and my dad shipped me out here rather than do the 'Dad' thing."

"Jesus, why here?"

She laughed. "I ask myself that every day." She shrugged. "He wanted me somewhere where I couldn't make trouble. What better place than Nowhere, Alabama?"

"We're in Georgia."

"Same difference."

I rolled my eyes. "So you're going to finish school here?" The idea of Juliet attending Hart's Run High was surreal. I couldn't picture her sitting in my homeroom. The walls would crumble to dust.

She frowned and looked away, as if the other diners were more interesting than my question. "We'll see," she said. "I'd like to try my hand at truancy."

"I'm sure you'll excel."

"As I do. Anyway, I'm not impressed so far with the kids I've met."

I raised my eyebrows at that. School hadn't been out for a week, and she'd already met my classmates? Then, in a fit of narcissism, I wondered if she'd already heard things about me.

"Except for you," she corrected. "Actually, give me your phone."

Amused, I handed it to her.

She was stymied briefly by its antiquated technology, but a few swipes and keystrokes later, she'd entered her phone number into my contacts.

"Here," she said, handing it back. "Now we're besties."

She'd entered her name as "Supreme Leader."

"Just like that?"

"Just like that," she said.

Pam came by with the check, and Juliet took it. "I got this," she said, and handed Pam a fifty. "Keep the change."

Pam made a face that meant she disliked Juliet but did like money, and cleared the dishes. I tried not to look boggled at the enormous tip.

"You want another cup?" Pam asked grudgingly. Juliet had bought us a lot of refills.

Just then, a car pulled up outside the diner. Even though the car's windshield was filled with the glare of the parking lot lights and the diner's neon sign, I knew who was in it. I could see my own half-transparent face on the diner window, small and scared. I looked away, my heart beating fast.

"We're good," I said abruptly. Pam nodded and took the cups. I tightened my grip on my backpack. "Let's go."

Juliet didn't ask me why my weather had changed. She just registered the shift and went with it. We left the diner quickly, crossing the parking lot to Juliet's car. I could hear my heart beating inside my ears, could feel all the ways in which my body was telling me to run. But I continued to walk, doing my best imitation of a generic diner-goer, with my face turned away. I kept my eyes on my feet and let my hair curtain my face. If you stand out, you just catch a predator's attention. I'd learned that the hard way.

We got into her car, and I looked behind us in the rearview mirror. Four boys got out and entered the diner. None of them looked in our direction. I took a deep breath and let it out. I was safe.

"Right," said Juliet. "You want to tell me what that was all about?"

"It's nothing."

"Nothing doesn't keep me from a coffee refill."

"That— The guy with the blond hair. He's my ex. Kinda."

"Kinda your ex, huh. Well, he's cute if you like that kind of thing."

"I wasn't really— He was just there."

"You don't look like you miss him much."

I laughed. It's hard to miss someone who's constantly showing up everywhere you go.

"No, I don't miss him."

Juliet narrowed her eyes, watching the four boys take seats at the counter. Jimmy handed them menus and even though I couldn't see Richard's smile, I could feel its sunny warmth, all the way across the parking lot. Even Dwayne, perpetual grump, seemed to bask in it a little.

In profile, Juliet's nose had a little upturn at the end, and her lashes cast shadows on her cheeks. She turned to me, and I blinked, feeling caught.

"That guy is a real dick," she said. "We should kick his ass."

I want you to know I thought she was kidding.

IN THE DARK HOUSE

The outside of my house was dark when Juliet dropped me off, and the inside was not much different. I came in the kitchen door and flicked the switch, blinking at the track lighting, sharp and direct. There was an empty TV dinner package on the counter, promising value and taste, so I knew my father had at least fed himself. Three months after my mother was gone, my father stopped hiding how much he was drinking, and by 6:00 p.m. most nights was passed out in front of the evening news, book open on his lap. He was still on the mostly functional side of alcoholism. He went to work and, as far as I knew, did a good job. When I saw his coworkers around town, they just gave me the standard pity looks for losing my mom—not the deluxe pity looks reserved for people who've lost their mom *and* had their father lose himself. Sure, he might not be paying our bills, but he could if he wanted to.

The kitchen counters were as clean as I'd left them, except for the open bottle of gin and some desiccated lime carcasses.

If he'd gone to the trouble to cut up limes and squeeze them, it was a fancy night indeed. I trashed the limes and wiped down the counters. If I didn't do this every night, the sticky residue would attract ants from the window above the sink. I could hardly blame them; it smelled like a party. I capped the gin and returned it to the sideboard in the living room. There was a round wooden tray there my mother had bought long ago. It used to hold two bottles, a brass shaker, a jigger, and four crystal glasses. Now it held my father's increasingly down-market gin, flat store-brand tonic, and one of the crystal glasses. The others had met sad fates. One dropped from his fingers late at night when he had fallen asleep in his chair, and shattered against a wooden magazine rack. He'd chipped his tooth on another and threw it away in a petty fit. The third had simply gone missing.

I found him asleep in the living room armchair. His reading lamp was still on, the usual book open in his lap, and his glass empty on the table beside him. He'd been reading that gardening book ever since her diagnosis, and I didn't think he would ever finish it. They'd been planning what to grow in the backyard when she'd gotten sick. The time for planting seeds was long past.

As I collected the glass, he stirred and opened his eyes. "Hey there, little rabbit. I was staying up to see that you'd gotten home, and I fell asleep."

I nodded. It was a fiction we were both comfortable with.

"Safe and sound," I said.

"Good Group?" He struggled a bit, trying to remember what day it was and where I'd gone.

"Yeah," I said. "Super helpful. I'm making a lot of break-throughs. Sheila says I can lead the meetings from now on."

He closed his eyes again. "That's great, honey."

I took the book and pulled a blanket over him, then turned off the lamp. The living room was dim, and my father's profile looked peaceful. He'd be gone to work in the morning before I got up. And we would resume this little play the next night and the next.

SWIMMING WITH THE KELLYS

In the morning, there was a text from Juliet telling me she was coming over, and I had just managed to put myself together in a reasonable fashion when she knocked on the kitchen screen door. She held up a box of Krispy Kremes, pointed at them, and then pointed at the door handle.

With a sinking feeling, I realized that it had been dark when Juliet had dropped me off the night before. At night, my house looked like any other house on our street, with white vinyl siding and a small green yard. But in the daytime, it was a case study in what happens when nature takes back its own. The lawn was overgrown with tall scraggly weeds, and honeysuckle snaked over the bushes. The mailbox had fallen off the house a few weeks ago, and since I was the only one checking the mail by then and didn't know what to do with the increasingly urgent-looking envelopes, I had let it stay where it was.

There was a pile of hospital bills even now on the counter. I flipped them over to hide the red Past Due stamps and tucked them out of sight.

The shame was hot in my cheeks, but there were donuts, and the damage was done. She gestured again for me to open the door.

I obeyed.

"I thought we should complete our culinary quest from last night," she said.

"God, yes," I said. Some deep ancestral Southern hospitality memory compelled me to shake off the shame and put two saucers on the counter for the donuts.

She snorted and shook her head, and commenced eating out of the box, the hard sugar shell flaking off the donut in icy curls, pinging the cardboard. They were day-olds, which were actually my favorite Krispy Kremes. In bigger towns where they have an actual shop, I hear people line up to get them straight off the conveyor belt. They're hot, soft, sagging with sugary goo. But I preferred them after they had been sitting in a gas station for a day, solidifying.

As she ate, I snuck glances at her. She was wearing a white ribbed tank top and high-waisted blue shorts. Her arms looked muscular, her shoulders golden from the sun. A thin silver chain hung between her breasts, the pendant out of sight.

"Want to hear my awesome plan?"

"More than anything," I said. We were both hunched over the kitchen island, leaning on our sticky elbows.

"We spend the day at the local swimming hole, drinking

cold libations and observing the local fauna." She affected an English accent that was half Monty Python, half Merchant Ivory film. Basically, what Americans think of when they think of England and assume everyone there is still wearing a top hat.

"I'll get my binoculars," I said. My accent was Doctor Who at best. "And a swimming costume so as to not offend the populace."

"Splendid," she said, "let us depart posthaste, henceforth, and so on."

First we needed supplies. Juliet assured me she had a swimsuit in her car, but that was it. The sunscreen was easy enough to find in the bathroom, and there were beach towels in the closet in the hall. More difficult was finding a swimsuit for me.

It's not that I didn't have any. It was more that I couldn't fathom where one could be. The only thing to do was to root around in my room for it. Juliet immediately followed me in because why wouldn't she, and my shoulders tensed in response. It sounds funny to say, but my room was one of the few places that I recognized as an accurate reflection of who I was. Or at least, who I was before my mother died. Some kids express themselves with fashion, with hair and makeup. They try on different selves until they find something that fits and feels right, and they wear it until everyone forgets they ever looked different. That's how style becomes identity, as near as I can tell. I'd never managed any of that. But my room—my room was me, the me I kept to myself, and the older I'd gotten, the fewer friends I'd let see it.

"Wow," said Juliet, her mouth open, taking it in.

At one point, my walls had been a pastel pink. I picked out the paint color with my mother when I was finally ready for a "big-girl room." But there were only a few slices of "Shell Pink Sunset" visible now because I'd papered every inch I could with movie posters, one right on top of the other once I started to run out of room. These posters were a record of my loves and obsessions, the movies that spoke to me and showed me who I was (or who I'd never want to be). Some had been presents from my parents, and some I'd tracked down online, and I had a few alternate versions of posters from different countries because I'd liked them better than the American ones.

Juliet's eyes swept over the room, taking them all in.

"What's your favorite?" she said.

An impossible question but answering it would say who I was, and I wanted to portray myself as someone Juliet would find interesting. I could say something arty, like *Mulholland Drive* or *Seven Samurai*. I loved *Breaking the Waves*, but suggesting Lars von Trier was my favorite director would reveal me as a broken human being. Films like *Carrie* or *Set It Off* or *Jennifer's Body* might appeal to her—she seemed like someone who'd enjoy a nice mix of feminism and violence. Is it feminism to destroy prom while coated in blood? I think so. If I said *Moulin Rouge*, she'd know I was secretly a dramatic sap, and that meant *The Incredibly True Adventure of Two Girls in Love* and *But I'm a Cheerleader* were out, too. *Rosemary's Baby* and *Get Out* were my favorite horror movies, but I wasn't sure I wanted to bring up violations to bodily autonomy this early in the friendship.

It was impossible to pick one. It could not be done.

"I love *The Apartment*," she said, nodding at its poster.

"It's so good," I said weakly. I'd missed my window. I felt relieved and disappointed in myself at the same time.

"'Some people take, and some people get took,'" she quoted.

I raised my eyebrows. She really did know it.

"I know a little bit about movies," she said. "Not as much as you, clearly."

Considering my room only needed some red string to look like a murder wall, I wasn't sure if that was a compliment or not. Embarrassed, I started rooting around in my dresser. I found a chlorine-bleached one-piece in my underwear drawer. It would fit, but why couldn't I have prepared for just this situation? Didn't Past Me have any sense of fashion or decorum? Also, when was the last time I'd shaved?

Juliet took a short tour around my room while I did this important emotional work. She booped my teddy bear on the nose and gave a cursory glance at the photographs I'd pinned around my mirror. They were all from middle school, when Sarah and Kelly Xu and I were inseparable. I could hardly recognize myself or them in those images. They'd changed a lot. I had changed more. Eventually, her eyes returned to the posters, and I was surprised to see that she looked uncomfortable.

"I promise I'm not a weirdo," I said, although, as I said it, I imagined looking around my own room as Juliet seeing this for the first time, and had my doubts.

Whatever it was that was bothering her, she pushed it away and gave me a sunny smile. "Don't promise that," she said. "It's why I'm here."

There were two ways to go swimming in Hart's Run, assuming you didn't have a pool of your own. There was the public pool, which cost a dollar to get in, and there was the state park entrance to the lake. The lake was free, but unless you had one of the houses with its own floating dock, you had to wade in. Wading in meant your feet sank several inches into the primordial ooze of the lake bottom. I could never do it without imagining decaying hands grabbing my ankles and pulling me down. We all have problems, I guess.

So we went to the public pool, bringing the supplies gathered from my house in a cheerful striped tote I'd found stuffed behind the bed linens. The smell of chlorine and damp concrete was immediate as soon as we entered the cinder-block alcove to pay our dollar. I paid for Juliet because she only had a fifty.

"Thank you, sugar momma," she cooed. The fourteen-year-old behind the counter widened his eyes, and we collapsed into giggles as soon as we walked out of sight.

I led Juliet to the bathrooms, and we changed in the stalls behind plastic shower curtains. The blue-painted floors were wet and smeared with dirty flip-flop prints.

Like I said, it was only a dollar to get in.

Despite the grim facilities, the pool itself was lively. It was hot out and the pool was crowded with screaming kids and their suffering families, septuagenarians glistening with tanning oil, and in isolated, squealing, and preening clumps, my classmates.

One of the best things about summer vacation was not being trapped in a classroom with any of them. One of the worst things was that they could just show up anywhere, without notice. In every direction I looked was someone I knew. Keisha Smith was sunning on a chaise lounge, half under one of the few umbrellas. We were in 4-H together as kids; I'd helped her groom her beef cow for the county fair. Alec Summers was in the pool with Jessie Slater on his shoulders. They'd been dating since they were embryos. Alyssa Gonzalez was helping Tori Butkiss put sunscreen on her back. I'd sat with them both at a table promoting the library reading club at the town's Fourth of July celebration. We were supposed to hand out flyers, but our fingers were so sticky from funnel cake sugar that we could only gesture at the papers in hopes someone would pick them up. That had been the summer before my sophomore year. Almost a year and a half had passed since I'd bothered speaking to any of these people beyond the smallest of talk. I was never popular, but I'd been well-liked enough. I'd had sleepovers in middle school where we froze each other's bras, and I'd counseled a few of these girls through breakups when we hit high school. But we weren't besties, any of us, and when I didn't want to talk about my mom and my life, they were happy enough to back off.

No one really wants to talk to a sad girl.

I took a deep breath and gave a wave in their general direction and got obligatory nods in return. That suited me fine. I wasn't much of a presence in my school anymore, but my position as a tragic figure gave me a kind of standing. By acknowledging me, they were acknowledging their own benevolence.

Then of course, there were the Kellys. The Kellys particularly liked to ask after my well-being, and to be seen doing so. They spotted me immediately, lighting up with well wishes and condescension, and I could tell even before we had crossed the length of the pool that I would have to suffer through a visit. Juliet watched the three girls with lazy interest, much like a lion surveys hyenas on the savanna.

We managed to snag two lounge chairs, which was astonishing luck, and draped beach towels over the backs to claim them. One of the towels had the Little Mermaid on it, and the other sported a giant Corona bottle. Let it not be said that I was cool. I'd painted half my face ghostly white with sunscreen by the time the Kellys surrounded our chairs. Perfect.

"Hey, Rabbit, how's it going?" asked Kelly Xu. She was flanked by the other two Kellys. Kelly Proud was wearing a red bikini with white stripes that made her look like a car, Kelly Xu wore a jungle print studded with yellow bananas, and Kelly Costa was wearing a white bikini and a pink net cover-up. I was pretty positive Costa's bikini would go entirely transparent if she got in the water, but I was also certain she had no intention of swimming.

"Fine," I said. I gave them a weak smile. I never knew what to do with these overtures. It was clear to me that they were not totally sincere, but they weren't exactly mean, either. Until my mom died, I'd just been a background player in their high school musical. But they had been the first at school to come up and express sympathy. That should have made me like them, but instead I resented them.

Costa and Proud were bad enough—Costa was as petty as she was pretty and Proud was very proud that no man had ever crossed her vaginal threshold—but Kelly Xu was extra hard to deal with in moments like these. Like I said, I didn't mind that she dropped me for the Kellys. Mostly. But the way she acted like we had no history was galling. She'd slept over at my place. She'd known my mother. She could do better than "How's it going?"

They looked at me expectantly. What did they want?

"I'm Juliet," said Juliet. The Kellys beamed.

Oh. Of course. They had wanted to know who Juliet was.

Introductions were made and pleasantries exchanged.

"You're over by the sanitariums, right?" said Kelly Xu.

I glanced at Juliet in surprise. The sanitariums were a series of small cabins on one side of the lake, built during the 1800s. It had been a wild time in America. In Battle Creek, Michigan, a quack named John Harvey Kellogg was working hard on administering enemas and cornflakes to the rich and sickly, while here in Hart's Run, Georgia, we had our own health nut. A doctor named Louie McCracken convinced a wealthy landowner in Hart's Run to hand over several acres and a good amount of money to build a sanitarium for well-to-do health seekers. McCracken believed swimming was the most healthful thing a person could do, so he had a lake made and alongside it little cabins so his clients could regularly swim, especially in winter, all while undergoing various other strange lake-associated treatments, like mud baths and rock massages. The cabins weren't used for spa treatments anymore and had been subsumed by the state park. You could still tour them, though, and read about "going Crackers." Since only rich white people had been crazy enough to believe him and had lost quite a bit of money in the process, the term was pleasing on several levels.

The properties next to the state park and the sanitarium were some of the most expensive in Hart's Run. Based off her car and her clothes, I would never have guessed Juliet belonged in that neighborhood. I thought she was more like me.

Then I remembered her huge tip in the diner, and that she didn't have anything smaller than a fifty to get into the pool, and I cringed at my stupidity.

"Yeah," said Juliet. For just a flash, she looked uncomfortable. Then it passed.

Kelly Costa squealed with delight. "I told you! Riley McKenna said he saw a girl drive into the Bergman place, and you're the only new face around."

Wow. Our very own Sherlock Holmes. Juliet looked offended at the flimsiness of Kelly's reasoning but said nothing to contradict her.

"Oh. My. God. I've always wanted to see inside! Are you Jesse Bergman's daughter?"

"It's just a house," said Juliet. "I'll have you over sometime."

The conversation continued without me, and the sounds of children playing and splashing seemed incredibly loud. I felt blood rushing to my face, roaring in my ears. I'd been ridiculous, thinking Juliet and I had some kind of connection. She wasn't like me. She was royalty, and soon enough she'd be an honorary Kelly. I felt foolish sitting beside her.

Jesse Bergman was Hart's Run's golden boy. Fifty years ago, he was born here, grew up, and then sensibly got the hell out. He went to Hollywood, but unlike anyone else in our town who had done community theater, he didn't just land a few commercials and then strike out. He got cast as Richard Donovan in *Saving Donovan*. It was a small role (it's more of an ensemble piece), but one that shot him into the stratosphere of fame. There was a good ten-year stretch when you couldn't finance an action movie without casting Jesse Bergman. Now he took more serious roles, and everyone was a little surprised he was good in them. Somehow you don't expect the guy who wrestled a giant snake to also be capable of moving you to tears in a small drama about a family farm, but Jesse Bergman had range. I loved his movies without shame, the highbrow and the low. I'd seen the Galaxy trilogy five times. There was something about an underdog story that really got to me.

He came back once to get a key from the mayor. He set up some scholarships for the high schoolers. But that was it until a few years ago when he bought a bungalow on the lake. He tore it down and then built a skinny glass house suspended ludicrously over the water. The neighbors hated it. It was utterly at odds with the homes around it. But we were all excited at the idea of him visiting Hart's Run. Only, he never did. The building just stood there, and after an initial flurry of furniture deliveries it became clear no one was actually going to move in. It seemed Jesse Bergman had bought a house just to abandon it.

Juliet's tolerance for small talk was low, and after making polite chitchat for a few minutes she pointedly told the Kellys she was getting a soda and asked me if I wanted anything. I gave her a ten and she walked off. They looked crestfallen, like petitioners to the queen who'd traveled a long way to go unheard. They longingly watched her leave, then turned back to me with disappointment.

"Rabbit," said Kelly Proud. Her tone was that of someone forced to acknowledge a social inferior at a dance in a Jane Austen movie. I resisted the urge to curtsey.

"Um, Kellys," I said. They exchanged looks with one another I couldn't fathom.

Kelly Costa closed her eyes for a moment, as if in pain. The last time we'd spoken about something other than my dead mom status was when she'd let me know in middle school that my puffy paint sweater was "not the thing." When she opened her eyes again, her voice was cheery and friendly, like we were opening a new chapter in the book of friendship.

"So, you and Juliet Bergman hang out," she said.

Bergman. So bizarre. I felt myself flush again.

"Yeah," I said. "That is a thing we do." I wasn't sure that the past twenty-four hours constituted a real pattern of behavior, but I didn't feel the need to explain any of that to the Kellys.

"Weird," she said. I nodded. I couldn't deny it was weird. She continued, "Why does she drive that old car?"

"What?"

"That Camaro. It's super old. Danny Elders said there are at least three Harleys and a vintage Mustang in the garage. His uncle delivered them back when the house got built. Why not drive those?"

"It's this whole thing Bergman has about staying grounded despite having money," I lied. "Remembering your roots."

That sounded good.

Kelly Xu nodded, then looked impatient with the entire conversation. "Look, Rabbit, can you just tell her we're having a party this weekend?"

She'd always been direct. I preferred it.

"It's my party," said Kelly Costa. "Tomorrow. But it's at Richard's house."

The Kellys watched me for a reaction. It wasn't a secret that Richard and I had dated—if you can call that dating—but I hadn't been a regular at his football games, and I didn't go to the parties he went to. I was a perplexing bit of data to most of his set.

A party at Richard's house sounded about as much fun as dental surgery. I kept my face neutral, determined not to give them any satisfaction.

"Why don't you just tell her?" I asked. I was genuinely

confused. The Kellys did not, to my knowledge, go through middlemen.

They collectively frowned.

Because she wasn't giving them the time of day, I realized. That's why. It must be absolutely maddening to them for the celebrity daughter not to care about their small-town royalty standing, to just walk off as if they were nothing and no one. If it wasn't for her father, they'd have written her off, but that house and that fame meant she should be one of them, and they couldn't rest until she was.

"You can come, too," said Kelly Costa. Grudgingly.

"Great," I said. "Cocktail dress okay, or are we talking full ball gown?"

Kelly Xu showed her teeth in the way that beauty queens do: broad and generic. She must have learned that from Costa. "You're too funny, Rabbit. You were always so funny."

I gave her a stony look and she had the audacity to blush, like I'd hurt her feelings.

They turned to exit, releasing me.

"I'm not telling her shit," I said to exactly no one.

RICHARD LOSES FACE

"**T**hey always that dumb?" Juliet said, returning with two watery Cokes. She put them down on the concrete and sat on the lounge chair beside me. Wordlessly, she pushed me to sit up so she could start smearing sunscreen on my back. She was not gentle.

"Depends on who they're talking to," I muttered. My brain was having difficulty switching between feeling betrayed that she hadn't told me who she was and feeling her hands on my shoulders.

"You're mad at me," she said.

"No," I lied.

She rubbed in the last traces of the lotion and gave my back a light slap like I was a horse she'd finished currying.

"I was going to tell you about it," she said. "People act weird when they know."

I nodded. My attention was only half on her. Richard had just come in with his two besties, Duncan Levitt and Caleb

Winters. They were wearing board shorts that showed off the muscles at their waist and made their legs look stumpy. Richard sported a pair of mirrored sunglasses, and I couldn't tell if he'd spotted me. I went as still as a stone.

I let my breath go when they got in line for burgers. If they were eating, they'd probably stay in the cafe area for a while, and I could see about getting us out. We'd have to walk by the cafe to leave, but with careful timing and misdirection it could be managed. I could survive this. I could escape.

"Hey, it's your boyfriend again," said Juliet.

"He's not my boyfriend," I said, disoriented. I'd told her about Richard the night before. Even if she didn't know all the details, she had to know I didn't want to see him. How could she think this was a good joke to make?

"Really? Can't take your eyes off him," she said.

I scowled.

Richard and his friends moved into the far end of the cafe area, no longer in my direct sight. I tried to distract myself by spraying my chest and arms with some perfume from Juliet's bag, the kind of thing that is either ironically trashy or sad trashy, depending on who wears it. On my skin, the scent started as plastic rose and then transformed into plastic watermelon. I smelled like a scratch-and-sniff doll of sadness.

Suddenly, ridiculously, I missed my mom. My mom would have squeezed lemon juice into my hair to give me highlights. She would have shot Richard and his friends a look that let them know she was absolutely going to call their mothers and bring hellfire down upon them. Moreover, she would never have let me date Richard in the first place, because more than anyone in our family she could see past a pretty package.

But she wasn't here.

"He's really got you spooked," said Juliet. She didn't sound sympathetic. She sounded judgmental. Juliet had probably never been afraid in her life. Money must insulate you from a lot of things.

I shrugged. She wasn't inspiring me to tell her the whole story.

Juliet was still watching the cafe area and showed no sign of forthcoming apologies for hiding her Bergman roots or for being an absolute bitch about Richard. I pulled my towel around me. Everything was irredeemably spoiled. Juliet was just some rich girl who wasn't ever going to really be my friend because that was impossible, the Kellys were still the Kellys and Kelly Xu was the worst of them, and Richard would haunt me until the day I died and probably hang around my grave asking me if I really meant it when I broke up with him.

"You know, I don't really feel like swimming," said Juliet. I nodded. Of course she wanted to leave. Why did I think she wanted to hang out with me in the first place? It was probably a fun game for rich people to just show up with cheap donuts, pretend to be your friend, and then leave. They probably all stood around in smoking jackets at the club, toasting with champagne and laughing about the last dumb rube who thought they were best friends. *Then I gave her half a BFF necklace! And she wore it! It turned her neck green. Can you believe it, Jacqueline?*

I shrugged on my cover-up and mechanically gathered the bag and towels. My cheeks felt hot, and I kept my eyes lowered. If I looked up, I was sure I'd see the Kellys watching me, shaking their heads. Poor Rabbit. Poor, poor Rabbit.

Juliet led the way, and I followed like a pack animal. She was wearing a peach bikini, no cover-up, and a pair of ratty Converses. Her brown curls were gathered in a loose bun and the escaping tendrils rose in the wind behind her. I could not imagine what it was like to stride in a bikini with that much assertiveness. In that moment, I hated her a little.

Our steps traced the long end of the pool, and she led us abreast the cafe area. My jaw clenched as I realized she was leading us right past Richard's table. This was further evidence Juliet was not really my friend. A friend would not put you in that situation.

Then something shifted in the way she walked, as if the motion of her body had brought her to some kind of decision. She quickened, and her hips lost their slight roll and became purposeful. She was a table away from Richard when she picked up a discarded tray, and it probably only took her three steps before she reached him. He and his friends were standing by the table, laughing, Richard a little apart. He fell back, snorting at something Caleb had said.

Then she connected the tray with his face in an incredible snapping arc. I dropped the sunscreen bottle and the cheap plastic shattered on the concrete with a loud pop, spraying everyone in my immediate vicinity with white goo. Juliet didn't even stop walking. Not when he screamed and grabbed his face, and not when he dropped to his knees, blood gushing between his fingers. She just let the tray fall with a clatter on the ground and kept going, not even looking back to see if I was following.

Did I follow?

Hell yes, I did.

SO MUCH FUN

"**D**on't run," Juliet called. She sounded like a lifeguard, and I was a kid running over slick concrete.

I obeyed, and gradually caught up to her as we emerged from the pool entrance. It was all I could do not to look behind me and see if Richard and his friends were in pursuit. My ears were pricked for sirens. My worldview insisted that the breaking of rules resulted in swift punishment. If the FBI had shown up right then, I would not have been surprised.

"Never run," said Juliet. "Remember, you're just a small girl in flip-flops with a beach bag. You couldn't hurt a fly. Why would you be running?"

"Because you just clocked Richard in the face with a tray," I hissed. We were nearly to Juliet's car. Juliet gave a friendly nod to a couple we passed.

"Richard doesn't know that," she said. She took the beach bag off my shoulder and put it in the trunk, then opened the passenger door for me like a chauffeur.

"I'm pretty sure he knows he got hit in the face," I whispered, sliding into the car. I remembered the moment in Group when I had tried to figure out if she was a beautiful idiot or an asshole. There was the same kind of willful obliviousness operating here, an insistence that I follow her down the rabbit hole of her own logic.

"Of course he knows *that*. He's an animal in pain," she said. She started up the car and backed out in a leisurely fashion. In my head, you were supposed to flee a crime with spinning tires in a cloud of dust; I'd seen *To Live and Die in LA*. But clearly Juliet and I didn't watch the same movies.

Richard and his entourage stepped out into the parking lot just as we were exiting. He was pressing a blood-soaked paper towel to his nose, wrapped around an ice bag. My heart clenched in fear. Surely he'd look at me and know I'd participated.

But he didn't even glance at our car. Mostly he was sniping at his friends and shrugging them off if they tried to touch him. There was a girl with him, too. I hadn't noticed her earlier. She felt familiar, but her back was to me and all I could really make out was that she had dark hair and was trying to comfort him. He was sullenly ignoring her.

"See?" said Juliet, leaving the parking lot and Richard's drama behind. "He doesn't know we did this."

I was stuck somewhere between stunned and angry and couldn't figure out how to express either. But sometimes the simplest words will do.

"What the actual fuck?" I said. Only I didn't say it. I yelled it. And then I yelled it again. It felt like all I could say. Juliet looked amused, and drove on, employing her turn signal when appropriate, driving the speed limit in a very responsible manner. Not at all like someone who had just enacted violence on a stranger without warning.

You can only yell for so long until you're all yelled out, and I was not in practice. I gradually wound down to a sigh.

"Better?" said Juliet.

I nodded wearily. "I just . . . He had to have seen us. You *hit* him."

She shook her head. "You don't understand. He didn't see you—you were farther back—and he barely saw me. At best, he glanced at my tits, which is understandable because they're glorious. He was bent over laughing, and his friends were focused on each other. To the extent that Richard ever thinks anyone could hurt him, it wouldn't be someone like me."

I shook my head. I was pretty sure that in most versions of the world there were consequences to your actions. You couldn't go around hitting people.

But what if you *could* do what you wanted? What if I'd always *assumed* there were consequences because I'd been *told* there were consequences? What if there was a little gray area at the edge of right and wrong where no one was really paying attention because who would expect it?

"Someone like you," I said. "You mean, a girl?"

She nodded, turning the wheel. "A girl, yeah. And I'm pretty in a way he understands. Hot, even. For Richard's entire life, he's been told that someone who looks like me doesn't hit some-one like him in the face."

"You're unbelievable," I said.

"Why? Because I see somebody is a pig and I give him what he had coming? Or because I know I'm hot?"

"Just—just the things you say." I rubbed my face. I felt like I was in an argument I didn't even understand and couldn't fig-ure out how to stop. All I knew was that she'd done something really wrong, and I wanted her to admit it. I wanted her to feel ashamed and apologetic because I felt like she should, because I did, and all I wanted was to go back and find Richard and tell him it was all my fault and how sorry I was.

"The world is unfair, Rabbit. Only children expect other-wise. So I'm leaning into it."

"Okay," I said, "okay, but why did you do it? That was crazy."

She parked the car. We were in the driveway of the Bergman house. In my head, I'd always called it Galaxy House. I hadn't even noticed we'd arrived.

She looked at me as if I was the crazy one. "He fucked with you. No one fucks with my friends."

I blushed. I couldn't help it. No one had ever declared them-selves to me like this. No one had ever defended me.

"Rabbit, a guy like Richard deserves what he got. He deserves worse. What's so wrong with making sure he gets it?"

"You don't even know what he did! You don't even know he did anything!"

"Do I need to? Was I wrong?"

I thought about Richard's face, and the sheer incredulity that crossed it right after the plastic tray dropped and the blood flowed. He couldn't believe it because nothing bad had ever happened to him. I shuddered. But in a good way, like in a horror movie when the monster slowly eats your least favorite character.

I thought about how powerful Juliet had looked as she'd advanced on him.

Over and over, I'd chosen the path of least resistance. I'd dated Richard because it was easier than not dating Richard, and I put up with my classmates' pity about my lack of a mom because it was all too painful to talk about. I'd been going to Group for three months because it made my dad feel better. I chose to clean up his limes rather than talk to him about his drinking. My mother had been dead more than a year and all I'd done was try to make other people happy, or at least not upset them.

What would it be like to be like Juliet, just a little?

"Okay," I said.

"Okay?" she said, grinning.

"Yeah," I said. "He deserved it."

"We are going to have so much fun."

And it was fun. Until it wasn't.

GALAXY HOUSE

Galaxy House was beautiful, expensive, and utterly wrong. There were the people in Hart's Run who had money, and they lived on the lake. Then there were the people who had *more* money and had a house on the lake but lived elsewhere. But even that kind of money was not this kind of money. That kind of money was oversize furniture and enormous stainless-steel grills. This kind of money was modern architecture, bold jutting lines, glass on glass on glass. This kind of money made for a house that looked like a sword belonging to a chiseled man who subsisted on a macrobiotic diet and high-tech supplements, and slept in a hyperbaric chamber.

It was mean and gorgeous. Perfect for Juliet.

"You coming?" she asked. She looked bored with the house and bored by my slack-jawed reaction to it.

I did my best to organize my face into an equally blasé expression. No big deal. Just standing outside the house of a movie star with his glamorous scion. As you do.

We entered through a side door that led into a mudroom bigger than my kitchen. Juliet hung our bags on brass hooks shaped like hands. There were several brass hands lining the wall. Some were open palmed, some were fists, each waiting for a bag or a hat or an umbrella. They were unsettling.

I was unsettled, too. Our conversation in the car replayed in my head. What did she mean when she said we'd have fun?

But like a terms of service agreement eighty pages long, I didn't linger on it. I was too distracted by everything around me.

After the mudroom was the kitchen, which had an island so broad I couldn't reach across it if I tried. There were two glossy pastel mint-green refrigerators, side by side, both of them labeled SMEG. Juliet opened one of them to hand me a bottle of coffee. The label promised me chocolate, cherry, and the deep satisfaction of being extremely in tune with the universe and ethical labor. The coffee delivered.

"You had *this* in your fridge, and I gave you diner coffee," I said.

She laughed. "I like to be among the common people. Come on, let me show you the house. I can tell you want to see it."

I squirmed a little. I did want to see it. But I also remembered what she'd said about how people could be weird when they knew who she was.

The kitchen had already made a dent in my blasé face, and the rest of the house utterly destroyed it. The living room was large enough to accommodate several couches, a glossy grand piano, and probably a church choir. Everything was in shades of blue and gray with an occasional pop of yellow by way of artwork or a throw pillow. It was nothing like my house, which was decorated only in the sense that my parents had gradually accumulated its contents over many years. When my mother was still alive, you couldn't find a place to sit because of her various half-abandoned craft projects. It was chaotic and cozy. This house was composed, deliberate, and beautiful. It gave me the idea that if I regularly sat on the couch and read *The Economist*, my life would make a great deal more sense.

"You haven't noticed the best part," said Juliet sarcastically.

Hanging on the wall was an enormous portrait of Jesse Bergman. It was full-length from floor to ceiling and took up a third of a long wall. It was a close-up of his face, painted in a photo-realistic style. I immediately recognized the image it was based on. How could I not? I'd watched the Galaxy series over and over. It was early in his career; he'd played struggling prizefighter Galaxy Tyrell. In the final fight, Galaxy is down for the count. But determined to save his mother's house and prove to his pregnant girlfriend he can be the man she needs him to be, he struggles to his feet and stands tall once more. His face is covered in blood and his left eye is lost in a sea of swelling and bruise. I might have had one of those T-shirts with that image in my closet, a fact I hoped Juliet would never discover.

It was iconic.

"God," I said, "sorry, it's just so small."

She smirked, and I took a chance she'd tolerate a fan question.

"So, what's he like?" I tried not to look like I cared.

Juliet studied the painting. Her lip curled the tiniest amount. "Galaxy is just like this. Two-dimensional."

"You call your dad 'Galaxy'?" I asked.

"What else would I call him? Sperm donor?"

Father talk was over. She walked; I followed. The rest of the house was just as tastefully and expensively appointed. Room after room commemorated Bergman's accomplishments with various plaques, trophies, and movie posters. There was a small library that Juliet assured me had never been used until her arrival. Half the books were just artful cardboard fakes, a detail Juliet revealed by sweeping several of them off the shelf. There was a game room with dartboards, two pool tables, four vintage pinball machines, and a nine-pin bowling lane. In the lower floor of the house was a small but well-appointed gym; Juliet said he was a proponent of weights and not much else besides constant, brutal dieting.

"This house is like a movie set," I murmured, awestruck.

"Or a shrine. To a god who doesn't visit. Have you noticed what's missing yet?"

We were standing on the back deck that wrapped around a third of the house and projected over the lake. The wood was a dove gray. We could hear the rhythmic lapping of the lake against the floating dock below, followed by a second, hollow slap. There was a small boat tethered at the end of the dock, knocking gently against the wood.

I shook my head. I had never been anywhere so thoroughly designed for leisure and enjoyment. It was so lovely, it was a little hard to imagine doing things like eating or eliminating bodily waste in a house like this.

She pointed at herself.

Then I realized. In the whole house, there wasn't a single picture of her anywhere. It was like she didn't exist.

She gave a tight little smile. "It's fine. If there were pictures of my ballet recital it would mess with the aesthetic."

"You must have been a terrible ballerina."

She smiled, a real one this time. "I was the worst."

I looked out over the water. In the distance, I could see people on Jet Skis, could hear their laughs as they bounced against and over a boat's wake. That kind of abandon seemed very different from the moment I was in now, which was contemplative. The contrast enhanced the sense that we were alone in our own space, set out from the rest of the town. I thought about telling Juliet about the Kellys' invitation. But the last thing I wanted to do was to spoil this moment.

"'Let me tell you about the very rich. They are different from you and me,'" I intoned. Probably the only thing I really remembered from Fitzgerald.

She snorted. "Really putting that public school education to work, aren't you?"

"Not all of us are beautiful, Juliet. Some of us have had to cultivate a personality."

She cocked her head. "You think I'm beautiful?"

I reddened and looked back at the lake. Save me, Jet Skiers.

"You're somewhere in the neighborhood," I said.

She tilted her head and cast her eyes upward, looking thoughtful. "I am, aren't I?" Then she laughed and I laughed, too.

We went quiet after that. A skier on the lake lost their grip and fell into the water, then bobbed in their life jacket like a wine cork.

"You are, too, you know," said Juliet abruptly.

"What?"

"Beautiful." She smiled at me, and something unfamiliar expanded in my chest. Something like happiness.

On her own, she was softer than I'd thought, gentler. There was a bravado about her when she was in public that she ceased to generate in private. Her cheeks were freckled, and little wisps of curls framed her temples.

"So. Now you've met Galaxy," she said, jerking her head back to the portrait inside the house. "What's your dad like?"

I shrugged. The sun slipped beneath the water and I felt a chill. "I don't know. Dad-like."

Juliet raised her eyebrows.

"Well, okay, not *your* dad-like. But you know, typical dad. Does dad things. Dads real hard."

"You know, Rabbit, the least interesting thing we could do with our time together is trade in stereotypes and equivocations."

Who talks like this?

"Okay," I said. "Fair. It's just— My life isn't— My dad's not a movie star."

"I assumed," she said. "But let's pretend I'm interested because I'm a girl with depth."

I tried again, feeling like I was pulling the cord on an old lawnmower. Sputter, sputter, start. "He kept things together. For a while. Got me into therapy when I needed it," I said, then paused. Why had I said that? Something about Juliet made me want to talk, to tell her everything.

"How did he know you needed it?" she asked.

I looked down. Inside me, tectonic plates slowly ground against each other.

"You don't have to say if you don't want to," she said. Most of the time Juliet seemed so commanding. Was this kindness, or a concession to my weakness? Or was she just admitting she didn't care enough to press?

But she held my gaze, her face open and lovely. I could read it any way I wanted.

I turned away from the lake to face the house, blazing gold light on us like a beacon. "This house is insane. It's so big," I said.

Coward. She wanted realness and I wanted to talk about real estate.

"Not that big. Just five bedrooms."

"Oh," I said. "Just five bedrooms." My house had two.

"Yeah, Galaxy is a really modest dude."

"Yeah, no trophy room," I said. "That's how you know."

She snorted. "There actually is a trophy room."

"Yeah, but it's a really *humble* one," I said.

She smiled, and then she looked sad. Maybe the jokes about Galaxy weren't that funny after all.

"My dad didn't get me into therapy, you know. Even when I clearly needed it," she said. She held out her wrist. There was a faint line running across it.

I took her hand and held her wrist. I wanted to trace the scar with my finger. It was impossible to think of Juliet ever being so vulnerable as to think of ending things.

I looked up and met her eyes. They were dark gray, storm colored and fickle.

She tilted her head a fraction, gave me a half smile.

I was still holding her wrist.

Oh Christ.

I let her wrist go.

"What happened with Richard, Rabbit?" she asked. Her voice was soft, gentle. She wasn't asking for much.

So I told her.

THE ABRIDGED HISTORY
OF SAD GIRLS

I hadn't told anyone, ever, so the story came out in dribs and drabs. It might not have made a lot of sense, but she kept nodding. Maybe she had heard the story before. Because most every girl has a story like this, and we all just go around confessing it to each other like it will turn out differently in the retelling. But the moment the story starts, we know how it ends.

A year and a half ago, my mother died. Cancer, quick and awful. She had a cold, only a little cough, but it wouldn't go away. She went to the doctor for allergies, and came home after lots of tests and bloodwork, looking shaken. It wasn't allergies. The cancer had spread and there was nothing to be done. On TV shows, brave doctors always find last-minute cures, reuniting families with their loved ones, hale and hearty again. There are hugs and flowers and upturned faces filled with love. But it turns out there are things doctors with symmetrical faces can't fix. All they can do is give you the bad news.

I didn't try to tell Juliet what that was like. I didn't have words for it then, and I don't now. How do you describe a black hole? Scientists are still working that out.

My father fell into that black hole.

I'm saying all this so you'll understand that there was, around me, a roiling miasma of misery, grief, and hopelessness. And there are some people in this world for whom that is a sexy perfume.

Richard Cummings was one of those people. I doubt he could have articulated why someone so clearly miserable was so intriguing. Maybe it was the contrast between his luck-kissed life and mine. He was a junior like me, popular, a football player, and one of those kids who looked like he was twenty when he was eleven. He was handsome, could and usually did date cheerleaders, prom queens, the girls whose mothers took them to salons to keep up their blond well past babyhood. Maybe he was slumming.

I wasn't looking to get involved. But I studied at the town library after school because I didn't want to go home to my dad, and day after day, Richard would show up and share my table. There were plenty of other tables, but mine had the sexy whiff of depression. He'd make weak jokes, I'd give weak smiles, but he wasn't unkind, and I was lonely. He'd ask me out to get pizza or take a walk, and I'd say no, and the next day he was there again. I didn't have the energy to tell him to take a hike, and maddeningly, he never did anything egregious.

I'd already figured out that telling a guy to get lost could be a scary proposition. You can pick that up just walking down the street.

So, I didn't tell him to leave me alone. Bit by bit, I got used to him, and then somehow, we were dating.

Romantic, I know.

We had some perfectly tolerable sex, which didn't do a lot for me but did make me feel I was briefly the center of someone's attention. There was something pleasurable and powerful-feeling about someone being so interested in my body, even if he wasn't particularly devoted to its responses. He looked so grateful during, like I was doing him a huge favor. It felt good to be generous.

But, like I said, his jokes were weak. There were times I'd realize we hadn't read the same books, didn't listen to the same music, didn't even like the same movies. I loved movies more than anything. I stopped finding his easy adoration so compelling.

There was also the way he would grab my arm tightly when we were out walking together and would pass another guy. Sometimes at the end of the day there was a quarter-sized bruise on the inside of my arm. I'm not sure he meant to do it. But he still did it.

I broke up with him over the phone because I didn't want to see his face crumple. It went about as well as a breakup can go when one person spends the majority of the conversation pretending not to understand the other person. He told me I didn't mean it. He told me I was confused. He cried over the phone, thick, wet-sounding sobs that made me want to hang up. To be clear, it's not because I think boys shouldn't cry. I'm all for emotion, regardless of gender. I just think everyone should cry in a non-snotty way, preferably in private.

An hour later he called me back and told me he was on the roof of his house with his dad's shotgun. He told me he was going to kill himself if we didn't get back together.

I hung up.

Maybe I'm not all for emotion.

For the next hour, my phone rang every five minutes. I muted the ringer and watched the notifications pop up, one after another. I didn't think he was going to do what he said. I didn't even think he was on the roof. But I was completely terrified that if he would lie to me about this, he was capable of more than I'd realized.

The phone silently rang and rang. I stared at it like it was a snake.

He didn't do it, obviously. This isn't that kind of story. What he did, instead, was show up everywhere I went. He started calling my home's landline and hanging up at least once a day. Sometimes I could hear him breathing. This went on for a few weeks. My father didn't notice because why would he? And I didn't have any friends left to tell. By the time Richard and I were sleeping together, I'd withdrawn from most of my friends at school. Some of them had tried to keep me in their orbit, but most of them had let me spin away. The last to go was Sarah Taylor, my best friend. I'd known her since elementary school.

She stayed the longest, but I eventually told her to go to hell when she tried to get me to go to church with her. I felt a little bad about that—her mom was crazy religious, and I knew that was where it was coming from—but not bad enough to keep her around. Really, there was no one left to tell, and I sure as hell wasn't going to tell my dad. Honestly, I didn't even think it was all that weird at the time. Richard was just having the natural reaction of a boy who'd never been told "no" in his entire life. He could call that love. He probably thought it was.

Anyway, obsession didn't look that different from love to me. The entire history of cinema taught me this.

Then one night when I was getting ready for bed, I had a strange feeling. I parted the blinds in my window and saw him standing in my yard, looking up. His face was cast in shadows from a nearby streetlamp and his eyes looked like dark holes.

Like any idiot in a horror movie, I walked past my father asleep in his chair and stepped outside into the night.

I would've loved to report to Juliet that I told him to fuck off, get off my lawn, that I stepped back inside and called the police and told them I was being stalked by a low-rent Jacob Elordi.

But that wasn't what happened. He closed the distance between us and pulled me to him. He kissed me and I let him for a moment. Kissing him felt good because I knew very clearly that I shouldn't. I had been scared of him for weeks, which meant I'd also been thinking about him for weeks. It was almost a relief just to give myself over to hormones because then I didn't have to wonder if he was nearby. The thing I'd feared was right in front of me, finally.

But only for a moment. Then I pushed him away, gently.

What happened next was boring to talk about. He tried again, I retreated. A few repeats of this and he was angry, the anger that had always been underneath his sunny facade. I'd been so compliant for so long—I was so good at just going along with things—I'd never gotten to see it.

It's hard to say how I felt. I know I must have been scared, but what I remember is how everything seemed surreal, ridiculous, even more so when he shoved me and I found myself on my back, looking at the flat, black sky of suburbia when Richard's unreadable face appeared above me. He did not look adoring. He did not look grateful.

There was a blank space that I retreated to, either because of my head striking the ground with a hard thwack that reverberated down my spine or because of my disinclination to be there anymore, as if I could step out of my body until all this unpleasantness was over. I was distantly aware that he kept kissing me and telling me he knew I didn't mean it, we could be together if I'd only *listen*. His body was heavy on mine, and my arms were frozen at my sides, as if I were a Barbie doll still in its clear plastic box. As long as I was in that blank space, I could almost laugh at him tugging at his belt. Poor dumb idiot. Doesn't know how buckles work.

I don't know what would have happened—okay, I have some ideas—had a car's headlights not appeared at the top of the street. Richard jumped off me, and, hilariously, helped me up, straightening my pajama top like it was all some kind of misunderstanding. *Ever so sorry.* He turned abruptly and headed to his car without a word, then drove off. I stood on the lawn, stunned, not sure whether I should laugh or cry.

He stopped calling after that. He pretended I didn't exist, which suited me fine.

Throughout my recitation, Juliet just listened. She nodded at the appropriate times, looked grim but unsurprised when I described Richard on the lawn. She knew the story. I could tell she had a story of her own, but I wasn't going to ask about it. She'd tell me in her own time, I was sure.

"Rabbit," she said. "No one's ever going to hurt you like that again."

ANIMALS

There are all kinds of ways people use to explain how humans and animals differ. Some call it "soul" and tell you there's a glowing cloud inside you that God put there. I always liked the idea of this, but after my mom died it was hard to stomach. Why would God put something so special inside us and then just snip it out? Anyway, my parents had never done much for my religious education other than one visit to a Unitarian-Universalist church a few towns over, so I found it all a little mysterious.

Those of a more scientific bent point to things like tool use as the difference between humans and animals. But every day, scientists are finding some chimpanzee or bird using a stick to scrape bugs out of a hole. Our tools don't make us that special. Plenty of animals learn to use a tool and then go on to teach it to their kids. That's just unsettling.

It's not memory, either. People will tell you that a goldfish doesn't remember anything, but it turns out that fish can learn how to get through a watery maze. Crows and ravens remember who has done them wrong, and bring trinkets to people who give them food, and dive-bomb researchers they don't like. They hold grudges and I like that about them.

Art is a reasonable criterion. Humans are definitely the only ones running around with boxes of paints trying to reproduce the world or making macramé key chains at summer camp. But for all we know, dolphins are arranging ocean rocks into nice little piles to impress the octopuses. Maybe coral reefs are big art galleries but we just don't know what we're looking at.

Violence isn't particular to humans, either. Animals kill all the time—for mates, for territory, for food, or for no discernible reason. Violence isn't a moral failing; it's just a fact. Animals don't stay up all night afterward thinking about how they'll explain it to the other animals.

They don't justify their actions. They don't make a story out of it.

It was because I knew how awful Richard was that seeing his nose get crushed was so satisfying. It felt like justice, of a sort. At least that's the story I told myself.

But Juliet didn't need a story to hit Richard. Juliet was pure.

THE PANDA AND
THE PRINCESS

When I woke up in the morning, I thought for one disorienting moment I was at home, and my father was in the kitchen preparing breakfast. But that couldn't be right. My dad hadn't made us breakfast for a very long time. He definitely didn't make French toast, which was what I smelled. I squinted against the morning light pouring in from the huge picture windows and the glare of the sun reflecting off the lake into my eyes. Right. I was at Juliet's, in one of the larger guest rooms. I'd called home Saturday night and told my dad I was sleeping over for the weekend, that I'd made a new friend named Juliet. Maybe he'd remember. He'd sounded bleary, but mostly he seemed confused I was seeing a friend. Fair enough. I was confused by that, too. Before my mom died, there'd been a calendar in the kitchen mapping all my activities. I'd been building a résumé I'd hoped would make a good college overlook a lousy high school. I ran the book club at the library, where we mostly read banned books. I was on the academic bowl team. And lest you think that I was only a nerd, I was also in band, where I played trumpet.

But when the calendar filled more and more with my mother's doctor's appointments, my commitments didn't seem to matter as much. I stopped putting mine in. I didn't have the energy to go places, much less talk to people once I was there. Besides, I could do math. At the rate the hospital bills were coming in, college was looking more and more unlikely. I was a fine student. But I wasn't anyone's first pick for a full ride.

But that was the past. Right now, I was in Jesse Bergman's house, wearing Jesse Bergman's pajamas. Not an event I'd ever foreseen. But life's all about change. I stretched out in the luxuriously large bed and if I could have purred, I would have. Turns out, thread count really does matter.

I found Juliet in the kitchen, wearing a long silk kimono with a blue-and-white latticework pattern. She was making coffee. To be more precise, she was using an espresso machine that looked like a Fiat 500.

She gazed at me disinterestedly. "Oh, you're still here."

The smile fell from my face.

"I— What?" I said. I froze, feeling like she'd caught me stealing something.

She gave me a stern look, then laughed. "I'm just fucking with you. God, you're easy."

I smiled weakly.

After confirming that I'd like a latte, she poured steamed

milk in a broad cup and swiftly patterned a panda in the foam. Hart's Run had only managed a Starbucks in the last ten years, so this was pretty novel to me.

I took the cup and cradled the foam panda. It looked up at me with trust.

"Where'd you learn how to do that?" I asked.

"Rome," she said. "The only place to learn it. This is very basic, though. Don't judge."

She wiped down the machine and expertly put away its components. Her actions had the thoughtless efficiency that comes from relentless repetition.

"You worked in a cafe?"

She gave me an indulgent smile. "Would the daughter of Jesse Bergman work in a cafe?"

"Probably not."

"It was a six-week course my father signed me up for while he was filming in Florence. Just a way to get me out of his hair and keep me off the set so I didn't cramp his style. It's very hard to bang teenage movie stars when your own teenager is around making everyone notice how gross the age difference is."

I grimaced. Jesse Bergman was just sounding better and better. I felt a little mournful for a moment, as I realized I was going to have a hard time watching his movies from now on after these little tidbits.

I followed Juliet into the beautiful multi-couch living room and stopped dead.

There was a girl sitting on the couch—a girl I knew *very*

well—looking at me with anger and disgust. An untouched coffee was on the low table before her.

"You remember Sarah, don't you, Rabbit?" I blinked stupidly. "I hit her boyfriend upside the face with a tray. It's getting cold," Juliet said to Sarah. "Drink it while it's fresh."

Sarah, her eyes still fixed on me, picked up the latte and took a dutiful sip. She was wearing a puffy white dress sprinkled with rainbow dots. She looked like a cupcake.

"While you were sleeping in, Sarah dropped by, all full of righteous anger," said Juliet. "As well she should be. I damaged something of hers. But we've been sitting here, talking it out like civilized folks. I think we've come to see we are not enemies."

Sarah and Richard? Since when?

Sarah smiled at Juliet in agreement, and then gave me a look that suggested this peace did not extend in my direction.

I couldn't tell if Sarah's active hatred of me came from the fact that I'd totally dropped her as a friend or because I used to date Richard. A little column A. A little column B.

It was very unfair. I should at least have been issued a Dead Mom pass when it came to the friendship—and if the friendship was *so* important to her, then she wouldn't be dating my ex.

Of course, if I'd ever been a friend to her, I would have known they were dating. I would have warned her.

"You talked it out," I said. Juliet sat across from Sarah and patted the couch cushion next to her. I sat, and the foam panda collapsed a little more. "You talked out how you hit Richard upside the face."

Juliet nodded, as if her action had been the only reasonable one.

I took another sip of the latte, sucking in most of Juliet's design. Bye, panda. The coffee was strong, and my heart was really starting to race, but whether in response to the coffee or the situation was unclear.

"We both agree that the only way to make this right is for Sarah to hit you in the face," said Juliet.

"Excuse me?" I said. My stomach dropped, and I suddenly became aware that I was sweating all over.

"Yeah. Because I hit him for your sake."

I looked at the two of them in bewilderment. "I never asked you to hit anybody!"

"You did," said Juliet solemnly, "with your eyes."

Sarah, whose face had been pretty straight up until this point, let loose a laugh.

Juliet also cracked a smile.

"You're both assholes," I said.

"I don't want to hit you in the face," said Sarah. Her voice was soft and sweet, just like I remembered. When Sarah and I used to drive around together, listening to music and singing, she gave Taylor Swift a run for her money.

"Good," I said, "because I am fond of my face in its current configuration."

Sarah put down her cup and rested her hands in her lap. Then she smoothed her dress once, twice.

"To be honest, I've been hating you for months," she said,

looking at her lap. "I'm sorry, but it's true. Everything Richard does with me is . . . it's about you. It always has been. It took me a while to realize that, but when I did, it made me so angry."

Anyone but Sarah would have kept that to themselves. But Sarah couldn't be anything but sincere. The only surprising part of what she'd said was that she'd been angry. She looked up at me, pained and heartsick. It was hard for me to imagine wanting more from Richard than he gave me, but I could imagine how much it would hurt not to get what you wanted. That was a feeling I was very familiar with.

I knew Richard didn't pick her because she looked like me. She was shorter, plumper, gentler. Her hair was dark, thick, and pulled back to the nape of her neck with a ribbon. She looked as though fat-bellied squirrels would start up conversations with her. I wasn't as boyish as Juliet, but no one was confusing me with a Disney princess anytime soon. My hair was ash blond—what's known as "dishwater blond"—and I tended to wear whatever looked cleanest on the floor.

No, Richard picked a girl because he wanted to grind her down. He'd worn away my disinterest. I had no doubt he was working on Sarah's virginity even now. Sarah's home was steeped in religion and morality. Whenever I ate dinner at her house, Sarah's mom would make us all hold hands for grace that took so long the food got cold. Unsurprisingly, we slept over at my house more often than not, where we were allowed to do wild things like play video games and eat Pop-Tarts.

Sarah was beyond sheltered. It was the kind of challenge Richard would enjoy.

I didn't know what to say. "I'm sorry," I said. "But you don't want his full attention, not really."

And because Sarah had been honest with me, I was honest with her. I gave her the CliffsNotes version of Richard on the lawn. Telling it a second time was easier, although the way Sarah's eyes widened and then filled with tears made me embarrassed. I found myself making jokes about how comfortable the ground had been, about my idiocy in meeting him outside, as if the whole thing was a hilarious story. *Can you believe he did that? And then he helped me up?* Comedy gold. But Sarah's horrified expression kept ruining the delivery, making it clear there really wasn't anything funny about it.

I suppose there wasn't.

"Thank you. For telling me." She gave me a little sad smile. It was a nice smile. It always had been, and I realized I'd missed it. I smiled back, but it felt weird on my face.

"I'm also sorry— I mean . . ." I said, then trailed off. I wanted to apologize for more than just Richard, but I didn't know how to get the words out. *I'm sorry I pushed you away when you tried to help. I'm sorry I made you feel like an idiot when you offered to take me to church. You didn't know what to do.*

I thought all that but I didn't say it.

She nodded anyway. Like I said, she'd always been sensitive.

Juliet's eyes flicked between our faces, looking a little cross. It occurred to me, maybe thanks to the panda coffee, that Juliet hadn't made the connection between this Sarah and the one I'd mentioned the previous night. Juliet hadn't realized we already knew each other and did not appear to enjoy playing catch-up.

"There's something else I need to tell you about," said Sarah. She shut her eyes and took a deep breath. "Something ugly."

SARAH SHARES A SECRET

She had our full attention, so of course she immediately clammed up. Juliet moved to beside her on the couch and took her hand, leaving me alone. I felt a little pinprick of jealousy. Only a tiny stab, but I already knew it would get worse.

"We were at his house, with Duncan and Caleb. We'd been at Duncan's, but his sister came home, and Duncan doesn't like the guys around his sister, so we left."

Juliet's eyebrow rose at this, but she nodded. My eyebrows didn't rise because that didn't surprise me at all. Duncan and Caleb sucked. They were just variations on the theme of Richard. They wore sherbet-colored polos and Madras shorts. The colors declared them to be fun, cool bros. I knew them. They were the guys Richard played *Call of Duty* with, and I was the walking ad for depression medication who watched them while quietly drinking. Richard didn't have to explain to his friends why I was there sometimes. They knew not to question him.

Besides, what could he have said? *There's something about this clinically depressed girl I find intoxicating?*

For all that Richard had pursued me, he never invited me to watch him play football or hang on his arm at parties. Maybe he knew instinctively I would have said no. Unlike me, Sarah would be the perfect girlfriend. She'd enthusiastically accompany Richard to all athletic outings and subsequent soirées: an exemplary showpiece. When they walked together, she'd probably hooked her arm in his and gazed up at him like he was the planet who tugged her little moon around.

Richard would take that adoration as his due. He wouldn't recognize how rare it is to find someone like Sarah, whose love was given so easily, so fully. He'd take in her Disney princess face and her cupcake dresses and it would leave no impression. For a guy like Richard, dating Sarah was like shooting your dad's good scotch; she was quality but he didn't notice or care.

Maybe that's why they got sloppy around her.

"So we were hanging out in the main house. Richard's dad was away on business and his mom had gone to bed, but it's a big house and she couldn't hear us. And everyone was drinking—"

I raised my eyebrows at this. Sarah never drank, or at least, I'd never known her to. When we were eleven, I'd suggested we steal a beer from my fridge. She'd let out a squeak like a mouse and looked fit to faint.

"I mean, not me," she said, catching my look. "Not really. I tried keeping up when we first started dating. I just got sick. And Richard says he hates a drunk girl."

I scowled a little bit at that, I'll admit. Richard had learned something from dating me after all.

Those standards didn't apply to him, however, so when he finished his beer, Sarah said, he gave her hip a slap and told her to get him another one.

She didn't have to tell us that this embarrassed her. She didn't need to tell us that her cheeks had pinked, that she felt foolish in her nice dress with her blown-out hair, for hoping the two of them were going to have an evening together instead of the night ending as it almost always did—sitting with his friends as they all got drunker and drunker. She didn't have to tell us because we could hear it in her voice, in the way she twisted a lock of her hair. Her story was taking shape in my head like a movie, a variation on that same story every girl tells. We were about to see the scene where the ingénue discovers the world is not what she thought.

Because the world won't let you stay an ingénue forever.

"Anyway, we were out of beer, so I walked out to the carriage house because there's a second fridge there, just for beer. Richard's dad calls the carriage house his man cave," she explained. Juliet looked heavenward a moment, but then returned to Sarah's face, attentive. Again, that little stab. "I was closing the door to the fridge when I saw something taped to it."

She paused, then looked at me. She looked apologetic.

"It was you. It was a picture of you," she said.

I frowned. I had always waved Richard off the few times he tried to use his phone to take pictures of me, or worse, the two of us together. I wasn't interested in documentation.

Juliet looked surprised. "Like, a picture-picture? Printed?"

"A Polaroid," Sarah said. In the last year, there'd been a fad for new Polaroid cameras in pastel plastic cases. They were huge with middle schoolers and used with showy irony by high schoolers. I was pretty sure the Kellys each had one so they could instantly capture their precious moments and then festoon them with stickers.

"Of me," I said. It made no sense. A queasy feeling unfolded in my stomach.

"Yeah," said Sarah. "You're—you're sort of half-dressed in it."

"That shithead. He took a picture of me sleeping?" Of course he did. That was pure Richard.

"You're not— I think you're passed out."

My brain did some quick calculations. After my mother died, I'd experimentally tried my father's gin, but drinking alone felt too close to what my dad was doing, and I hated the taste. But Richard had a steady source of beer from his dad's supply, and when he'd have one, I'd have one. Sometimes I had too many. But I didn't remember passing out. Of course, I wouldn't, I guess.

"It wasn't just you. You can see Caleb and Duncan, like, carrying you."

I went cold all over.

"What are you saying?"

Her eyes widened. "I don't know! I don't know what the picture is of, not really. But it was you, and you're wearing a bra and jeans."

Beside her, Juliet's face had gone still and blank. She raised her eyes and fixed me with a look I couldn't fathom.

"Okay," I said. "Okay, I don't know what to do with that."

I could feel my brain making connections that I didn't want it to make. I tried to disengage. I tried to shut it off.

"I know," said Sarah. "I'm sorry. I just— I thought you should know."

"Do you have the picture?" Juliet asked intently.

Sarah shook her head. She'd been shocked, confused, and traveled back to the house with the beer. She'd acted as normal as possible, which wasn't hard, in a way. She'd wanted to believe she hadn't seen it. So she did her best to believe she hadn't. And when she'd returned, Caleb had looked at her very hard. *Had she seen it?* his eyes seemed to say.

No, said her shoulders. *No*, said her easy smile. *I saw nothing, and I remember nothing, and I'll say nothing.*

And Caleb had relaxed, she'd relaxed, everyone was more relaxed and had more beer and the night went on. She sat on Richard's lap again, but she wasn't just uncomfortable this time. This time, her skin was crawling.

But she didn't leave. She didn't leave him. Weeks went by and she maintained a holding pattern, unable to break free because if she did, she'd have to do something about what she'd seen. And she couldn't. She couldn't.

That's what she told us.

"And," she said, her voice full of shame, "I still loved him. And I still wanted him to like me. I told myself the picture didn't mean anything. You were drunk. Just really drunk and it was one more reason to hate you. Then I saw Juliet hit him, and I knew—I knew he'd done something really, really wrong. But I still came here, mad like I was going to defend him. I don't know. It's all mixed up."

Juliet took Sarah's hand, gave it a squeeze.

I barely registered it. My brain had finally finished its calculations and arrived at the inevitable conclusion.

"I wasn't drunk," I said. "I was dying."

ARE THERE MORE?

I did it a few weeks after Richard showed up on my lawn. I waited, because I didn't want him to think for even a second it had anything to do with him. I don't like to be misunderstood. But I'd been carrying the pills around for longer than that, much longer, shoved into the bottom of my backpack. I'd stuffed a tissue into the pill bottle so it wouldn't rattle. Every day I walked around with that bottle, a little secret. I just wanted to know it was there if I needed it.

Without Richard to distract me with his bad jokes and his adequate sex, the black hole in my chest had expanded. It spilled over my edges and everything it touched lost color, lost joy. Whenever I talked to people, which was rarely, I felt as though I was watching myself from the outside, marveling at the workmanship it must have taken to build such a realistic automaton, a perfect pretend girl. Nothing a girl like that did could matter. Nothing was of consequence, but also, none of it would *stop*, which was the real hell of it.

Ultimately, no one thing pushed me over. It was still the same world that had seen fit to take my mother, to send my father to the bottle, to gift me with a stalker. But I couldn't stand to look at any of it anymore. I don't know if I wanted to die, not exactly. I don't know if I meant it. But I felt pretty sincere when I pulled the pill bottle out of my bag one night and swallowed each tablet with a swig of vodka. My father was in Atlanta that weekend for a conference, learning more about how Verizon could further dominate sales on the eastern seaboard. Fascinating stuff. I didn't like the idea of him finding me, but I also wasn't thinking too much about that. There was no sense of an aftermath in my mind. I just wanted to go to sleep and not have to wake up again.

In the movies, the failed suicide wakes up with a renewed sense of gratitude for the miracle that is life. That wasn't me. They gave me naloxone and I woke up in a hospital bed, vaguely surprised to be alive. Surprised, and tired. I'd have to go on living, a realization that exhausted me through and through. The hole in my chest didn't shrink its borders. I just got better at carrying it.

My father was sitting beside my bed, angrier and more worried than I'd ever seen him. It was almost nice to see he cared. That was when he signed me up for Group.

But no one had ever been able to explain how I'd gotten to the hospital. I'd suddenly appeared in the emergency room in a crumpled pile. I suppose I should have wondered more about that, but the whole thing was so embarrassing and stupid, and

I wanted it all to disappear. I was out of school for a week and a half. My father told them I had the flu. I didn't want anyone to know I'd tried. And I didn't want anyone to know I'd failed, either.

In the end, I decided that if the pills weren't the way out, I'd at least escape Hart's Run. I went to Group. I earned high grades. Better, even. I worked on college application essays, and I did everything I could to be good enough to be ignored. I'd graduate high school, I'd go to whatever school would fund me the most, and I'd leave this town behind. That was my plan. My mother's plan had been a little different. When I'd told her I was thinking of Duke University in North Carolina for college, she'd laughed, as sick as she was.

"You'd better go farther than that," she'd said. "Or I'll haunt you." She was thinking beyond college. She wanted me to go to New York City, or Los Angeles. She thought I'd eventually end up in film somehow, because all I did was watch movies and talk about them. I didn't know how to tell her that I was just a spectator.

Liking movies isn't the same as making them. To make movies you must be able to make things *happen*. And that wasn't my strength. Instead, things happened to me.

Anyway, that's the story of my suicide attempt. My adorable cry for help. How basic and boring.

I didn't like this new version, though.

Had Richard come by my house? Did I owe him and his shitty friends my life?

But Sarah said I wasn't wearing a shirt in the picture. That chilled me.

I boiled the story down as best I could for them. They listened without interrupting. Juliet rubbed the thin line on her wrist absently.

"Are there more pictures?" I asked. "You said you drink with him. If there's one of me, why wouldn't there be one of you, too?" The words sounded as ugly as I felt inside. I was mad at Sarah suddenly, for changing the story on me. I wanted her to feel like I did, like everything in the world had shifted a few inches to one side. Like everything she knew was just slightly off.

Sarah's eyes widened and she gave a sharp little inhale, like a cute cartoon chipmunk learning its favorite nut was stolen.

"I—I hadn't thought of that," she said.

Juliet squeezed Sarah's hand again. It looked like it hurt a little.

"If they took a picture of Rabbit, they could have taken a picture of you. Of any girl."

Sarah shook her head. "No, I don't get drunk like that. I'd remember."

"You sure?" said Juliet. "You don't have any funny gaps? Did you ever fall asleep around them? Drank just a little too much?"

Sarah blinked rapidly, then she looked down at her hand, at Juliet's.

"I don't know," she said. "Like I said, I couldn't keep up. They drink a lot. Richard teased me. He said I was a lightweight."

She looked shattered just thinking that a picture might exist. Juliet put her arm around Sarah.

But I was the one who now *knew* there was a picture of me. It wasn't a hypothetical. And no one was squeezing my hand. No one was hugging me.

"I want that picture," I said. "He doesn't get to have that."

Juliet looked up at me, and I knew I had her full attention. Sarah had started to cry, very quietly. She looked pretty doing it. But at that moment, there was just Juliet and me. Juliet nodded. It was a promise.

SLEEPOVER

The sleepover, unfortunately, was easily expanded to include Sarah. Of course, I was fine with that. Sarah was *wonderful*. She'd let me know there was a compromising photo of me floating around in a carriage house. That was a gift, wasn't it?

It was a hot day, so we went down to the dock and stretched out on towels in our underwear and bras. Sarah was annoyingly buxom and lush, but was mortified to be half-undressed, which was some comfort. Juliet was all long limbs and angles, nothing soft about her. Whenever one of us got too hot, we would dip our feet in the water. Sometimes Juliet would dangle her whole head over the edge and get her hair sopping wet, then flick it over us so we screamed. If that wasn't enough to cool off, we'd get a can of cold iced coffee or soda from the little cooler we'd brought down from the house and put the can against the base of our necks before we drank it. These actions transformed the heat into a kind of luxurious suffering, and the late morning bled into the afternoon.

We didn't talk about the picture of me, or the other, hypo-thetical pictures. That was too raw and fresh. Instead, we talked about fireflies and when we could expect to see them come out, and whether it was worth it to try to find a mason jar with a lid in that upscale house. As fancy as Galaxy House was, it did seem to lack some of the basic necessities of summer. My father had always been ready to walk barefoot into the backyard, try-ing to swoop fireflies into a jar. He was a pro at catching new ones without letting the old ones out. By the end of the night, he'd be holding a jar of light that out-blazed my poorly pop-ulated one. Then we'd let them all go in a stream of dazed, bumbling glow.

Juliet said out of nowhere, "What we need is football."

"Excuse me?" I said. Meanwhile, Sarah was nodding as if Juliet's statement made total sense in a conversation about lumi-nescent bugs.

Juliet pushed herself up from her towel. As we were still lying down, she eclipsed the sun.

"It's not football season, though?" said Sarah.

Sometimes Sarah seemed a bit dim.

"Not to watch. I mean that if we ever expect to be president, we need football."

Again, Sarah nodded as if this made perfect sense. Good for you, Sarah. Way to follow Juliet into the illogical wastelands.

"I'm going to need a little help getting from A to B here," I said. I was feeling cross and overheated. I didn't like feeling out of the loop, I didn't like how Sarah was in the loop, and I didn't appreciate Juliet's impatient look.

"What is the point of football?" said Juliet.

"Fuck if I know. Brain damage?" I said.

"Come on," said Juliet, "seriously."

"To score points on the other team. To get the ball from one side of the field to the other. To demonstrate entropy and futility at the same time."

"Don't forget Uh-muer-icah," said Sarah, in a pretty good imitation of a good ol' boy accent. I laughed until I saw Juliet grin at her, and then I felt my face twist a touch.

"Sarah is closest. But no. The point of football is to teach boys to ignore pain, their own or someone else's, to listen to authority, and to move as one. It teaches Us versus Them."

"Football makes you into a rule-following drone," I said. "Got it."

I couldn't see Juliet's face against the glare of the sun, but I could still see her narrow her eyes to focus her attention solely on me.

"This is serious, Rabbit. Boys are taught how to do violence as a group and then they teach each other how to cover it up. It's how they know they're men. We aren't. We're only taught to see each other as competition. We end up unprepared."

Next to me, Sarah sat up and stared at Juliet. She looked spooked. I sat up, too, scowling. My back felt hot and burned, I was sweating, and I didn't like being lectured, even if my own uncharitable thoughts about Sarah proved her point.

"It's just a game," I said. "And yeah, I've known some shitty football players—Richard for one—but some of them are okay.

Most of them, probably." I was thinking about Alonzo Rivers, who was on the football team. Right when my mother first died, and most people were either avoiding me or giving me platitudes and pocket copies of the Bible, Alonzo had come up to me after the last bell while I was unloading my locker. All he said was, "It just sucks. It really sucks and I'm sorry." And then he walked away.

It wasn't poetry, but it did make me cry.

Juliet did not like me disagreeing. With her head backlit by the sun's corona, looking like an angry goddess, she said, "I'm trying to tell you something important. If you want to haul up every exception to the rule and waste our time, you're welcome to do so. But I'm trying to tell you a fundamental truth. It's not just football. At every step along the way, men learn how to move and hurt in groups. They go to college and join fraternities. And from there they form networks that open doors to them for the rest of their lives. Have you ever heard of Skull and Bones? Go take a look at the portraits of US presidents and tell me there's not a link between those kinds of organizations and real power."

"So football makes you president," I scoffed.

"That's the short version." Juliet smiled sweetly.

"Look, I'm not saying you're wrong, exactly, but there's got to be a way to be president without hurting other people or joining a weird brotherhood." I pulled my legs in close. I couldn't explain why, but this conversation was upsetting. There was some kind of fundamental difference between the way Juliet and I saw the world, and I wanted more than anything for us to agree.

"Women play sports," said Sarah in a conciliatory tone.

"That's not the point, Sarah," said Juliet. "When men play a sport, it's about destroying anyone on the outside. When women play a sport, it's all about in-group support, girl power, rah rah rah."

I gave up, shaking my head. I didn't have the words to say what I wanted to say, to explain how it sounded to me like we were trying to trade places. I didn't want to be like the boys she described. I didn't want to play their game.

Sarah spoke up. "It makes sense. I mean, it's not like guys are going to stop doing what benefits them."

Her voice was soft, and she sounded sad and a little scared. The tops of her shoulders were starting to pink. She was thinking about the photo, I knew it. So was I.

Juliet looked at her triumphantly. "Exactly. We can't pretend the world isn't what it is."

I rolled my eyes.

Juliet's phone rang and she answered. Sarah and I listened, not very covertly.

"Not much. Yeah, okay, that sounds good. Ha. Right. Oh, yeah, she did. Okay. I'll see you there."

She hung up and looked at us, pleased.

"Well?" I said.

"We're going out tonight."

I blinked. "Going out" wasn't something that had been in

my vocabulary for a while. The last party I'd gone to had been at Kelly Xu's. This was after Richard, but I'd known he was out of town. I also knew it was a pity invite but went anyway. Kelly Xu made a big fuss over me when I arrived, then quickly abandoned me for the other Kellys when I failed to make small talk. I'd spent about an hour drifting from group to group, trying to laugh at the appropriate times. It was excruciating for everyone involved.

I had a suspicion as to where we were going.

"That was Kelly Xu, the best Kelly. She's inviting us over to Richard's house. Seems when the parents are away, the boys will play. It will be, and I'm quoting here, 'raging.'" She smirked.

I absolutely, positively, did not want to go to Richard's house. One, he was my ex; two, he had a photo of me; and three, Juliet had recently hit him in the face. Even though she swore he only saw a plastic tray approaching him at terminal velocity, I was afraid his memory would get jogged if he saw us. I wanted to stay where I was, sitting on a private dock outside a beautiful house where my every coffee need was anticipated.

"I don't have anything to wear," I said weakly.

"Yeah," said Sarah. "Me either. Plus, I told Richard I was going to go to a church lock-in." Sarah's mother loved signing Sarah up to be incarcerated with God. Her father wasn't religious but was a pushover. It basically meant that when Sarah wasn't with Richard, she was in church.

Juliet raised an eyebrow. "Surprise! God wrote you a rain check. Leave the clothes to me," she said.

Even though Sarah didn't look thrilled about attending the party, she perked up at the idea of clothes. Juliet turned to me expectantly.

"Fine," I said. "Have it your way."

"I always do," she said cheerfully.

Sarah walked off to call her parents and explain that she had a ride to the lock-in and they needn't worry about her. Juliet watched her go, then picked up my canned coffee.

"Wait, I'm not done," I said.

She leaned over, and her lips brushed my ear. "If I hear again that you failed to tell me something—a party invite, anything else—you're out."

She turned my coffee upside down and poured it out on the dock, crushed the can in her hand, and left.

THE OBLIGATORY MAKEOVER

I guess somewhere in my mind I'd thought Juliet would have one of those enormous walk-in closets where every article of clothing gets its own special cubby. You know, a room full of nothing but shoes, with special skinny drawers set into the wall that reveal beautifully arranged belts and scarves. But this wasn't Juliet's house. It was Jesse Bergman's. The closets were empty, but even so, it was clear they were designed for him and him alone. Special drawers awaited a sizable watch collection. An acrylic lazy Susan for folded pocket handkerchiefs. All of them empty.

Juliet had carved out a little space for herself in one of the bedrooms. Not for the first time, I thought about what a narcissist Jesse Bergman must be to not even pretend to designate a room for her. The one she'd chosen for herself wasn't even the primary bedroom, although in a house like that it was still pretty darn huge. Her things had barely made a mark against the room's smooth veneer. There was a duffel bag peeking out from behind the bed, and a pile of dirty clothes in one corner.

"Let's see what we can do about this clothing situation," she said. She rummaged through her bag. A strange collection of oddments poured out. Tank tops, flannel overshirts, jeans, but also a sequined off-the-shoulder top, a skirt of violet tulle, long socks festooned with cat faces. It was like grunge fairycore.

For Sarah, she picked out the sequined top to go with her jeans. I could tell immediately that Sarah did not want to look like a disco ball. A wild outfit for Sarah was stripes.

But there was no arguing with Juliet. Sarah put on the top, and it really was something. Was it Sarah? Not at all. But she did look pretty great, I had to admit. Juliet fussed over her, fluffing up her hair and smudging a little eyeliner around her lashes. The effect was striking. Sarah's Disney princess look was transmuted into something much more sultry. A Disney villain maybe. Sarah looked in the mirror, torn between shame and delight. She was probably watching the angel and the devil argue across her shoulders.

I found myself hoping there was a sequined top for me. Something with a little flash, a little different from my usual style, which was not so much a choice as it was resignation.

Maybe I was also hoping she'd show me a little favor, a little reassurance. Her words on the dock were still whispering in my head. I couldn't connect that coldness to the girl I saw now, gleefully rooting through clothes and promising us transformations. I tried not to think about it, but the words lingered.

Juliet didn't hand me sparkles or tulle. Instead, she looked at me speculatively and then snapped her fingers. "Got it," she said. She went over to a pile of dirty clothes and pulled out a gray T-shirt.

I must have looked crestfallen, because Juliet smiled, with just a touch of mockery, daring me to protest. I didn't.

When I put the T-shirt on, I could catch just a hint of a spicy smell, like an orange studded with cloves. And under that, something a bit animal. Juliet.

It was just a gray V-neck. Nothing special. I'm ashamed to say that for one terrible moment, my eyes welled up before I got them under control. Sarah tentatively primped in front of a full-length mirror in the corner. I felt drab.

I had seen so many teen comedies where a judicious application of makeup and the removal of eyeglasses with a showman's flourish had metamorphosed a nerdy girl into a shy femme fatale. I'd been fully prepared to live that trope. This was not it.

"Chin up, Cinderella, I'm not done," Juliet said. "Sarah, can you go grab me that pair of scissors from the kitchen, just in case?"

Just in case?

"On it," said Sarah, and left.

"Come over here," Juliet said, and pulled me over to the bathroom. "Where I can see you."

She sat me down on the toilet lid and took my chin in her hand, moving my face into the light. I tensed up, remembering her words on the dock. Closer, the spicy orange scent from her was stronger.

"I think we need to play up those eyes," she said. She rummaged around in a makeup bag on the counter until she pulled out a dark green-and-gold eyeliner. "There we go. Suitable for Cleopatra, suitable for Rabbit."

Then, she straddled me.

I mean, she sat down right in my lap, face-to-face. To say I wasn't expecting her to do that was an understatement. I thought she was going to stand beside me, like she had for Sarah.

I couldn't breathe.

"Look up at the ceiling," she said. She sounded amused.

I swallowed, then obeyed.

"Open your eyes wider, you baby," she said.

In the periphery I could see her, intent on her work, dabbing gently at my eyes with the tip of an eyeliner pencil she'd warmed on the inside of her wrist. I could feel her breath on my cheek.

I wanted this moment to hold me in it forever. I also wanted to bolt from the room.

And then she was done and pushed off me lightly. I took a deep breath. Was I disappointed? Relieved?

She looked me over and frowned.

"Nope, just like I thought. It's not enough," she said, narrowing her eyes. Then she grinned. "Do you trust me?"

I shook my head and laughed.

"Fair enough," said Juliet.

Sarah was in the doorway, holding the scissors. How long had she been there? The scissors were long and thin, like the beak of a waterbird. Sarah handed them to Juliet, handle first.

"Close your eyes, little Rabbit," said Juliet. "And take off that T-shirt or you'll itch all night."

Once again, I obeyed. What else was I going to do? Leave?

So I sat there in my bra while Juliet cut my hair. I hadn't had a proper haircut in a long time. I'd pretty much let it do whatever it wanted after my mom died. It had grown long and heavy, and most days I put it in a ponytail and forgot about it. I only remembered it when it was in my way.

She hacked off my ponytail. The scissors, sharp as they were, struggled to make their way through. When she'd finished, she dropped the ponytail in my lap. The sudden weight felt gruesome.

"Better keep it for spells," she said. She was joking, but Sarah's eyes widened all the same. Growing up in a religious household must make you very concerned about supernatural dabblings.

Then she snipped and snipped, tugging on the ends, and comparing lengths. She twisted the hair in front of my eyes and before I could say a word she'd cut it again, carving out bangs. I hadn't had bangs since I was a kid.

"Faith, Rabbit," said Juliet warningly. I kept my mouth shut.

She kept returning to my bangs, cutting into them and fussing. Finally, she was done. My head felt light. My hair covered the bathroom floor, my feet. Sarah brushed at my bare shoulders with a towel, brusque and soft at the same time.

"Perfect," Juliet said, pulling me up and turning me to face the mirror.

"Oh," I said.

A stranger looked back at me from under heavy bangs. My eyes were golden and warm against the bronzed green eyeliner. My hair was *short*. The ends curled toward my mouth in a bob.

I didn't look like a Disney villain. I most assuredly didn't look like me. But maybe I looked like my older sister—if I'd had an older sister, and she'd spent a year in France smoking tarry cigarettes and drinking green liqueurs out of tiny glasses, thumbing through a copy of—God, what do French people read? Sartre or Simone de Beauvoir or the guy who likes madeleines.

Madeleine the cookie, not Madeline the schoolgirl.

Anyway, I looked like that. *This* was the makeover promised.

"Holy fuck," I said.

Sarah clapped her hands like she'd just seen a magic trick.

"Praise be," said Sarah.

Juliet squeezed my shoulders.

"Perfect," she said.

THE OBLIGATORY HEIST

Even though his parents were loaded, Richard's house wasn't on the lake, but a mile out of town. It was a big blue farmhouse gutted of any actual farmhouse characteristics, its interior replaced by a Pottery Barn catalog. Juliet drove us down the winding driveway and then pulled the car off the pavement to park alongside the other cars in a field. When we stepped out, our feet sank into the muddy grass. At least I hadn't worn nice shoes.

But instead of heading toward the front door, Juliet tugged me to the side, toward the back of the house. "This way," she said. Sarah looked as confused as I felt. If we were there to attend a party, didn't it make sense to go through the front door? Maybe I wasn't up on party procedure. Okay, then, back door it is. I didn't particularly care. The less noticeable I was at Richard's, the better. I felt queasy being on his territory again. Sarah didn't look thrilled, either. Only Juliet looked excited, like she'd just reached a new level in her favorite video game.

Juliet walked us around the back fence, then quietly opened the gate. We stepped inside the immense backyard, under a canopy of pecan trees. The immediate back of the house, and the pool, were ablaze with light. We stood in the shadows. There were only a few partygoers milling around the back of the house, mostly smokers. The night was hot, and the party wasn't quite at the point where people were ready to jump into the pool with their clothes on. The smokers lounged on deck chairs near the back door, letting the music from the house slam into them with waves of bass. I could smell candy-scented vape alongside skunky pot.

Juliet pointed to the carriage house, set back from the pool area. The Cummingses had built it as a mother-in-law suite, but the mother-in-law had passed before she could move in, probably to everyone's relief. Since then, it had been annexed by the men of the household. Richard's dad ran a monthly poker game and Richard used the space to practice his electric guitar and entertain friends. I'd spent many an hour there in the church of *Call of Duty*. It was always off-limits during Richard's parties, probably because of Mr. Cummings's liquor cabinet.

Now I had a pretty good idea why we were here.

We sidled up to the carriage house and tried to look invisible as we approached the door. We were out from under the shadows now and relying on the smokers' obliviousness. Luckily, they were a lot more concerned with discussing Bitcoin than paying attention to their surroundings.

There was a hand-lettered sign taped to the door of the

carriage house, declaring emphatically: Do Not Open. Underneath this warning, someone had penciled: official jerk off room.

Juliet tried the handle. Locked. I glanced at the smokers like an idiot; there was no way they could hear the knob turning, but my nerves were on high alert.

"Okay," whispered Sarah. "We gave it a fair try." She looked terrified. I wondered if she was more scared of getting caught, or of whatever was on the other side of that door.

Juliet shook her head. "C'mon, Sarah, show some American sticktoitiveness," she said.

She pulled a card from her wallet and wedged it between the door and the frame, sliding it down. Then she gave the knob a turn and pushed with her shoulder against the door, all while gently jiggling the card back and forth.

The door popped open, and Juliet said softly, "Ta-da!"

Having shut the door behind us, Juliet pulled a small flashlight from her pocket and swept the room, careful to avoid the windows. The carriage house was a ways back from the house proper, but we could still hear the thumping music. It wouldn't be impossible for the smokers to notice lights in the little house when it should be dark.

The inside was a love song to a certain kind of masculinity, one that needs constant reassurance from leather sofas and mounted deer heads. The air was thick with Cool Water and boy funk, a scent I remembered with queasy nostalgia. There was a painting of flying mallards on one wall, and a large pinup of a woman wearing a red feather bikini. The poker table had a silver case of chips in the center of it, with two decks of cards awaiting players. Richard's amps were tucked in one corner, his electric guitar hanging from a hook on the wall. He knew three chords.

The photo wasn't on the fridge anymore. I'd known it wouldn't be, but I still felt disappointed. Sarah looked relieved by its absence, then anxious when we didn't immediately leave.

Juliet stood in the center of the room, turning slowly to survey it. She paused with interest when she saw there was a gun rack with two shotguns hanging on the wall, then kept scanning.

"I'm a teenage boy and I've got something incriminating. I'm smart enough to hide it but not smart enough to burn it. Where do I put it?" she said.

"In my bedroom," I said.

"Nope," said Sarah. "They've got a housekeeper, and Mrs. Cummings is a snoop."

I know that, I wanted to say. It irritated me that Sarah was acting like an expert on the Cummingses. Then again, she probably had been to dinner at their house, unlike me. *She* was someone you could show off to your parents.

"My locker?" I said.

"Drug searches," Juliet said. "Also, it's summer, genius."

"Fine, here. You want me to say *here*," I said, annoyed. I didn't like playing Watson to Juliet's Sherlock, especially since she didn't seem to want to do the deducting.

"Right. But Daddy shares the space. And even Mr. Cummings would ask about this."

Sarah nodded. Daddy would indeed ask.

There was no answer, so there was nothing to do but search. All the best heist movies have a search, and we were a cracker-jack team. We started with the obvious—various drawers, underneath the couch cushions—then got more creative. Sarah ran her hands along the underside of the poker table, but only found an ancient wad of gum. I lifted the bottom corners of the pinup poster, but there was nothing behind it but aging adhesive putty. No *Shawshank Redemption* hidden tunnel here. Luckily, it adhered back to the wall with pressure.

We'd searched for almost thirty minutes by the time my anxiety about being caught expanded to unmanageable levels. We hadn't found anything but a pile of vintage *Hustler*s and an incredibly detailed fantasy football chart. Boys are so cute with their hobbies.

"It's not here," said Sarah.

Juliet ignored her. She stood in the center of the room and turned slowly, taking in everything from a distance. Then she stopped her turning and walked over to the deer head mounted above the couch. She stepped onto the couch and stood eye to glassy eye.

"Hey there, Bambi," she said.

She grasped the antlers and lifted the deer head off the wall. It was heavy, and she swayed but steadied herself. She spun around so the head's backing was facing me.

"Do we have it?" she asked.

Taped against the wooden base was a manila envelope.

"Winner winner," I said.

"Not bad," said Juliet.

She put the head down on the couch and I peeled off the envelope. Sarah stepped back. She was realizing what I'd known instantly—the envelope was bigger than necessary for just one Polaroid.

Juliet unclasped the envelope and we squatted beside her as she dumped the contents on the floor. The light from the flashlight made it seem like we were gathered around a fire.

There were fifteen Polaroids. I already knew what I'd see. Passed-out girls posed like blow-up dolls, the boys fondling them, mocking them, egging one another on. And a few that were even worse—ones I couldn't stand to look at. Mercifully, I didn't recognize those girls but I saw myself in their vulnerability. I did recognize the Kellys, myself, and Sarah, however.

Sarah rested her fingertips lightly on the photograph of herself. In it, she was asleep—or more accurately, passed out—on the couch just beside us. Her shirt was unbuttoned to the waist. Richard was sitting beside her, propping up her limp body. His arm was around her neck, his hand grasping one of her breasts possessively. He looked at the camera with a grin on his face. It was very funny, what he was doing, wasn't it? He was inviting the viewer to laugh.

Sarah pulled her fingertips away, as if burned.

The picture of me was less composed. There were two guys in it, Richard's inner circle: Duncan Levitt and Caleb Winters. Caleb and Duncan were holding me between them by my arms and legs. I looked boneless, my head lolled to one side and my hair dragging on the ground. I wasn't wearing a shirt, just as Sarah had reported. Caleb was laughing like it was the funniest thing he'd ever seen. Next to the leather couch, there was a beer can on its side in the very corner of the frame, like a PSA about teen drinking.

I suppose Richard was the one taking the photo.

"What am I looking at?" I said. Although I knew, even then. I was trying to pretend I didn't, just like I was trying to pretend I hadn't noticed that the leather couch in the picture was the same one Juliet had stepped on to retrieve the photo. But I'd taken the pills in the comfort of my own home, not here.

"The usual tragedy," Juliet said. Her face was a strange mixture of satisfaction and disgust. She took the photo from me. I relinquished it gladly; it was something ugly I wanted no part of.

But we were a part of it. Juliet would make sure of that.

She tucked the picture into the back of the stacked Polaroids, my unconscious body shuffled in among all those other girls. Girls who were naked, girls who were posed, girls whose eyes never opened.

Juliet handed the envelope to Sarah, the only one of us carrying a purse. She then stood on the couch once more to return the deer head to its post. It gazed mournfully ahead, its glass eyes still watching us when we left and closed the door.

THE OBLIGATORY HOUSE PARTY

We didn't leave, not immediately.

Instead, we circled back around the house to the front, and walked up the steps to the porch. There were people milling about, but no one seemed too concerned we'd come from the wrong direction, if they noticed at all. A few partygoers waved at Juliet as we ascended, as if they knew her.

Juliet opened the front door and walked in as if it was her house, not Richard's. Sarah and I lingered for a moment on the threshold, like sad vampires awaiting invitation. Even from the doorway, we could smell yeasty beer fumes sluggishly wafting through the air. The room was dimly lit by a few table lamps and strings of Christmas lights that pooled around the floorboards like electric kudzu. I could make out people dancing, people draped on furniture, people stumbling and laughing. Shades of *To All the Boys I've Loved Before* and *Mean Girls*, with a sprinkling of *The Perks of Being a Wallflower*. Richard kept to the old traditions. My body was a tuning fork humming in response to the deafening music. *This* was a party.

It was absolutely not where I belonged.

"Oh, for fuck's sake," said Juliet when she realized we hadn't followed her in. She turned and grabbed me by the wrist and pulled me in front of her, straight to the kitchen, where people congregated around a sticky counter covered in bottles. Sarah followed in our wake.

"Poison?" asked Duncan Levitt. Duncan, who had slid his hand up my back every day for a month in sixth grade to let everyone know that I still wasn't wearing a bra. Duncan, who'd apparently carried my unconscious body by the arms. Duncan, who I'd now seen with his pants unzipped, pressing his crotch against Kelly Xu's cheek. The hairs on my arms lifted.

"You the bartender?" asked Juliet. She smiled at him, the picture of friendliness. Sarah and I followed suit, instantly putting on our best party faces. *Look at all the fun we are having! Look at us, laughing and singing at all the right parts of the song!* It was easy to be an actor, I thought. I wondered if I could do this for the rest of my life—pretend to be someone else so I didn't have to be me every morning.

Duncan gestured expansively at the collection of bottles before him, a hodgepodge of liquor scammed from the unlocked cabinets of parents all over Hart's Run and the discards from beneficent siblings. There was a lot of Goldschläger and Jägermeister. With a magician's flourish, Duncan set down three

Solo cups and scooped ice into them from a bucket with his bare hands.

I tried not to think about where his hands had been and kept beaming friendliness.

Too much. He cocked his head at me, as if trying to place me. I froze, waiting for him to say something, but the moment didn't come. My new hair and makeup, I realized, combined with my avoidance of nearly everyone for months, meant I was effectively in disguise. Besides, had Duncan ever said two words to me, besides calling me a surfboard? Whenever I'd been at Richard's, Duncan had at most given me a nod. I'd existed to him, but barely. Whatever notice he'd afforded me was at Richard's insistence, and Richard didn't insist on much.

For the first time, I wondered what Richard had told his friends about me, if he'd said anything at all. Did they wonder why I was around for a while, then wasn't? Did they know how Richard spent his spare time keeping tabs on me?

Or was I just one of the many girls that they had their fun with, photographed, then filed away behind the carcass of a deer?

Duncan peered more closely at me. "Hey there, what's your name?" he said. He was feeling no pain. His bloodshot eyes flicked over me, coming to rest on my breasts like heavy hands.

He was drunk. Maybe I wasn't all that well disguised.

"Natasha Romanova," I said.

"That's a name. Hey, Natasha," he said. "You Russian?"

"No, I'm too lazy," I said.

He looked at me blankly, and then correctly decided this line of questioning was not worth pursuing further. "What do you want?"

My mouth opened, then closed. I emphatically did not wish to tell Duncan about my recent journey to sobriety.

"She's the driver. Give her a Coke—let's keep her awake," said Juliet.

I gave her a grateful look and she winked.

Duncan shrugged, unimpressed. "Your choice," he said, and handed me a cup filled with brown liquid from a crumpled two-liter. The label declared it "Genuine Cola," a name that seemed like it had something to prove.

"And I'll have a screwdriver, my good sir," said Juliet.

"Excellent taste, madam," he said, and poured several healthy glugs of vodka into a cup, followed by a whisper of orange juice. He swayed a little but managed to make it look intentional.

"And you, my dear?" he said to Sarah.

"I'll have a sea breeze," said Sarah. Maybe something she'd heard in a secular TV show after her parents went to bed. Her voice was as bold as her new look. This wasn't church mouse Sarah.

"Excellent, excellent," he said, and handed her a cup with a sad, smashed orange slice hanging off the side. "After-dinner mint?" he concluded, offering us a small bowl holding a collection of petite white pills.

Juliet said no thank you, graciously, as if there was nothing she'd rather do than take mysterious pills but alas, her schedule was booked. We waved our drinks in thanks, and he bowed theatrically at our departure.

"No lime? He could have at least made you feel fancy," she said, peering into my cup.

Sarah raised her drink to her lips and Juliet took it from her. "Are you a complete idiot? You're going to drink anything these assholes give you?"

Sarah flushed, ashamed.

Juliet dumped the drink out into a potted plant. Sorry, begonia.

"So what are we—" I said.

"Oh, I love this song! Let's dance!" Juliet took our hands.

I protested that I didn't dance, had never danced, would never dance. I tried to tell her that dancing and I didn't know each other. But I couldn't get the words out. Maybe it was my Juliet-designed disguise, but I found myself beside her and Sarah in the living room, swaying to the music. I'd always thought everyone who danced knew some set of steps I'd never been privy to, but most of them just shuffled and swayed to the beat, with a few outliers providing actual moves. Juliet was one of those outliers, and we all just rocked in her eddies.

The secret to dancing was to realize no one was thinking as much about you as you were.

For the entire span of "As It Was," I forgot everything. I forgot I didn't like dancing or parties, and I forgot the photographs.

But then Caleb Winter, bleary with drink, sidled up to Juliet and attempted to grind against her backside. Caleb, whose spotty face was harder to see in the photograph where he held up my legs, but still recognizable, still smiling. He was lanky, with big hands and feet, like a puppy not fully grown. His buzzed red hair made him look like his scalp was rashy.

Juliet danced her way over to me and away from his invasive crotch and circled her arms around my neck. She drew me close.

"Sorry, I gotta dance with the girl I came with," she said to Caleb. She trailed one hand down my lower back and under my shirt for a moment, then retreated. My breath hitched in my chest.

Caleb took her words as a suggestion to grace both of us with his attention, and for a moment the two of us were blessed with a standing lap dance. Sarah spun away, lucky to escape.

The music was loud, but I could still make out what Juliet said to him next.

"If I feel your tiny mouse dick against my ass one more time, I'm going to rip it off and pick my teeth with it," she said, as sweetly informative as a weather girl.

At first he couldn't process it. But then comprehension drifted across his face, and he said, dully, "Bitch."

I grabbed Juliet's shoulder just as a delighted smile crossed her face and she made a fist. I shook my head and she pouted at me, then relented. As we left the dance floor, she pointed her fingers in a V at her own eyes, then out toward him.

"What the fuck does that even mean?" shouted Caleb after us.

Sarah giggled. "You weren't really going to hit him, were you?"

"No, no, I wasn't going to hit him," said Juliet reassuringly. "I was going to murder him."

THE GOLDEN BOY

It had been a while since I'd seen Richard up close. He was easy to pick out of the crowd. He was a little taller than the guys who surrounded him, and his blond curls caught whatever light could be found in the room and reflected it back golden. He wore an unbuttoned Henley that exposed a few blond chest hairs, and the sleeves were pushed up to display his forearms. At some point, Richard had walked into an Abercrombie & Fitch store and was irrevocably changed. The look suited him; he had a boy's face, a man's body, and a petulant expression you could confuse for sexy if you didn't know better.

I couldn't see any evidence of Juliet's assault, which seemed fitting. Nothing could mar Richard. Nothing could touch him.

He was drunk, holding court in the sunroom like a middling Louis XIV. Sarah shook her head and gestured that she'd be waiting in the living room. She had no desire to explain to Richard why she wasn't at the lock-in. I hung behind on the periphery of his circle, keeping my face turned away. It wasn't hard to hide—most of the guys surrounding him were on the football team and essentially formed a wall of broad shoulders. Juliet walked up to him, bold as brass.

"Great party," she yelled over the music.

Richard paused in his conversation and turned to look. Seeing Juliet, he was pleased indeed. I wondered if the Kellys had described her to him; if he knew she was Bergman's daughter.

"Thanks, it's Xu's party. But her parents were unhappy after the last one, so here we are," he yelled back. A freshman— Danny Carballo?—stepped in and handed Richard a Solo cup. "Wait a sec," he said to Juliet, "*don't* go *anywhere*." He lifted the cup and raised his other hand to signal attention.

"Friends, Romans, countrymen, lend me your beer!" he called out. The crowd gave a resounding cheer, while his posse chanted, "Chug, chug, chug." *Animal House* has done terrible things to the youth. He downed the beer in one seamless gulp. The freshman took the empty cup from him, a dutiful attendant.

He turned back to Juliet, triumphant. I could only assume this was the same inspiring leadership he showed on the field.

"*Julius Caesar*," he said helpfully.

"Wow," said Juliet brightly, "drunk *and* literate. Please, share with me more selections from AP English."

Displeasure passed over his face briefly like a cloud before the sun, but his smile returned soon enough. Nothing could disrupt Richard Cummings's good time. Anything that threatened it must be a misunderstanding. He just needed to show Juliet how things worked.

"You're the Bergman girl, right? Glad you're here. The Kellys won't shut up about you," said Richard.

Juliet stepped a little closer. Richard, tall as he was, barely had an inch on her. "Oh, when I heard *you* were the host, I had to come." She pitched her voice higher, breathier, and looked up at him through her lashes. The ghost of Marilyn Monroe took a bow. Geraldine Danvers, who would have been happy to inform you that she'd been an understudy for Cosette in a theater camp production of *Les Mis* last summer, looked sour at this display.

Richard laughed. I had to admit, his laugh was pretty good. It was big and generous and felt like a sunlit meadow. I suppose I'd liked that about him.

I really hated that Richard was handsome. Good-looking people are very hard to deal with.

"That's some grade-A bullshit, but I'll take it," said Richard.

She smiled and dropped the dumb blond act. They understood each other.

By then I'd been detected. Kelly Xu was standing before me, a Solo cup in her hand, blocking them from my sight.

"Rabbit, you came," she said. "You look . . . different." She took me in, her eyes flicking between the new length of my hair and the lined eyes with interest.

Clearly my disguise couldn't work on a Kelly. Or at least not a Kelly Xu. I frowned, waiting for the inevitable cutting remark.

"Different good, I mean," she said. "It suits you."

I blinked and said "Thank you" in surprise.

"It's really awesome to see you out," she said.

"Um, thanks. Yeah, I'm trying to—" I stopped. I had no idea what the rest of that sentence would be.

She nodded. "Yeah. I mean, I know you had that—that whatever with Richard and all, but that didn't seem great."

"It wasn't."

She hesitated, her eyes glancing his way and back, and for one terrible moment I thought maybe she knew just how not great it had been. Maybe everyone knew.

But no, Richard wouldn't have told everyone the whole story. Not when it would paint him in a bad light.

Probably he told them just enough to make me look crazy.

Probably no one had bought that I'd had the flu.

"Anyway," she said, and looked self-conscious.

"Yeah," I said.

Please let this moment end, I thought. For both our sakes.

"I'm— I want you to know I'm glad you're here," she said. "That's what I'm saying."

I nodded, confused. "Yeah, I got it."

"Because of your mom and all," she said.

Jesus, she was so close to being decent and then she had to keep talking.

"That's not necessary," I said.

"I mean— No! I mean, I'm sorry I didn't—I didn't say much. When it happened. Not really. And I wanted to tell you—I'm sorry about that," she blurted.

I took a deep breath. This was, I told myself, the best Kelly Xu could manage. And maybe it was the best I could expect.

And it did sound sincere.

"Thank you," I said. And I guess I meant it.

Relief spread across her face. It made me uncomfortable.

I thought about the Polaroid of her. Her passed-out face, and Caleb grinning while he ground his crotch against it. Kelly Xu had always been a bit of a romantic. In middle school she'd made a vision board about David Blott, her crush. She was no Kelly Costa—her virginity or lack of it was no one's business—but she had firm ideas about love and its relationship to all things sexual.

That picture would destroy her. She couldn't know about it.

She squeezed my shoulder—do people actually do that?—and said she'd talk to me later. We both knew she wouldn't, but it was all right. She left looking like she'd just received communion.

Richard and Juliet were still talking. I feigned deep interest in watching one of Richard's court demonstrate how many push-ups he could do with a girl sitting on his back, and stood near them with my back turned. I was pretty sure that Richard wouldn't recognize the back of my head, due to booze and my new disguise as a cool French girl, but I didn't want him to look at me twice. Luckily, I was experienced in being overlooked.

"So, your dad's really Jesse Bergman, huh?" he said to Juliet.

"That's what they tell me. The one and only."

"He teach you any of those Galaxy punches?" Richard did a quick bob and weave.

"A few," she said.

"That man had *moves*," he said. "You don't look much like him. Maybe the mouth."

"Well, I'm the real deal. There were paternity tests and everything," said Juliet.

"Gotcha. Everybody wants a piece," Richard said.

Juliet's mouth tightened a little.

He raised his hands in a gesture of peace. "Hey, hey, I mean no harm. I'm just saying sometimes it's like that."

"Sometimes it is," said Juliet, all agreeable again. "Well, Richard, I'm going to depart now. It's been smashing."

Richard looked disappointed, but magnanimously gave her leave to go. Another girl took Juliet's place, and another Solo cup was delivered.

We backed away as the chant began again.

We picked up Sarah on our way out. She looked worried, but we grinned at her. We'd been successful. I hadn't been discovered, Juliet had gotten to meet Richard face-to-face, no one had remembered her in connection with a plastic tray, and the sickening photographs were in Sarah's purse.

Sarah smiled in return, and with a shy, proud look, showed us a final triumph tucked into her purse: a pastel-green Polaroid camera she'd found in the living room, stashed under a side table.

Then we left, we were free, spilling onto the moonlit lawn

from the front door with our hands over our mouths, barely suppressing our whoops of delight.

"God, what an asshole," said Juliet, still laughing so hard she could barely catch her breath. "He deserves everything that's coming to him."

IT'S FINE, SILLY

The next morning, I woke up to the sounds of laughter and the smells of maple syrup and bacon. I wrapped Jesse Bergman's robe around me as I walked from the spare bedroom to the kitchen.

Juliet was standing by the immense kitchen island, a spatula in her hand. There was a glass stovetop built into the island, which gave me the distinct impression that she was magically cooking pancakes on the counter. She wore a ribbed gray tank top and a pair of men's boxers, and her hair was knotted on the top of her head, tendrils escaping around her temples. Every now and then, she paused her cooking to take another bite from a peach. I tried and failed to imagine Juliet grocery shopping at the Piggly Wiggly. It was impossible. This food had simply materialized in the fridge.

Sarah sat on a tall barstool alongside the island, happily watching Juliet's cooking show, sipping her coffee. Sarah, like me, was still in pajamas and a robe. Horribly, her perfect complexion was not the result of makeup. There was no God.

"I'm assuming you eat of the pig," said Juliet. She gave a plate of bacon and paper towels a shake and waggled her eyebrows.

"I eat of the pig," I said. I had tried being vegetarian once and had made it for approximately two weeks before I lost control at a barbecue. I'm not proud.

I sat down on another barstool. I was exhausted. After the party, we'd stayed up till 3:00 a.m., talking. Not about the pictures. I wasn't ready to talk about them, and neither was Sarah. But we talked about everything else.

Sarah talked about how her parents were getting a divorce. Her mom, always religious, had joined a new Baptist church and went all in, hence the uptick in lock-ins "for the teens." Her mom had signed her up for yet another one that weekend, which at least had given her an excuse to avoid Richard. But it was one lock-in too many for Sarah's father. He pitched a fit over the whole thing and accused her mother of trying to brainwash their child. They'd both started yelling while her father ineffectually slammed all the drawers in the kitchen. It was around then that Sarah decided she needed to get out of the house.

I'd taken this in with some amount of guilt. Sarah's mom had always been . . . intense. She'd once called my house at two in the morning, asking my mom to put my dad on the phone because she was worried about his soul, all because Sarah had mentioned to her mother that he liked to read *The Lord of the Rings*. The religiosity had always been there. But it sounded like her father had finally had enough. Too little, too late, I thought. I was likely always going to alienate Sarah after my mother died, but it hadn't helped that she'd tried to get me to go to church with her. Probably her mother's suggestion, I now realized, with a sinking feeling. Or her demand. Poor Sarah.

I'd talked a little bit about my mom.

I didn't mean to. I was trying to talk about Group. Not about why I'd been in it, even though they knew now. Mostly I wanted to talk about what a terrible waste of space Sheila was, which Juliet was happy to corroborate. But talking about Sheila's self-help rigmarole made me remember how my mother loved to read self-help books, but for humor. She'd pick the worst ones—like that one about washing your face—and read passages aloud to my dad and me while we made dinner. She didn't do it with the really serious ones, the ones about awful trauma and abuse. Just the ones that were made for reading on airplanes when you were thinking about leaving your lousy boyfriend but weren't really going to do it. The ones that suggested the key to self-actualization was creating a capsule wardrobe.

Sarah had laughed at this.

"Oh my god, yes, remember when she was reading that one about how to use your astrological sign to find the best sex?" Sarah said. I remembered it vividly. Sarah had been embarrassed and tickled pink. It was not the kind of conversation that ever happened in her house. Or if it did, an exorcism would immediately follow.

It was easy to slip back into our shared memories, our old ways of talking to each other. I'd forgotten how comfortable I was with her, when I wasn't being envious.

"Oh noooo, I remember! There was that bit about how a Virgo man would be mopey in bed but—"

"The girth of him would make up for it!" completed Sarah, then clapped her hands over her mouth, scandalized at herself.

We'd giggled so hard that Sarah slid off the couch to roll on the ground.

After a while, we'd pulled ourselves together, and mostly stopped laughing, at least until I made a circle with my hands and mouthed "girth" at Sarah, which set her off again.

Juliet had watched the two of us laughing, a small smile on her face. I felt a little bad, realizing we'd left her out.

Juliet had talked about the French coast and California wineries. She'd talked about craft services tables and movie trailers. She'd talked about which star was sleeping with which other star and which third star didn't know about the first one. And somehow, she'd managed to do all that without saying much about her father. It was impressive, really.

Talking like that had been exhilarating. It also made me feel naked. I wrapped the thick robe tightly around me, like I'd shown too much last night.

"Good," said Juliet. "I mean, I want to respect people's choices in religion and whatnot, but I also want to have crispy edges on my pancakes from bacon fat."

"Priorities," I said.

"Here," said Juliet, "eat of my body." A series of fluffy discs slid off the hot pan she held over my plate. One, two, three in a tidy stack. She handed me a bottle of syrup. "And drink of my blood." Sarah's eyes widened, then she giggled.

"You are so weird," I said.

"Thou shalt have no gods before me," said Juliet sternly.

"And also sacrilegious."

Juliet just smiled. Clearly, she was not worried.

She poured me a cup of coffee, and Sarah passed me a pitcher of cream that looked like it belonged in a design magazine. I smiled, feeling very taken care of by the two of them. After our talk last night, Sarah seemed more like the friend I remembered, and less like competition for Juliet's attention. Juliet was the benevolent spirit that had brought us all together.

My smile faded when Juliet laid the Polaroids out in a line down the center of the kitchen island like a spread of solitaire. She placed the mint-green camera beside them. Just your typical breakfast scene: coffee, pancakes, sordid evidence.

I immediately averted my eyes, preferring to eat breakfast until I died of clogged arteries rather than talk about those pictures, but Juliet wasn't going to let me get away with that. She tapped them purposefully until I looked up.

"So, what are we going to do about these?"

Sarah took another bite of pancake to avoid answering.

"I dunno, aren't we just . . ." I trailed off. I knew I was playing dumb, but I didn't want to answer her question the way I knew she wanted it answered.

"Just what?" said Juliet.

"Well, I mean, aren't we just screwing with them? They're

going to freak out when they can't find all this. And now they don't get to keep their weird trophies."

Juliet looked at me like I was a new species of stupid.

"That's the limit of your imagination? You think we took this to make them feel *anxious*?" It was early in the morning for scorn, but Juliet managed.

Sarah looked between the two of us like a kid whose parents were fighting. I suppose she'd had practice.

"We don't really know what these are pictures of, not really. I mean, everyone in these pictures is drunk, everyone's being stupid." It sounded ridiculous as I was saying it. I knew it was a lie.

"I wasn't drunk," said Sarah quietly. "There's no way I was that drunk."

I swallowed. I didn't even know how I'd come to be in that picture.

"You know what these are pictures of," said Juliet. "These are pictures of guys doing what they want, without consequences. These are pictures of guys treating girls like props in their sick little scenes. We don't know what happened after these were taken, but it wasn't good."

Sarah closed her eyes. I suspected she was a virgin. Or, had thought she was. Now she didn't know what to think.

Did I? When I woke up at the hospital, I felt like I'd been hit by a truck. I hadn't felt like I'd had any physical damage other than what I'd done to myself.

I shook my head. I wasn't going to go down that path unless I had to.

I looked at the photos.

"We should burn them," I said. Nothing felt more right to me in that moment. I wanted to destroy the evidence and the story about myself that I hated. If these photos didn't exist, neither did the nights when they were taken. Kelly Xu would never have to know. And I could forget.

Sarah looked interested.

"The boys?" said Juliet. "That's an option."

"The *pictures*."

She looked at me like I was simple. "Absolutely not," said Juliet. "We need them. I've told you what we're doing. I told you from the start. We're going after them. We're going to show them what they've done. They need to be fucking punished."

"No," I said. "That's crazy. If we don't burn these pictures—we should take them to the police." Even as I said it, I couldn't imagine Chief Powell wrapping his mind around what these photographs showed. He called marijuana the "devil's salad" and wore a blond bowl cut that made him look like an overgrown child.

Sarah shook her head violently. "No," she said, "no, no one else sees these."

"They aren't just of you two," said Juliet. "You don't get to decide. There's other girls here, too. They can't say yes to us sharing these pictures with the police. And what if they don't want to know? Don't want others to know, like Sarah here? Besides, it's not like the police would help, not really. You know that."

Juliet wasn't wrong about the police. It was a small town, and if you hadn't noticed that people with money and connections were treated differently than people without, then you weren't paying attention. There were kids at my school who should have been issued DUIs or possession charges but weren't because the officer recognized their name and knew their parents. Kelly Costa's brother had once been tossed in the drunk tank for impaired driving and was looking at a license suspension or worse. But then Costa's mother—the scourge of the PTA—had descended on the police station in a cloud of self-righteousness and threats, and before anyone knew what had happened, Chief Powell was somehow apologizing to her for throwing her son in lockup.

Costa's mother was terrifying, honestly, in a way that you couldn't help but admire. Kelly Costa got a lot of her personality from her. In another time and place, they'd probably have ruled an Italian city-state.

But Richard's family was the richest in town. They'd get a lawyer out of Atlanta immediately and before we knew it, we'd be the ones in trouble somehow.

The pictures were gross, but I could already think of things the guys would say to explain them. Worse, I knew the ways the adults would excuse them. *They were such promising young men, really, and what had all these girls been doing to end up in those photographs in the first place? Why were they at a boy's house alone? What were they wearing?*

Sarah nodded, and I couldn't help but agree. Juliet was right.

I'd mostly been thinking about Kelly Xu, but the other girls . . . I hadn't thought about them. The two of us couldn't decide for them what to do about the photographs.

But I don't know why I never questioned why Juliet could.

"What do you want to do?" Sarah asked Juliet.

"I want to hit them. I want them to suffer. I want them to hurt." Juliet said all this calmly, like listing activities for a summer day. Juliet had goals.

Sarah looked shocked but also like she'd go with whatever strong wind swept her along. It was up to me to say the reasonable, rational thing.

"That's crazy," I said. I shook my head. "I understand what you're saying, but there's no way we're doing that. I'm not going to hit someone."

I looked at Sarah and willed her to agree with me. Slowly, she nodded.

There was a beat while Juliet registered our rebellion. Then, she smiled, all sunshine. "Okay, I hear you. That makes sense."

I held her gaze, not believing her.

"It's fine, silly," she said. "Finish your breakfast and we'll figure out the day." *I won't be rash*, she was saying. *I am listening.*

I believed her.

THE BOAT

The day was pure summer, warm and lazy, and like all summer days was over far too soon. I called my dad to confirm I'd stay one more night, but he didn't pick up. Replacing the phone in its cradle, I had a brief flash of worry. What if he'd drunk so much he'd fallen? He'd never been a stumble-around drunk, but that could change. What if right now he was bleeding out on the kitchen floor?

Then a sour thought came along to displace that one: Serves him right.

I joined Juliet and Sarah out on the deck that wrapped around the back of the house. It looked out over the lake, now impossible to distinguish from the night sky. I could just make out the dock below extending from the property out onto the water, and the small, elegant boat tied to it, reflecting the house lights off its glossy surface.

"You want to take a ride?" Juliet said.

Of course we did. Growing up near a lake, you get to know

boats whether you own one or not. There are the pontoon boats, low slung and slow, and canoes with their hard metal seats. You recognized the motorboats of the visiting families with money, all oversize and accessorized like SUVs, cream-colored pleather seats and fake wood burl. They thrummed along the water like fat, imperious swans. You could clock a townie boat, always a ramshackle affair, puttering, smoking, and held together with zip ties and hope.

My folks didn't own a boat, but once or twice every summer we'd borrow the neighbor's canoe and paddle around until we were tired, sunburned, and a little cross. The neighbor—Mrs. Albertalli—kept the life jackets outside in a derelict shed frequented by a family of skunks, and I always felt like a brown recluse spider was going to crawl out of the folds of the vest and bite me in the middle of the lake. But other than that, it was a great time. 10/10.

The boat tied to the dock outside Galaxy House was like nothing I'd ever seen. It was a four-seater, two buckets in the front and a bench in the back, and the cockpit was front forward, nearly at the bow. The body looked like it was carved from a single piece of honey-colored wood—even in the low light I could tell the wood was real, polished to an expensive gleam.

It looked like a javelin, ready to be thrown.

"Hop in," said Juliet. "I'll push us off."

There were no life vests visible. They were no doubt hidden behind a cunningly disguised panel, but Juliet didn't offer, and we didn't ask. Sarah looked a little sick at this flouting of protocol; we'd both had water safety drilled into us from a young age. Just standing on the deck without a vest felt transgressive.

I gave Sarah the front seat next to Juliet. I didn't want to. I wanted to be near Juliet. If I let myself, I could feel her weight straddling me again, her fingers on my cheek as she applied the eyeliner. Whenever I thought about it, I pulsed from head to toe. But I didn't know what to do with that feeling. I was grateful for the darkness, for the cooling air against my burning cheeks. Still, when Sarah took the seat, I was jealous. Juliet untied the boat, pushed us off, and then clambered in beside Sarah. I wanted to kick Sarah's seat.

Yeah, I was doing just fine.

Juliet turned the engine over and the boat started. It was not a putterer or a thrummer. It purred, stretched, and then leapt. We were in the center of the lake before I knew it, having zipped around some of the small islands that had grown up over the years around fallen trees and debris. The lake stretched out around us infinitely; I could barely make out the lights of Galaxy House behind us.

For a moment after Juliet killed the engine, we just breathed and listened. The silence of the night minus the engine's noise felt heavy. Then slowly, little signs of life made their way to our ears. Music from a party onshore drifted to us, the high notes skipping across the water. A fish splashed against the surface, disturbing the faint hum and buzz of cicadas.

Juliet stood up in the boat, which swayed, then righted easily.

"Let's swim," she said. Her face was hard to see by moonlight. Was she smiling?

I felt uneasy. There was a correct response here and I didn't know what it was.

Sarah shrank. "I didn't bring my swimsuit. I didn't know—"

"You see anybody?" said Juliet. Quickly and assuredly, she peeled off her clothes and tossed them into the boat. She dove naked from the boat, and we swayed in her exit.

Sarah whimpered audibly. Juliet surfaced and heard it, and I could just make out her lip as it curled. If there was some kind of accounting happening here, Sarah was definitely in the red.

That was all I needed. I stood up. Under my unsteady feet, the boat swayed. I clumsily shucked off my top and jeans, then my bra and underwear.

I took a deep breath, closed my eyes, and stepped off the edge of the boat.

Even in the center of the lake, the first three feet of water were warm and lovely, like a bath. It was summer, after all, and the top layers were heated day after day by the sun. But jumping in took me well past that comfort into the cold center. The water tightened around me like an icy fist. For what felt like forever I was clenched in its grip, then came to my senses, kicking up and breaking through.

"Fuck! That's cold!" I yelled. I could hear Sarah sniffling in the boat, and Juliet's scorn for her washed over into me. Sometimes Sarah was so mousy.

Treading water a few feet away, Juliet laughed. "What's that they say? Colder than a witch's left teat?"

"It's tit," I chattered. "And yeah, just the left one. The right one's where she keeps her heat."

I could hear scuffling in the boat, and then Sarah stood, naked, her arms trying to block her breasts and crotch from view.

"Ain't nothing there I haven't seen before," said Juliet. "C'mon, girl, get in. The water's—"

"Fucking terrible," I finished, laughing. Even Sarah laughed then, forgetting her modesty, and leapt into the lake.

She came up with a scream, then laughed and gasped, pushing away the brown strands of hair that had gathered like a net on her face.

"There you are!" said Juliet. "That's the girl I wanted to meet."

We chatted for a while, then fell quiet. We took to feeling the water and listening to what came our way. After a while, I floated on my back and went quiet. Back in the warm top currents, I'd mostly stopped shivering. The mumble of Juliet and Sarah talking carried through the water, just barely. In the clear sky above us, I could make out the smoky Milky Way, dotted with brighter stars. There are some advantages to living in the sticks; we didn't have the light pollution you find in bigger cities.

My mother and I had counted stars together. It probably started as a game to keep me busy as a child, but we'd kept it up. When she got sick, I'd walk around the hospital parking lot, trying to make out the stars against the glare of the hospital's lights. It was soothing. I had this crazy idea—there's a lot of magical thinking when someone is really sick—if I could just count enough of them, it would save her somehow. I tried to mentally divide the sky into quadrants, to make the task doable. But every night the stars shifted, because nothing stays still. My mother was gone, and the stars were always dead light anyway.

I closed my eyes against that memory until I was just floating in space. In the dark lake, I didn't have to be anyone, much less me.

Not being me felt amazing.

Through the water's muffle, I heard Sarah yell.

I lifted my head. I'd drifted about twenty feet away from them. Juliet was back in the boat, laughing and pulling her shirt on. Sarah was at the side of the boat, rocking it, trying to pull herself up and failing.

At first, it just looked funny. I thought Juliet was playing a joke. But Sarah was crying and yelling, her voice teetering on the edge of hysteria.

"What's going on?" I said.

"I can't get up! She won't let me get up!" cried Sarah.

Juliet sat in the driver's seat and rested her hand on the wheel. She wasn't laughing anymore. She was watching Sarah's panic with cool interest.

"Calm down, Sarah, Jesus," I said, rolling my eyes for Juliet's benefit, even though she couldn't see them in the dark. I closed the distance and came alongside the boat. I tried to hoist myself, but the boat didn't have a ladder. I tried to scissor kick myself up but couldn't get the height. The boat rocked and slipped under my hands, and Juliet began to laugh again, harder this time.

It was ridiculous and frustrating, and I kept trying, sure I'd be able to do it. But I couldn't, and some of Sarah's panic began to expand inside me, a slowly inflating balloon.

"There's a trick to it," Juliet said.

We released the boat and waited to be told what to do, docile idiots bobbing in the water, embarrassed and relieved. We'd started to get a feel for her. She liked to test us, that much was clear. This was another test. She'd scare us, and then she'd relent.

"The trick is, don't get out of the boat. The house is that way." She pointed south, where I could barely make out the light-filled windows of Galaxy House.

And with that, she turned the key and the boat purred awake.

"What the fuck are you doing!" I yelled. "This isn't funny. Help us get up."

"Swim hard," she said cheerfully.

She waved, the boat thrummed with power, and she was gone.

SWIM

I cried first.

You'd think it would have been Sarah, but no, it was me.

I believed Juliet would turn the boat around. She had to. We were having a sleepover. We should have been sitting in front of a scary movie with popcorn, for god's sake. We were supposed to laugh like girls on TV do, big smiles, sharing crushes and sneaking beers.

Not treading lake water in the pitch black.

But the dark outline of the boat kept shrinking, then disappeared.

She wasn't coming back.

All we could do was save ourselves.

So, I cried. Because when in my experience had "saving yourself" worked out? My mother wasn't able to. My father couldn't or wouldn't. I hadn't been doing a bang-up job of it. Hell, I'd done the opposite.

Crying and swimming at the same time isn't easy. I tried to

stop, but only sobbed harder. It was all I could do to keep my head above the water. There was a weight inside me pulling me down. She's left you. She's left you, you fucking idiot.

"We need to swim," said Sarah. "Seriously, Rabbit, we've got to go. We're going to get too tired." Sarah's voice was as quiet as ever, but urgent. She was pleading with me.

"I'm already too tired," I said. "This is insane. She has to come back."

"She's not coming back. Come on, let's go," she said, and turned to face the distant shore.

Someone had to lead, and it was her, so I followed. I guess all it took for Sarah to grow a spine was for me to lose mine.

We swam. We swam freestyle, we swam sidestroke, we backstroked and dog-paddled. I hurt all over. My arms and shoulders were the worst, but my legs were useless weights dragging behind me. I had stitches running up both sides, and my lungs burned. I had never been a strong swimmer, had never been one of the kids who took to water like it was air and made it look so effortless. I'd hated the athletic kids and I'd hated my body.

Now my body was going to kill me.

But I didn't die, and time got weird. Sometimes I felt like we were almost to the shore, and other times it stretched farther away. We started to fall into a rhythm. Every time I surfaced, I looked for the back of Sarah's head, smooth and wet like a surfacing seal, took a breath, and went back to it. As long as I saw her, I knew we were both still trying.

Slowly, the panic receded. This was work, and work could be done. The weight that was pulling me down lessened, then let loose.

I laughed when my feet finally brushed the mucky bottom of the lake. Sarah put her arm around me to pull me to my feet, and together we staggered onto the sand, every last grain of which had been imported to give rich vacationers the sense that they were at a real beach, not in Georgia.

Once out of the water, I fell to my knees, and Sarah sat down heavily beside me. We both spreadeagled onto our backs, our jagged breathing synchronized.

Juliet appeared above us, hands on her knees, looking down. She was dressed again. Hell, she looked like she'd showered. Her face was in shadow. Her wet curls looked silver in the moonlight.

"I knew you could do it," she said.

That's when Sarah lost it.

Sarah leapt up and lunged at Juliet in a spray of leaves and sand, but Juliet slid away, laughing. Sarah yelled, then wildly barreled into Juliet, knocking her to the ground. For a moment, all I could see was their two bodies grappling, Juliet clothed, Sarah naked. Juliet was laughing, as if this was a funny game. Sarah was growling, not even using words, clawing, and hitting.

But even on her back, Juliet had no trouble fielding Sarah's attacks. Eventually, as if Juliet had been letting a toddler tire herself out with a tantrum, she swung her leg around to shift herself on top of Sarah and pinned her to the ground. It was an efficient, almost professional move. Sarah tried to free herself but couldn't.

"There. I knew you could do it! I knew you could! That's some good energy," said Juliet. "But you know why you can't beat me?"

"Because you're bigger and stronger," I spat out. Sarah was still struggling fruitlessly. I tried to stand—I don't know what I thought I was going to do—but I fell back down to the sand. My limbs were useless.

"That helps," she said. I could hear the grin in her voice, even if I could only make out the shape of her head. "But no. The difference is I know what I'm doing, and you don't."

"Well, thanks for making that clear to us," I said bitterly. "This has been a really illuminating night. We're so thankful for this educational experience. Best sleepover ever."

Sarah stopped struggling and started to weep.

"Let me teach you," said Juliet.

"What?"

"Let me teach you how to fight," she said to Sarah. "Your whole life you've been small and weak and sitting on the sidelines. You go to school, you follow the rules, you do everything you're supposed to—and what? Does anybody notice how damn good you are? Do they know how hard it is to be perfect? For parents who don't care what *you* want?"

Sarah stopped crying, the tears and snot shining on her face. I struggled to a sitting position to listen.

Juliet turned to me. "And you, Rabbit? Where's your gold

star? Where's the parade for the good girls who stay quiet? There isn't one. There is no reward coming. Richard stalked you for months and no one cared. He'd do the same to you, Sarah. And those pictures—no one stops them. No one steps in and says, 'Might isn't right.' That's not the world we're in. They say, 'Boys will be boys.' They say, 'Old enough to bleed, old enough to breed.' They call you jailbait, like your sole purpose is to trap them."

She released Sarah's wrists, but Sarah didn't move.

"People like Richard and his shitty friends take what they want. And it doesn't stop in high school, or college, or when you finally get the shitty desk job you've spent your whole life working for. Because then there's a Richard Cummings coworker, there's a Richard Cummings supervisor, Richard Cummings is the head of HR and Richard Cummings owns the goddamn company. You're not blessed because you're meek. That's just what you tell yourself when someone's got their boot on your neck. Don't you want to know what it would feel like to punch a Richard Cummings in the face?"

I thought about Richard's bloody face after Juliet had slugged him with the plastic tray. How stunned and stupid he'd looked, like a steer after the bolt gun fires.

Sarah pushed herself up on her elbows. Juliet was still straddling her and made no move to get off. But she reached forward and brushed Sarah's hair off her face. It looked like tenderness. It looked like possession.

"Yes," said Sarah.

Is that when Sarah stopped being Sarah? I don't know. Her voice sounded different. She wasn't so Disney princess anymore.

It's hard to look back and tell. Everything happened slowly, until it all happened very, very fast.

"That's my girl," said Juliet. She leaned forward and kissed Sarah's forehead solemnly and smiled. Then she rolled off Sarah and helped her up. Sarah's legs were still shaking from the swimming like a newborn colt's.

"And you?" Juliet said to me.

"I hate them. But I just want to graduate and get out of here. I want to go to college and forget this place," I said. "Nothing ever happens to guys like them."

She squatted down next to me.

"Don't you think something should?"

I looked at her, my mouth open to speak, but all I could do was nod.

She bent over me. Her hair was a curtain between us and the world. She smelled like expensive shampoo, and under that, spiced oranges, leather. The weak light from the moon disappeared and I was in the blue darkness with her. She kissed my forehead, just like she had Sarah's. It felt religious, and my eyes closed reflexively, as if God could see.

As she pulled away, she touched her index finger to my lips, like she was gently shushing me.

I felt her long after she'd pulled away.

I never stood a chance.

We walked back to the house together, Juliet in the center.

The wind picked up and whipped our hair. She was dressed and we were naked, but it didn't matter. We were in a space defined by moonlight and the pain of our exhausted bodies, of Juliet's strength and certainty. There could be no more secrets. All that mattered was our joined hands.

PROCURING SUPPLIES

The next day, Juliet said we needed supplies, and we didn't even ask her what for. We piled into her Camaro and drove to Walmart. After nearly drowning, fighting naked on the beach, and vowing to somehow wreak revenge on Richard and his friends, it was a welcome diversion. Once we were in the car and driving, it felt like all that ugliness and fear had happened to some other girls, some other day. We could have addressed the forced swim and the fight, I suppose. Juliet could have apologized, though the very idea makes me laugh. But we didn't talk about any of it. We just cruised down the road into the new normal. If you tell yourself your actions are in service to a greater cause, it doesn't matter much what you've done to each other.

The Walmart had opened about six years prior, and its impact was profound. Like a lot of small southern towns, Hart's Run centered around the courthouse building. You couldn't even drive straight through town without circling the square because of the one-way street signs, and there were any number of small businesses lining the way. But when the Walmart came in, there was less reason to go to Knickerbocker's shoe store or Elsie Dee's Sewing Shop. They were still there, but there was a ragged look to them as they struggled year after year to make it to the next.

I wish I could tell you that I thoughtfully supported the local businesses and avoided the mega-corporation. But I didn't really see the value in a sewing shop or understand why it might be important to have a druggist who knew you personally. Everything at Walmart was cheap and shiny and immediate. I loved it without reservation.

Those who live in bigger towns might find this a little hard to understand. But for me to even go to the movies was a forty-minute drive. My parents subscribed to *The New Yorker* and some other magazines that assured me there was life beyond our little town. I think my mother needed that reminder. I read about museum openings and restaurants that served asparagus and foie gras, about film festivals playing indie movies that would never stream on Netflix. I learned about play openings and ballet companies. It all sounded amazing and vibrant and utterly out of my reach. I'd close the magazine and I'd still be in my little town, hoping and praying for a Taco Bell. You know, real culture.

Walmart, God help me, was the closest glimpse I had of the world outside Hart's Run.

It was strange to see Juliet under the glaring fluorescents.

Her golden complexion looked washed out, and she seemed a little overwhelmed by the whole experience.

"There's . . . so . . . much . . . stuff," she said.

"Welcome to peak capitalism," I said. "Behold our wonders."

We picked up a cart, and Sarah and I dutifully nodded to Mrs. Plainsong, the elderly greeter who once gave me a toothbrush for Halloween instead of candy. A monster, basically.

Supplies, it turns out, meant cleaning agents. This was not what either Sarah or I expected, but there we were in the cleaning aisle with Juliet, surrounded by jewel-colored bottles that promised fresh breezes, spring meadows, and seaside waves.

We watched quizzically as Juliet loaded up the cart with all-purpose cleaner by the gallon, along with three sets of rubber gloves, two mops, three buckets, and a jumbo pack of microfiber towels.

"Juliet," said Sarah, "what—"

Juliet looked up. She was crouched down to read the bottles on the bottom shelves.

"Purple or blue?" she said.

"Purple," I said. "Purple is always the answer."

"Royalty," said Juliet. "Got it."

Sarah tried again. "Why are we—"

"It's to clean, obviously," said Juliet. She stood up with a jug of purple cleaner called the Purple Stuff. I liked the straightforward name. More things should just say what they are.

Sarah continued to look puzzled. I was also confused, but I'd decided to go along with it. We were starting to get interested stares from passersby. The cart was almost full of cleaning products, and Juliet had shoved a jumbo pack of paper towels up underneath it.

"To clean up the blood. After all the murder."

Sarah, adorably, gasped.

Juliet laughed. "You are such a sweet mouse, Sarah. It's for a little project I'm cooking up. With your help."

I shrugged. I could clean. It was hard to imagine Juliet doing so, however. Juliet's presence in Galaxy House troubled its magazine-ready surface. She didn't like washing dishes, even though there was a dishwasher, and her clothes had started spilling outside of her room. But sure, she was feeling domestic.

We also picked up a case of Clear American sparkling water (black cherry), a bottle of bug repellent so we could smell like lemons gone wrong, and cheap battery-powered desk fans.

"You, uh, starting a maid service?" said the checkout clerk, passing bottle after bottle over the scanner. I didn't know his name, but I faintly recognized him. He had been a senior when I was a freshman. Now he was another example of someone unable to break out of the gravitational pull of this collapsing town. There's nothing wrong with working at Walmart. I know that. But to never leave the town you grew up in? That was misery.

"Yeah," said Juliet. "One of the ones where we wear skimpy little outfits and cat ears."

Sarah flushed and actually covered her eyes. I tried and failed to keep a laugh from barking out of me.

The clerk—Chad? Chadly? Chadocracy?—took that image in stride.

"Cool," he said. "That's a good idea."

Juliet gave him a stern look. "Don't steal it."

He snorted and gave her the total. $251.45.

Good lord.

Juliet paid for everything with three hundred-dollar bills. I didn't mean to, but I did a double take when I saw them. Of course, I've seen a hundred-dollar bill before. But not that often, and not in the hands of kids my own age. Maybe I hung out with the wrong people, but everyone I knew used ApplePay these days.

Juliet gave me a little smirk, which I shyly returned. Money made me uncomfortable. I couldn't help but think of the unpaid bills in my house. Juliet's whimsical purchase was our utilities and phone bills, or one of the many laboratory bills for my mother's care that we continued to receive from the hospital, even now.

There was also something about the way Juliet handled her money that bothered me—first at the diner, now here—though I couldn't put my finger on why. She liked using the large bills, and she liked people's reactions to them. I got that she came from money, but I didn't see why she had to flash it around like she did.

In the parking lot, the sun was hot and merciless, and heat was already rising off the black asphalt. I squinted, looking for Juliet's car. Sarah pushed the cart, which wasn't easy since one of the wheels intermittently locked.

We unloaded it all into the trunk of the Camaro, and it barely fit. We rolled down the backseat window and let the mop handles dangle out.

Mission accomplished. We'd bought every bottle of Fabuloso in the state of Georgia.

"Here," said Juliet.

She handed me and Sarah each a pair of sunglasses from her pocket and put on a matching pair. All three were rose gold and oversized, like we were the aviators of a luxury plane.

"You didn't pay for those," I said stupidly. Sarah hesitated to put them on. Forbidden sunglasses.

"I did not," she said. "But if it makes you feel better, the markup on them is ridiculous and they were assembled by children."

"How is child labor supposed to make me feel better, exactly?"

"Don't you like them?" she said, sounding a little hurt. "I got them for you."

The problem was, I loved them. They were somehow both trashy and fancy at the same time, and I adored the fact that we all had matching ones. So, no, I didn't return them to Walmart. I was not a person of principle. I was a person who liked shiny things. Morally, I was a raccoon.

I nodded, and she beamed with pleasure.

I put them on, and we saw ourselves reflected back in her image. Golden and rosy and gorgeous. We peeled out across the heat-shimmering parking lot like discount goddesses. Nothing could slow our unstoppable beauty.

CABIN IN THE WOODS

Back at Galaxy House, Juliet was a cat with the cream, full of secrets. She refused to tell us what we were up to or where we were going, even as we loaded up plastic bags full of cleaning supplies onto our backs and under our arms. We followed her on foot away from the house, into the surrounding woods, a strange caravan of girls, buckets, and mops. Our path was abreast of the lake for a time, then deeper, farther into the trees. The more pine trees there were, the clearer the forest floor, save for clumps of tangled blackberry bushes, high-bush blueberries, honeysuckle vines, and fallen branches. The dropped needles made a springy rust-colored mat under our feet. The sun dappled the ground with warmth, and I felt my clothes begin to stick to me as we walked. The house was long gone, and without the lake line visible I started to feel more and more that I was in uncharted territory. After a time, I wondered whether I'd be able to find my way back alone.

"Here it is," she said triumphantly.

There was a weathered gray log cabin before us, its roof heavy with pine needles. The surrounding trees were thick and close and cast it in shadow. It looked like a witch's house, and we three were children who'd wandered off the path.

"It's a McCracken cabin," I said, suddenly realizing. "But bigger." The cabin looked the same age as the sanitarium cabins in the state park, but more spacious. That wasn't the only difference. The ones in the state park were maintained, their roofs patched, their wood treated to prevent decay. This one wasn't falling down, but repairs looked sporadic. Green moss carpeted the stone path leading to it and crept up the cabin's north-facing chimney.

My house would probably look like this in another year or two, once the kudzu had its way.

Juliet smiled.

"It's not just a McCracken cabin," she said. "It's *the* Mc-Cracken cabin. This was his. He had the largest, unsurprisingly."

"Wait, what do you mean?" I asked. I was confused. I'd seen the cabin that had belonged to Louie McCracken. All the school kids in our town took a tour in elementary school and learned about our town's famous crackpot. I'd seen his bed, neatly made with a diamond-patterned quilt. His desk, where he drafted his book, *Healing Waters*, was there, too, safe behind a velvet rope.

"The other ones are all real. But that one is a re-creation. They don't like to mention it, but McCracken didn't enjoy being too close to his patients. His was farther off. We're a good fifteen-minute hike from the other cabins."

"Wait, are we in the state park now?"

"Nope," said Juliet, happy to be the font of knowledge. "This is still Galaxy's property, though if you head east, you'll hit a park road. All the cabins were supposed to go to the state park when the government bought it. But the farmer who owned the land played fast and loose with property lines, and this one ended up cut out of the deal. Everyone thought he did it to take them for more money later—holding the crown jewel hostage. But nope. The farmer just kept it standing, made repairs, and every time the state park offered him money, he told them to go to hell. So finally he died, and my dad swooped in to buy this land and, bonus, the cabin of one Louie McCracken."

"And your dad didn't give it over to the state park."

"Nope," she said, pleased. This seemed to be an aspect of Jesse Bergman that she appreciated. "He outbid them, then he kept up the tradition of telling them to go fuck themselves."

The door was unlocked, but it took force to get it to swing open on the rusty hinges. The inside of the cabin was as gray as the outside, dimly lit by a south-facing window, grimed with years of dirt. Long-abandoned spiderwebs wafted in the newly moving air from the low, oppressive ceiling.

The cabin was a kitchen, a study, and a bedroom, all in one. There was a desk just like the one in the re-creation, sans the velvet rope. Any remaining papers had long since moldered away. There was only an empty wooden bed frame, and beside it a sizable wooden wardrobe with one door fallen to the ground, its interior empty and dark. In the kitchen area, the fireplace was full of old ashes, and hanging on the wall above it was a series of frying pans of graduating size, along with some other iron tools I couldn't quite identify—nineteenth-century toast sticks, probably. The tour I'd had of the other cabins, long ago, had stressed how the rich socialites who'd come for the McCracken cure had struggled to adjust to the lack of luxuries. McCracken practiced what he preached, apparently.

Juliet tossed her cleaning supplies to the floor and put her hands on her hips, looking resolute.

"Are we . . . going to clean the cabin?" I asked. I knew the answer, just as I knew that somewhere, a historian was swooning from disapproval, shock, and horror.

"We are," she said. "This is ours now. We're going to need it."

I didn't ask her why. I mentally pushed the horrified, protesting internal historian off a cliff, along with the saner version of myself who wanted to know what we needed the cabin for, exactly.

We spent the day cleaning. Even though we ran the battery-powered fans until they died, our shirts grew wet with sweat, and eventually we stripped down to our underclothes. I peeked at Juliet under my lashes as I worked. Sometimes when I looked, her eyes met mine, as if she was doing the same thing. Whenever that happened, I tucked my head down and scrubbed harder, as if I could cleanse my thoughts through good works.

The grime was incredible, and there was no water to aid us. Mostly we dusted and swept, using the rags to drag out years of dirt. By the end, it wasn't clean by a long shot, but it felt a little less like a horror movie set. I ached all over and sat down without thinking in a straw-caned chair. It held up under my weight despite the years; they knew how to build a chair back in the day.

Juliet grinned at me and sat down, then lay on her back on the freshly swept floor. I cringed at the thought of the dirt still there, now plastered to her sweaty back. Sarah sat down cross-legged beside her, looking wilted.

"Happy now that we've cleaned your clubhouse?"

"Oooh, a clubhouse! Yes, no boys allowed!" Sarah perked up enough to shake her almost empty bottle of generic multi-purpose cleaner in a festive fashion.

"Very. Now this is our space, just ours. And next time," said Juliet, "I'll bring water so we can do a better job."

"Wait," Sarah interjected, "we could have had water?"

"I thought this would be more of a team-building exercise if we didn't. Next time we'll do it better."

"But not right away," said Sarah. She looked as if an answer in the affirmative would break her.

"Not right away."

Sarah nodded at that. I didn't.

"I hate you." I found a stained rag near my hand and tossed it at her. "We've lost half our brain cells to huffing undiluted Pine-Sol."

"You smell great, though," said Juliet, and laughed. Sarah joined in, and eventually I did, too.

"God, McCracken was such a weirdo." I looked around. Though cleaner, the cabin was still disgusting, and still a dump. Once word got around about McCracken's water cure, the socialites had poured in, some for real health concerns and some because it had become fashionable. It gave them a good story to bring back to New York City. Despite making money hand over fist, McCracken hadn't done anything to improve his own living situation. What money he made, he'd poured back into his sanitariums, and by the time the fad ended, and the rich ladies stopped coming, he had no reserves. He died penniless, unable to leverage his fame into a cereal empire like his competitor, Kellogg. "Almost as weird as you."

"Well, sure," said Juliet from the floor, "but he believed. He was convinced he was doing the right thing."

"There was no water cure," Sarah said.

"No, but he thought there was."

"No," I said, "he made it up to ride the fitness craze. There are letters to his sister where he talks about it. It was a scam."

"Sure, in the beginning. But then he started to believe it himself. And that's when it really took off. You have to believe your own bullshit."

I laughed. "Okay, so he was a sincere weirdo."

"McCracken was a genius. He saw a bunch of people—mostly women—who had been ignored over and over by medicine and told it was all in their heads, and he offered them hope."

"But it wasn't real," Sarah said.

"It was," she said, "for a time. Because hope is powerful. Being seen is powerful. He gave them that. And in return, those ladies would have done anything for him. They worshiped him." She sounded admiring.

"Till they didn't," I said.

She shrugged. "There comes a time when you have to change course. You can't run the same con forever. He didn't get that."

Grimacing, I lay down on the floor next to her and was immediately enveloped in multiple layers of artificial lavender and "fresh breeze" scent. Sarah did the same, a little farther away from the two of us, her eyes shut with exhaustion. My skin crawled to feel the grit under my back, but I suffered through the disgust until it passed. It was worth the filth to feel my shoulder pressed against Juliet's. Every time she breathed, I was achingly attuned to the retreat and return of her body. The sweat on her freckled arms mingled with mine and evaporated in the heavy heat.

For a while, we were quiet together, listening to the blue jays cussing outside.

Then Juliet's hand brushed against my hip.

I thought it was accidental. But she slowly traced her fingers on my skin, then rested her hand lightly on the top of my thigh, impossible and exquisite. My breath caught and I pulsed in response. I almost wanted to push her away, to leave and never come back, to escape the intensity of her touch. Sarah was only a few feet away from us, could easily open her eyes and see.

"But if he believed it, was it a con?" Sarah asked.

Juliet's hand retreated, leaving me feeling like I'd imagined the whole thing.

"The best cons are the ones you run on yourself," said Juliet.

A CHARMING
DOMESTIC SCENE

"**H**ungry?" asked my dad from the kitchen when I finally came home from Juliet's. If he noticed my new haircut, he didn't show it. He was standing over the stove, sautéing onions. He had a kitchen towel thrown over one shoulder like a pictorial for *Dad Cooking* magazine. My dad was slender but was starting to get a little bit of a paunch. Probably the booze. He favored plaid shirts and jeans that were a little too big; he was the kind of guy who a makeover show would love to get ahold of. Just some basic grooming, a new suit, and an addiction recovery program, and you'd have a handsome guy.

What I couldn't understand was why Dad Cooking was happening. The kitchen looked fractionally tidier. There were some grocery bags from Ingles folded on the counter. Ingles was the nicer of the two grocery stores in town; the Walmart's grocery section was all wilted lettuce and floppy cucumbers. I wondered if he paid for his groceries with his credit card. They'd been sending notices, too.

"I could eat," I said cautiously. A home-cooked meal did sound good. I felt like I was made of pizza, pancakes, and coffee, the three food groups at Juliet's.

"I made my special sauce," he said.

My dad's special sauce wasn't actually special. It was jarred pasta sauce that he doctored with onion and sausage, and if he was feeling really fancy, some fresh herbs at the end. It tasted like home, though, our home, and I liked it a lot. It wasn't much effort, but it was an effort, and that was something I hadn't seen much in our house for a while.

"Great," I said. I put my house keys on the table by the door and hung up my bag on its hook. The hook was relatively new. When my mother got her diagnosis, she started cleaning and ordering the house. She still had energy then. She read multiple books on organization and household management. It turns out there are tons of these, all with covers of sun-dappled white kitchens and moms holding up freshly baked pie and not dying of cancer.

Our house had always been comfortably messy due to the way my mother had five to six craft projects in progress at any given time, my father's habit of leaving books open wherever he went, and my own inability to put things away after I was done using them. Post diagnosis, it became organized and neat. It wasn't a bad thing, really. It was nice to know where my keys were every morning. I liked the alphabetized bookshelves, too.

Cleaning the kitchen at night did make for a nicer morning. But I couldn't shake the feeling she was getting things ready for her departure. I missed seeing a pile of embroidery hoops in the kitchen or finding a stack of quilting squares tucked between couch cushions. I missed the evidence of her presence.

For a few weeks after she died, I'd still come across a stray crochet hook or a hoop, and for a moment, she'd be there in front of me again, puzzling over a dropped stitch, a pattern booklet open on her knee like a treasure map. When she worked on her crafts, she twisted her hair into a messy topknot, which made her look younger. In the last year of her life, she'd started wearing readers while she worked. Every time she put them on, she'd laugh at herself, and tell me aging was ridiculous.

Whenever I found a scrap of her, my father would take it and return it to her crafting room.

It had been over a year, and she was almost tidied away.

I frowned and opened the fridge. Actual groceries.

"How've you been?" asked my dad. He tried to keep his tone neutral as he ladled the special sauce onto bowls of spaghetti, but I could tell he was curious. Maybe he'd noticed the hair after all. I took a seat at the kitchen table after putting out the water glasses.

"Good," I said. *Been going to parties, breaking into buildings, stealing illicit photos, and oh—my new friend tried to drown me but I'm sort of okay with it? Oh, and we're going to beat up my ex-boyfriend, the one you didn't notice stalking me. And his friends. They suck, too.*

Typical teen stuff.

"Shaky cheese?" asked my dad, offering me a green canister.

"All of it," I said, and shook a mountain on top of my spaghetti. I liked to watch it turn from powdery white to oily orange.

For a little while, we just ate in silence. I didn't know how to do dinner conversation without my mother. I didn't know how to do it with this version of my father, who hadn't shown up like this for months.

"Sadie, I wanted to talk to you about something," he said. He was looking at his pasta remnants like they'd just become very interesting, pushing them around on his plate.

I stopped eating and took a swallow of water. My dad had his "serious talk" voice, and that was never good. He never called me by my real name, either.

"I'm still going to Group," I lied.

"Good, good. But it's not about that."

My dad's face was a weird combination of scared and hopeful, which was not an expression I'd seen for a long time. Not since we'd gotten the diagnosis.

My mouth went dry. I did not want to know what this was about.

"I've been talking a lot with—with Sheila."

"Sheila, my group therapist Sheila?"

"Right," said my dad, then paused and licked his lips. My blank face was making him nervous, and I didn't do anything to ease that. "So, we've been talking a lot—at first about your care—just that you were okay!—but then, you know, she's lost someone, too . . ."

"I do know. That's why she leads my grief group. The one where I receive substandard therapeutic care."

"We talked about that—Sheila's going to step away from that, if— I just want to know—"

"You want to date her," I said. I looked away. I'd known dating might happen eventually, but I didn't think it likely when he was so hell-bent on pickling himself. And not with my pseudo-counselor.

I pushed the idea away like a box full of maggots.

"I—well, we're already dating, actually," he said. I carefully lowered my fork to the plate. "Only for a little while! Not even a few weeks. Nothing serious. Just getting coffee. I didn't want to say anything because I didn't know if—but I'm thinking this has potential, but only if—only if you're okay with it."

There was a long silence during which I stabbed some sausage and chewed it to a paste.

Unbelievable. For months he'd been a gin-soaked ghost haunting the house. And what gets him to clean up and make dinner? The hope of getting laid.

"I'm okay with it," I said. "It's been *ever* so long. Mom would want you to move on." I gave him a smile that was mostly sneer.

"I'm not—I'm not moving on, sweetie. Your mom is always with me," he said. He put his hand to his heart.

That move really irritated me.

"It's fine," I said. "It's great. I hope you're very happy together."

"Well, I don't know if—"

"Maybe you can have a little baby. Start over. Like it never happened," I said, my voice falsely cheerful.

He stared at me, his eyes wide.

I hated seeing the hurt on his face, knowing I put it there, knowing he was still so vulnerable to it.

But what was pain for if it wasn't going to make us harder? Some of us didn't have the luxury of shutting down, much less falling in love.

I picked up our empty dishes and put them in the dishwasher, because that was what my mother would have wanted. Then I left him at the table.

Everything in its place.

MONTAGE THEORY

My favorite movies always have a montage. Whenever my family and I watched movies together—back when we were a family—we'd raise our arms together and yell "Montage!" the second one started. Montages are magic. A scrappy street fighter transforms into a heavyweight champion via shadow boxing, jogging, and hitting a bag over and over. A naive World War I recruit hardens into a bitter, wounded soldier through a series of closeups on his face. Every explosion, every death, leaves his eyes more haunted. Small actions build into something larger.

The same thing happens with friendships. Give us a few scenes of two people laughing over a joke we can't hear, sharing a bowl of chips, walking through a park, and we will understand they are becoming friends. We know the signs.

This visual shorthand conveys so much. Time can be compressed and sped up.

But when you're in those moments, you don't recognize them.

You can't step outside of yourself and say, *Here is the moment where I knew we were friends.* You don't notice the moments stacking one on top of the other to build something greater.

The truth is, I don't know how we three became friends. It felt instantaneous. I didn't question how fast things went. Juliet had decided we were going to be friends. So, we were. It wasn't something I could argue with.

The thing to remember, though, is that a montage is a crafted thing. Someone makes decisions about what goes in, and what's left out. The same footage can be cut and reordered in so many ways to tell the story you need.

When it comes to memory, you're your own editor. You can take the pieces of your life and fashion them into a new story, one where you are the victim, the hero, the misunderstood genius. Or the unloved, the fuckup, the villain.

What story do you need?

It's your choice. And who's to say that's not how things were?

THE GOOD TIMES

"**J**ust hit it. It doesn't matter how good of a job you do yet, just hit it," said Juliet. It was a few days after the boat incident, and we were in the Galaxy House gym, where we'd be spending most of our free time together in the coming month.

"Yet?" I said.

"First, we start small. We learn to defend ourselves. Then we overthrow the patriarchy," she said cheerfully. Just like that.

According to Juliet, the first thing we needed to work on was our endurance. We'd started with jumping jacks, pretended to skip an invisible rope, and punched at the air repeatedly. In addition, we'd established that I could barely do a push-up, I *really* couldn't do pull-ups, and I was not secretly a great boxer. It was hilarious. Sarah and I giggled at the silliness of it all, and Juliet had even joined in.

None of it seemed very serious, and it was important that it didn't. We knew Juliet wanted to teach us how to fight, and we knew we wanted to punish Richard and his friends. But if Sarah and I had really considered the intersection of those two ideas, we might have realized it was insane. We might have stopped. And we didn't want to stop, not really.

Besides, since the forced night of swimming, both Sarah and I had moved like old women. Juliet's exercises, although awful to start with, eased the pain. The more we moved under her instructions, the looser our limbs were.

Juliet was holding a red padded mitt straight out with one arm, the other tucked behind her back, her legs planted like tree roots. Sarah was facing her, knees slightly bent, her left foot forward and her right behind. It was supposed to be a stable way to stand, according to Juliet, but Sarah still wobbled. She managed to keep her fists in front of her face, but no matter how Juliet coaxed her, Sarah wouldn't move them any farther.

Behind her fists, Sarah's lip trembled. She'd been weepy all day. She'd broken up with Richard, finally, unable to stand his touch after seeing the pictures. She was better off without him, but she still cried. He didn't call her incessantly like he did after he and I broke up, which I perversely took a strange pride in, as if his obsession had been a testament to my irresistible beauty.

I'm aware how screwed up that is.

"Oh, come on, cupcake. It's just a little punch," Juliet cajoled. Her patience, never abundant, was fading. "It's not going to bite you."

"Shouldn't we be wearing big pillowy gloves?" I asked. I

wanted to break the tension, just a little, to remind us we were doing something fun.

"You're hitting mitts," said Juliet. "They give. Besides, you won't be wearing gloves when it's for real."

At this, Sarah's eyes widened.

"Look," said Juliet, in a tone both stern and understanding, "I just want you to throw a punch so we can make sure you won't break your hand, okay? Just *try* so we can move on."

Sarah let out a nervous, strangled sound. She raised her hands even higher, completely hiding her face.

"Talking about hand breaking isn't helping," I said softly. I was trying to keep it light, but I did feel a little like Sarah might have a breakdown before our very eyes.

"I'm telling her the truth," said Juliet defensively. She looked at me until I looked away. Then she softened. "Come on, Sarah. Just one punch. I'm trying to take care of you. I want to make sure you don't get hurt."

She gave Sarah's shoulder a squeeze, like a big sister. She felt like that sometimes, older, wiser, helping us to survive.

"I—I can't," said Sarah. "This is so dumb, but I can't. I feel stupid." Sarah stepped away from Juliet and the mitt apologetically. She laughed nervously, trying to make it okay.

It wasn't. Juliet's face took on a cool expression, and her big-sister energy evaporated. When Juliet was warm, it felt like stretching out in a patch of sunlight. When she withdrew that warmth, the contrast felt like nuclear winter.

She looked at me speculatively. "You're up?"

"Sure," I said, though I felt nothing like it. I knew, however, that I didn't want to be on the receiving end of the same disappointment she'd leveled at Sarah.

I tried to assume the same stance Sarah had, and I was pretty sure I looked even worse. Sarah was more graceful than I was, quicker to catch on. Whether that was because of her years of dance training, or because I piloted my body like an automaton, who's to say.

"No, no, that's not it," said Juliet. She dropped the pad and stood behind me, then grabbed my right thigh in her hands and pushed my leg out. "Distribute your weight."

At her touch, my eyes fluttered and an electric warmth spread up my thigh. *Oh, stop, stop, stop*, I told myself. She released me, and I could breathe again.

My adjusted stance felt weird, but maybe not as stupid. I still felt where her hand had pressed, like she'd left behind a mark.

"There you go. Now, what I mostly want you to do is be ready to move. You don't need to bob and weave or any of that fancy stuff. Whatever happens, you keep standing."

Out of nowhere, Juliet shoved me. I caught myself from falling and glared. Pushing me felt like a cheap move, like a schoolyard prank.

"There you go. Some people take a long time to recover like that. You're a natural," she said, and gave me a radiant smile.

Unwillingly, I felt myself glow. Goddamn it, I thought. There's no need to be this delighted with nothing.

Sarah had sat down on the mat a little ways off, and she

pulled her legs in close at Juliet's praise of me.

I felt bad for her, but not very. It just made me want to do even better. Maybe if I got good enough, Sarah would decide this wasn't for her and I'd have Juliet's attention all to myself. I mentally went through the checklist of things Juliet had told us as she'd demonstrated a punch. The hips were involved. The jab was quick. Don't throw your weight behind it or you'll be off balance. It was a lot to run through; trying to keep it straight in my head was overwhelming. It had been easier when we were just jabbing at the air.

Juliet held up the padded mitt again with a crisp wrist flick.

I didn't move.

Oh god, I was going to freeze up, just like Sarah. What the hell was my problem?

"One hit," said Juliet softly. "Show me what you've got in there."

I've got a black hole, I thought. That's all I've got.

Did my fist snap forward, darting quick like a snake's strike? Did I hit the pad and win Juliet's approval?

Did I discover that inside me all along, there'd been something graceful and deadly and ready to be free?

Nope.

I punched with my whole body, and barely clipped the mitt. I tried to follow my own fist to the ground and caught myself gracelessly. I made a sound like a cow stuck in barbed wire.

"Congratulations," said Juliet, "that was pathetic. But it was still a punch."

We smiled at each other, and I felt bathed in her good graces.

This was the first time we trained, and for the next four weeks we'd meet every day we could, and Juliet would run us through the paces. Most days, you'd find me cursing and wheezing, trying to keep up. But eventually, I did a little better, breathed easier as we jumped rope, skipped, held planks, and did mountain climbers. Jumping jacks and burpees and squats. Running in circles around the room. I never found any of it easy, but there was progress. I finally managed real push-ups, which were embarrassingly hard for me and so felt like a triumph.

We developed a routine. After conditioning, we drilled on the bags. The first sessions left my hands feeling bruised, my arms and shoulders so sore I'd want to cry lifting a jug of milk. I learned to keep my wrists straight, to twist with the hips as I punched for greater power. My jab was adequate, my cross a travesty, but I improved. I loved the sneaky hook and the sudden uppercut. Imagine all this scored to something kickass, and a little cheesy, like Imagine Dragons.

When we weren't punching, we were kicking. Balance and strength are almost the same thing, so it wasn't so much whether we could kick, but whether we could do so without falling down, or without someone knocking our supporting leg out from under us.

Real power wasn't in keeping still like a rock. It was motion that gave us mastery. If I wanted to keep upright, I had to learn to shift and adapt. Sarah was ultimately better than me, but I didn't hate her for it. Instead, I was happy for her, which was weird in itself. Since we'd started training, I'd felt like some-thing was opening up inside me. A little more generosity for her, for myself. I'd spent so much time wandering around in my head—it was a relief to concentrate on my body.

And my body was amazing! By the end of the month, I could run faster, I could jump higher, I could lift and toss medicine balls. I'd thought I was small, but I filled out. My arms weren't soft anymore. My leg muscles showed when I flexed. I'd catch my reflection in one of the mirrors lining the walls and almost stop what I was doing. Who was that girl? She couldn't be me. She looked like the main character.

Those were the good days. The days when I felt everything was possible and could still ignore why we were doing what we were doing, what exactly we were training for.

Those are the days I want to remember. Those are the scenes I keep in my montage.

ESTABLISHING SHOTS

The opening scene of Coppola's *The Conversation* is a three-minute-long take that just blows your mind when you realize there's no CGI stitching it together. With excruciating slowness, Coppola zooms in on the establishing shot of a San Francisco city square to focus on a mime. The mime's silent act is unsettling compared to the rising sounds of people talking and street musicians, not to mention that a mime is a form of clown and clowns are the devil's entertainers. And then there it is—a little bit of electronic noise, like a glitch in the sound. The first time you hear it, you think it's an error—even though you know Coppola doesn't make errors. Then a little while later it happens again, and then again. By the time the camera finds Gene Hackman, looking schlubby and doing surveillance work on a young couple in the crowd, you're well prepared for a movie that's all about watching and listening.

It's also a movie about thinking you know the story, and then realizing you've had it totally wrong from the start. I love a film with a twist.

So let's borrow from Coppola here and start with a wide angle of Hart's Run's annual July Fourth fair. The town square was much smaller than a San Francisco block, but the people milling around, chatting, eating, and listening to music are interchangeable. The fair was one of the town's most beloved events; there was a picture of the fair organizers from every year dating back to the '40s in the chamber of commerce building. As we slowly zoom in, notice the tables surrounding the courthouse, each one decorated with red, white, and blue tablecloths, streamers, and handmade signs. There was the 4H club, the Boy and the Girl Scouts, the Daughters of the American Revolution (creepy), the horticulture club, Kiwanis and Key Club, Friends of the Library, and about fifteen tables representing various churches, because that's as many as would fit. There was also a guy passing out flyers about chemtrails, and on the opposite side of the square, a lady wearing a sandwich board with a picture of the Twin Towers on one side and "Jet fuel can't burn steel beams" on the other. The conspiracy theorists in our town were very plane-focused. Add a few food trucks and kids running around with American flags and sparklers, and you're just about ready to focus in on Juliet, Sarah, and me, doing some surveillance work.

Or at least, that's what we said we were doing, assuming that Richard, Caleb, and Duncan would make an appearance. Mostly, we were goofing off. June had slipped away, and while

Sarah and I were more assured in our bodies, we were also getting a little sick of the whole training project. It didn't seem particularly real. We were teenagers, not soldiers, and though we liked the abstract idea of messing up Richard's face, the work to get there was repetitive and slow. Juliet wasn't oblivious to our burnout; when we mentioned the fair to her, she immediately said we should go, and the three of us met in the square on Saturday afternoon, after the passing of the parade kicking it off and before the local cover band started their set to close out the night.

The first thing we did was get our faces painted by Ms. Bardo, the middle school art teacher. She was wearing what she liked to call her "art uniform"—a forest-green jumpsuit, a teal scarf knotted around her hair twists, and multiple strands of a necklace that appeared to be made of hard candies. The colors changed, but the outfit components were always the same. She made a fuss over me and Sarah, called us her favorite students, gave Juliet a warm hello, and refused to charge any of us. We came out of her booth even cuter than we went in, if that's possible. We'd asked her for something matching but not too heavy, because I knew that in ten minutes, I'd be trying to scratch my face off if it was fully painted. After a little thought, she gave us a mischievous look and theatrically declared, "I see three queens before me! Three sisters ruling three kingdoms!"

With that, she painted a pink heart on both of Sarah's cheeks because "you're the loving one." On my cheeks, she painted blue clubs "for luck." I hadn't known clubs were clovers, but I could see it once she pointed it out. And on Juliet's cheeks, she painted red spades. Juliet frowned a little at this choice—she thought spades were for digging—but Ms. Bardo explained that spades represented pikes, or halberds, medieval weapons. Then Juliet was much happier.

We thanked her profusely, and she told us to "be good rulers," and gave us a curtsey before releasing us into the fair. Never change, Ms. Bardo.

"She's adorable," said Juliet.

"She is," I agreed. I was happy that Juliet recognized Ms. Bardo's specialness and that she got to see a little bit of what I liked about Hart's Run, when I let myself. It wasn't all bad; I could admit that when I wasn't actively trying to escape.

"And she got us right, too. We're sisters, and we're queens," she said. We were walking three abreast, and she bumped her shoulder into Sarah's, then mine. We bumped back and giggled.

"The only kingdom I want to rule is that of the funnel cake," I said. So even though it was a hot day, we got ourselves some sizzling dough with powdered sugar.

Juliet held hers gingerly in its thin cardboard tray and said, "Is there . . . a fork?"

"Use your hands," said Sarah, "like God intended." She broke off a piece of hers and popped it into her mouth, scattering powdered sugar down her front.

"This is a nightmare," grumbled Juliet, trying to extract a piece from the twisted mass of fried dough without getting powdered sugar everywhere. She failed.

"You live like an absolute goblin, and you can't handle sticky?" I wiggled my sugary fingers at her.

"It's not that. Some of us had etiquette lessons."

"Hard to believe," I said. She stuck her tongue out at me.

"Wait till we get some shaved ice. No spoons," Sarah said.

"What?!"

As usual, the city had blocked off the surrounding streets and brought in some carnival attractions. Moving from booth to booth, we tossed rings, we squeezed hippo-handled water guns at yellow duck targets (not sure of the narrative there), and we did not successfully convince any of the carnival workers to give us stuffed animals. It was incredibly fun, and we capped it off by sharing a bag of cotton candy, staining our fingers and tongues a vivid blue. Our engines ran entirely on sugar.

While we walked, Juliet quizzed us on Richard, Caleb, and Duncan. What were their families like, did they have siblings, what kinds of cars did they drive, how connected were they to the town, to the police? We answered as best we could. Sarah had picked up more than I had about Caleb and Duncan because she'd been in less of a depressive stupor when she'd been around them. She knew that they each had a sister, that they harbored dreams of being professional athletes, despite mostly mediocre performances on the field. She also noted that Duncan had a stepdad who sometimes roughed him up, but no one talked about it, a bit of news I promptly cast aside. I didn't particularly want to feel bad for Duncan, or consider what forces made him who he was. About Richard, we had much the same information: athletically gifted, adequate student, capable of inspiring easy adoration from most everyone he encountered. Richard had charisma; I had to give him that. We told her about his parents, who were the closest Hart's Run had to royalty, after Jesse Bergman. His father had made a killing before the dot-com bubble burst and still "consulted," whatever that meant, and his mother was involved in charities across the state—the kind of philanthropic work you can do when you don't have to work at all. Why they lived in a small place like Hart's Run was a mystery to me, but some people think small towns instill good values.

"All that money can't buy you class, according to my mother," said Sarah.

"How much do you think—" started Juliet, but Sarah interrupted her.

"Speak of the devils. Tweedledum and Tweedledee."

We followed her gaze and immediately saw who she meant. Caleb and Duncan were by the balloon pop booth, chatting up a girl who had just completed her dart throws.

"Look at them trying to pick up girls," said Sarah. "Creeps."

"She looks young," said Juliet quietly.

I sized her up. A freshman, maybe, if that. She was on the small side and her hair was in braids. I didn't know her.

The girl talked with them a little, then returned her darts and moved to leave the booth. Duncan stepped out and blocked her path. The guy running the booth paid no mind; he took another kid's money and handed them their darts.

Juliet immediately tensed and pushed the bag of cotton candy into my hands.

Oh shit. Whatever she was going to do, I was not ready for.

But just then an older girl stepped forward from the passing crowd and took the smaller girl by the arm. She had the same honey-colored hair as the girl with braids. An older sister who was none too pleased by the situation.

We couldn't hear what she said to Caleb and Duncan, but there was no mistaking her body language. She was angry and pointing her finger in their faces. The younger girl looked stunned and embarrassed, trying very hard to melt into the ground. Caleb and Duncan immediately put up their hands and stood down, looking as conciliatory as a couple of morons could. The two girls disappeared into the crowd, and Caleb and Duncan moved on, shaking their heads. *Bitches*, they seemed to be saying.

"'Sorry, lady, didn't know this was *your* underage sister,'" I said, putting new words in the boys' mouths. I couldn't help but try to make a joke to shake off the remaining tension of whatever had almost happened.

Sarah laughed, relieved.

Juliet smiled, then sobered. "Those guys are a menace. But we knew that."

I nodded and returned the cotton candy bag to her. I felt a little sick; too much sugar, too much heat. Now that the moment had passed, I realized I knew the older sister. Tamryn Fellows, whose sister was definitely in eighth grade at most.

We retreated from the crowd to find a bench in the shade. Sarah pulled some water bottles out of her bag and distributed them to us like a mother hen, clucking about heatstroke. Ms. Bardo was right about Sarah being the loving one. That's something I lost sight of, eventually.

We didn't say much for a time, just watched the crowds pass, the carnies calling out their rules and their prizes and the fantastic odds ever in our favor. One guy promised to show you the world's tiniest horse if you paid him two dollars. Three years ago, I'd paid, and he'd revealed to me a rather downtrodden miniature horse hidden in a small enclosure behind his gaily painted sign of a horse standing in a human palm. I'm not sure what I expected, but P. T. Barnum wasn't wrong. I had to respect the persistence of the grift; it couldn't be easy to separate kids from their money every day, every year. You get used to it, I supposed.

"We have to be like that sister," said Juliet.

"She was impressive," said Sarah. "I was terrified of her, and I wasn't even in trouble."

"Right," said Juliet. "A protector, a Valkyrie. But we have to be that sister for the girls who don't have one, or whose sisters aren't there."

I took a long swallow of water, then poured a little in my hand and splashed it on the back of my neck. It did nothing to cool me. I hadn't had a sister to watch out for me with Richard. I'd thought of Kelly Xu and Sarah as sisters, once upon a time, but Kelly had faded away and Sarah had been easy enough to alienate. I tried to imagine Juliet as an avenging angel stepping in between me and Richard, wielding a blazing sword and sweeping in on powerful wings, rescuing me on my front lawn, stomping his camera, talking me out of sleeping with him in the first place. But somehow I didn't see Juliet as preventing damage. She was more like the fixer in *Pulp Fiction*, the person you called to help you dispose of a body.

"And sisters to each other," said Sarah.

"That more than anything," said Juliet solemnly. "We keep each other's secrets. We keep each other safe."

"'Keep it secret, keep it safe,'" I intoned.

"Are you quoting *The Lord of the Rings* at me?" said Juliet.

"Scene six. Seven in the extended edition."

"You are a huge dork," said Juliet.

"It is known," Sarah drawled.

"Real sisters would accept me for who I am," I said pointedly.

"Fair point," said Juliet. "I accept you. In all your nerdy glory."

"That's all I ever wanted."

She smiled at me, and Sarah joined in, laughing, the three of us a matched set with our painted cheeks.

That was the last time I remember things among us making sense.

THE NOT-SO-GOOD TIMES

One night in mid-July, training in the gym, Sarah and I were goofing around, half wrestling, laughing. Whenever she'd get the upper hand, I'd tickle her, and she'd fall over laughing. Ever since we were kids, she'd been easily defeated this way. My mom would accuse me of trying to kill Sarah through giggling.

We'd been getting along, which is to say, I'd had fewer jealous thoughts, been less of a jerk, and had taken Juliet's words about sisterhood to heart.

But I suppose we weren't being serious enough for Juliet.

Juliet said, "Sarah, Rabbit, come over here." She was standing by the open area where we did our high-knee drills.

I had an odd sensation of being in trouble but not knowing why, like when the principal calls your name over the intercom. We stood side by side in front of her, curious, a little confused.

I don't know what caused it. Sometimes it seemed like the better things were among all three of us, the more likely Juliet was to try to stir things up.

Then things would slowly smooth out.

Then she'd disrupt them again.

But that couldn't have been right—she'd said we were sisters.

"Sarah, hit Rabbit," said Juliet.

Sarah gave Juliet a double take, as did I. For all we'd done—running, punching drills, even wrestling—we'd never hit each other. Juliet had said we weren't ready yet, and after a while, we forgot about the possibility.

"Like, *hit her* hit her?" said Sarah.

"Did I stutter?" said Juliet.

Sarah looked at me. She wasn't questioning Juliet, though. She was seeing if I was ready. The shift in energy felt jarring. We'd only just been playing together. It had felt friendly.

Now she looked at me as if I was a stranger.

Out of habit, we each assumed a wary stance, but then we both paused, not sure what to do next. Then Sarah advanced and I stood my ground. My hands were raised like I'd been taught, but when she jabbed, I didn't block. I just let it come, square on my cheekbone.

I'd led a lucky life. I'd had good parents until recently, and the bullying I'd experienced had mostly been mental.

Getting hit in the face was a whole new game. The bridge of her knuckles struck me like a hammer, and my head followed the blow, whipped to one side. I stayed standing, but I dropped my guard, instinctively cradling my face. My cheek and eye throbbed with heat, and whatever internal alarms my body had for injury cranked up to eleven.

I glared at Sarah. Once, she'd braided my hair. Once, we'd whispered to one another late at night, under the pale green light of my bedroom's ceiling stars.

"Fuck, that hurts!" I yelled.

"Of course it does," said Juliet incredulously, coming over to me. She put her hand on my back. "Good lord, Rabbit, what was that?" Concerned, worried even. It was a sweet moment that I couldn't enjoy because of my swelling cheek.

"What? You said for her to hit me."

"I did, yeah." She was bemused. "Did I say for you to let her?"

I thought about it for a long beat, like a full-on moron.

"No," I said.

"So why'd you let her hit you?"

"Because you didn't say not to!" I yelled.

Juliet paused, then laughed. "Your dad tell you to put on your clothes every day?"

"No," I said.

"Does anybody tell you to breathe?" Her voice was softer when she was patronizing.

"No," I said. My head was pounding.

"I'm not going to be with you every second of the day, telling you what to do. I don't want a robot. I want a girl who can hold her own."

She helped me to my feet and then gently held my face, gazing intently. I looked away, conscious of the warmth of her hand, her gray eyes scanning me, heady with her proximity and the perfume of her skin and breath.

I nodded, and she released me.

"And Sarah, you hit someone on the cheekbone again, you're gonna break your hand."

Sarah flushed, then nodded.

"I feel weird hitting someone," I said. "It was a lot easier when it was just the mitts."

Juliet nodded. "I know. But that's why we're practicing, so you won't freeze up. You've been conditioned your whole life to hold back, to push down your anger, to solve things with words. I'm asking you to ignore all that." She took a few steps away from me and raised her hands. "Give me a try. I won't hit back. I'll just dodge."

I laughed. As impossible as it had been to imagine hitting Sarah, hitting Juliet was a whole new level of unthinkable. The last thing I wanted to do to that face was rearrange it. I wanted to hold her face as tenderly as she'd just held mine.

She easily blocked my first two strikes with her arms, giving me a lazy grin. We both knew this wasn't her best effort. She wanted me to feel like I'd worked for it and come away with some success.

I could live with that.

The next time I tried, I ignored her face entirely and went for her stomach. She didn't block me, but her stomach was tensed in anticipation. I didn't knock the breath out of her; I nearly knocked the breath out of myself with the surprise of making contact.

"There you go. See, it's not that big of a deal." She was

holding her stomach, mostly to make me feel effective.

Right. Easy. I can do this.

"Let's try you two again," said Juliet.

So we went again.

Sarah circled me, warier now, knowing that I wasn't going to be such an easy target the second time. It was hard to reconcile this steely version of Sarah with the one who'd put up with watching way more Wes Anderson movies with me than anyone should.

My blood was singing in my ears. I knew what was about to happen wouldn't be as easy as it had been with Juliet, would be more of the real thing than I was ready for. I felt like two people. One of them thought she knew what she was doing. The other one was yelling *Run*.

That second person seemed a lot more sensible, really.

What happened next was chaos.

Juliet had told us that there was the theory of fighting and then there was the practice. That she could teach us form and drill us until we puked but all that would fall away as useless ritual in a real fight. Despite this warning, I'd thought somehow that all the training we'd done meant I'd know what I was doing once I was doing it, like the dreams I had sometimes that I could speak perfect Spanish even though I never studied, and Mrs. Olivera sighed every time I spoke. I had visualized punching Richard so many times while Juliet looked on approvingly.

In my head, I was very, very good at hitting people.

In reality, I looked like a drunk badger. I tried taking a swing

183

at Sarah and before I knew what had happened, she'd lunged under my arms and tackled me, her head knocking the wind out of me. I went down gasping and had just enough time to see Sarah's foot swing back to kick me. With speed that surprised even me, I pulled one of her arms away from my midsection and managed to grab her standing leg. Sarah windmilled and fell, and I staggered to my feet. Sarah touched the back of her head, wincing.

I looked at Juliet.

"I didn't say stop," Juliet said.

I had to work myself up to it. I can say that, at least. I thought about how every time I looked to Juliet to share a joke, there was Sarah, waiting to join in. Every time I had an idea, Sarah had another, competing idea. Worse, Sarah was sweet, and her sweetness just highlighted how petty I was.

For every time I'd been small and vicious, I could remember Sarah being generous and kind. She'd let me rail against some social slight (like when Valerie Newsom rolled her eyes at me for raising my hand too much in class) until I finally ran out of bile, then gently suggest I let it go by reminding me that Valerie still had to be Valerie every day, and wasn't that punishment enough?

Once, I was mad at my mother for volunteering me to ladle hot chocolate at a Friends of the Library bake sale. How dare she commandeer my Saturday? But Sarah had said it sounded like fun and asked if she could join me. And with her there, it *was* fun.

That was Sarah. I was a better person around her.

Maybe that's why I didn't want her around.

I'd forgotten all this. I'd let myself slip into our old patterns, our shared jokes. But underneath it all, this envy remained. It was highly motivating.

And so, I kicked Sarah in the stomach.

I did that.

Sarah gave a gasping yelp and balled up.

Juliet nodded, and I sat on the ground, panting. It was over.

The whole thing had happened very fast, and none of it had felt natural. I wasn't good at this. I didn't like it. I felt scared and it hurt to breathe. My body was one giant pulse.

Sarah gradually came out of the ball, and wiping her eyes, sat up. Juliet came over and helped her to her feet.

Sarah wouldn't meet my eyes.

Practice was over, and it was time to go home. Sarah had parents who expected her, and I had—well, I had massive inconsistency waiting for me. As Sarah and I stepped out onto the front porch to leave, Juliet asked me to stay a moment.

Sarah paused, her face blank, then walked down the steps to her bike and rode off.

Juliet waited until the sounds of Sarah's bike faded. I could probably catch up with her if I rode fast, but I didn't know if I wanted that.

"So, you didn't fight back because I didn't tell you to."

"Yeah."

"That was stupid," she said.

"Yeah," I said. I touched my cheek, feeling the swelling rise. I'd have to cover it with makeup.

"But I like the loyalty."

I looked down, suddenly embarrassed, pleased.

"Would you do anything I told you to, just because I told you to?" she said. It wasn't teasing. She looked genuinely curious and stepped closer. I could smell the sweat on her, the remnants of perfume and deodorant and the citrus scent of her skin. She was taller than me, and I had to raise my head to look at her.

I met her eyes. I couldn't say what I was thinking.

That I'd do anything she asked of me.

Anything.

Everything.

"And what if I told you to kiss me?" she said, amused.

My stomach pulsed and my heart skipped.

Was it a joke? Was it real? I couldn't tell.

She held my gaze. Daring me. Mocking me. Both.

And I—

I looked away. I couldn't bear the possibility that it was just one more test. I couldn't bear her rejecting me.

Biking home, I replayed the scene again and again, trying to find an ending that worked. But in every scenario, I turned away. I was always a coward. And she always smirked, stepped back into the house, and shut the door.

DAD TRIES TO DAD

"You've been coming home later," my father said as I entered the kitchen. He said it casually, in the manner of someone just making everyday conversation. But we weren't really having a lot of everyday conversation anymore and so it was immediately bizarre. I had been spending most of my time at Juliet's for weeks and had barely seen him.

I blinked, and several pieces of the morning fell into place for me. One, my father was actually awake before 9:00 a.m. on a Saturday. Two, he had brought out a box of cereal, two bowls, and two spoons and placed them at the kitchen table. Three, he had already poured me a cup of coffee.

This was a special effort. That didn't bode well.

I sat down, wary, and poured myself a bowl of Cinnamon Toast Crunch. We'd had a regular supply of name-brand cereal in the house for at least a month. There was a fresh quart of milk on the table, too.

"Not that much later," I said. "I'm not staying out all hours like a hooligan." It had been a week since I'd hit both of my friends, and since then, I'd made a regular practice of it. But I still got enough sleep for a growing girl.

"I know, I know, you're keeping reasonable hours and I'm proud of you. You've always been responsible."

I nodded. I didn't really like compliments on how responsible or independent I was. The people who compliment you on how good you are at taking care of yourself are usually the ones who were supposed to be taking care of you in the first place.

"You, uh . . . you got a boyfriend?" he asked his cereal.

I laughed. The entire time I had dated Richard, my dad had been oblivious to the relationship. Then when we broke up and Richard wouldn't let go, my father was just as oblivious. Now, when I still had the yellow trace of bruise on my cheek that I could barely cover with concealer, he finally asked about my dating life.

"Well, I had to ask," he said. "It's my job."

I just stared at him. I wasn't even angry that after months of benign neglect and, in general, being a gin-sodden lump, my father was now claiming to be on top of his paternal duties. I was just befuddled.

"Nope," I said. "No boyfriend. I have not developed a drug habit. I am not hanging with a bad crowd."

"Okay, okay!" he said, raising his hands in surrender. "I just . . . uh . . . I just wanted to make sure you were all right."

I stiffened and gave my cereal a stab with my spoon. "I'm fine."

"Still going to Group?"

"Yeah," I said. "It's been really helpful."

"Because, uh . . . Sheila mentioned you hadn't been going."

Fucking Sheila. *Real* therapists have patient confidentiality.

"I still go. Sheila probably just hasn't checked in with the new group leader," I said. I had no idea who the new group leader was, assuming there was one. I wasn't even attempting to be convincing, just staring at him and daring him to contradict me.

My father rubbed his face. He looked deeply uncomfortable. It had been a long time since I'd seen him have much of a facial expression at all, and I had no issue with letting him suffer. He'd have to ask me.

So, he did.

"Are you thinking about hurting yourself again?" The words tumbled out of his mouth quickly, as if the only way for him to say them was all at once.

"God, no," I said scornfully. It had never been about hurting myself. The whole point of it had been to *not* hurt. If I could have quietly blinked out of existence, I would have. I'd just wanted to turn myself off, like a light.

"Are you depressed?"

The question took me off guard. It seemed like a softball after the first one.

"No? I don't think so. Or if I am, I'm not really feeling it? Maybe that's progress."

He raised an eyebrow but didn't say anything.

I ate the last few spoonfuls of my cereal and then wiped my

sweating palms on my shorts. I needed to make sure my father didn't start watching me more closely. If he paid attention, he might start asking questions, making demands on my time. Or worse, he'd make me see someone more serious, someone with degrees who knew what they were doing. And I was pretty sure that would interfere with seeing Juliet. I could already tell mental health and Juliet did not go hand in hand. I'd fall by the wayside, and it would just be Juliet and Sarah and I'd be that girl who was almost part of something.

He opened his mouth to say more, and I jumped in with the only defense I had.

"I've been with friends," I said.

He looked surprised, and then he looked . . . happy for me? This was a little hard to bear because it meant that he had noticed how alone I had been, how isolated, and yet still poured himself a drink every night anyway. Cleaning himself up for one morning and giving me ultra-processed cereal didn't really make up for that.

"That's great, honey. That Juliet girl?"

"Yeah, Juliet Bergman. Me and Sarah and her have been hanging out a lot."

"Sarah! Oh, good. You two used to be so close," he said, and trailed off, not wanting to say when that had changed. He didn't fully register Juliet's last name, though he would later.

I nodded, pleased with myself. Invoking Sarah had been smart. Nothing untoward could happen if Sarah was involved.

"Actually, Juliet invited me over to her house tonight for a sleepover. Sarah, too. I was going to ask you about it," I said.

Juliet had not actually invited me to her house for the night. But I was already learning from her that if you sense weakness, you should take advantage. My father was putting up a front and both of us knew we couldn't maintain it. I was offering him an escape and I was getting something I wanted. It was a win-win.

"Yeah, absolutely. Is she going to pick you up? Do you need a ride?" He looked eager to meet my friend, eager to help out. I wondered if he'd had a drink that morning or if he was still feeling it from the night before.

The thought of my dad outside the Bergman house was inconceivable. I didn't want to see him try to take in that level of wealth. I didn't want to see how shabby he and our car would look outside of it.

"I'll bike," I said. "It's not far."

Before my mother died, there would have been a phone call placed to the parents of any friend, a brief talk to establish that everyone had the same understanding on alcohol and guns in the house and what have you, if I was staying at theirs. My mother would have dropped a few names to see if they had friends in common, or if they ran in the same circles.

I guess we didn't do that anymore.

"I'll see you tomorrow?"

"Yeah. Although she did ask if I could stay the whole weekend."

"Oh?"

"Yeah," I said, "she's got this whole spa idea while we watch a movie."

He brightened a little when I mentioned movies. I used to have regular movie nights with friends, or with him and Mom. He'd suffered through my Miranda July phase (I love her). Then I stopped. I tried watching movies when my mom was sick, but it was a ritual with all the magic leached out. The problems on the screen were solvable, but mine weren't.

I'm sure my dad thought this meant I was on the mend.

"Are you coming home with pink hair?"

"I hope so," I said.

Just a little flashback to the kind of humor we used to have in our house. It was a peace offering and he took it gratefully.

"You'll be safe?"

I stood up and put my bowl in the sink and gave him a hug from behind. There it was. Just a little juniper and ethanol.

"I'm always safe," I said.

TALISMANS

As dusk fell, I was back with the girls at the cabin. I helped Juliet gather brush, sticks, and wood, while Sarah swept out the fireplace and opened the flue. We stacked the larger pieces of wood on an ancient iron grate, and tucked pine cones beneath it for kindling. I was relieved to see Juliet hand Sarah a lighter; I half expected her to insist we create a flame with two sticks and our fervent belief. The fire licked the damp wood with little enthusiasm. Nonetheless, our mild success was pleasing, like we were pioneer witches.

I left Sarah to tend to the fire like it was a beloved pet, feeding it additional twigs whenever it faltered. Juliet had slipped outside while we were rediscovering the secrets of the cavemen. I found her behind the cabin, in what had perhaps once been a backyard but was now mostly a tangle of blackberry bushes. Juliet had stepped her way into a thicket by carefully stamping down blackberry canes. In the gathering dark, she ate one blackberry, another, plucked from the bushes.

It was strange to see her, unaware of me, unguarded, simply eating with the thoughtless hunger of an animal. Even stranger when she paused and dropped a berry to the ground, uneaten. Her hand rested in the air for a moment, as if waiting for someone to clasp it in theirs and lead her in a dance. Then she reached out to one of the blackberry vines and wrapped her hand around it and squeezed it tight.

My stomach seized in response; I knew those sharp and vicious thorns well. The pain she was feeling had to be immense, but she barely flinched. She held it a while longer, then released, flexing her fingers open and closed a few times. She ran her hand across her jean shorts, wiping off blackberry juice, blood, one impossible to tell from the other in the dark.

I called to her then, afraid she'd see me first and know how long I'd watched her. "We've got the fire going," I said.

She nodded in response, not meeting my eyes, shadowed and silent. She looked like no one I knew.

Then she turned, and she was Juliet again, lit up with energy and enthusiasm, and there was no trace of that other girl who ate blackberries in the dark.

Back in the cabin, Sarah and I sat down in front of the fire, our knees almost touching, like children ready for storytime. I shivered a little. Summer nights were mostly warm, but this one had a chill to it. Juliet kneeled and poked at the fire with a stick, and a flock of red sparks swarmed up, then blinked out one by one.

"Beautiful fire, Sarah."

I hid my scowl and rubbed my arms, and Sarah, almost like she knew my petty heart, handed me her sweatshirt, and squeezed my arm. I smiled weakly at her. God, why was I so quick to judge? There was more than enough Juliet to go around, wasn't there?

Juliet sat down, completing our circle.

"We trust each other, right?" she said.

If Sarah thought this was out of nowhere, she didn't show it. "Completely," she said. She looked it, too. Her eyes were bright and wide. There. That was the real thing I envied. Sarah didn't have doubts.

Trust. I thought of Juliet straddling me, of her hand on the small of my back when we danced, of her tracing her fingers up my thigh, and I ached. Then I thought about her mouth so close to me, telling me that if I kept information from her again, I was out.

Did I trust her?

I trusted her to be her. I didn't trust myself when I was around her.

Being certain that nothing was certain was close enough, wasn't it?

Juliet smiled, pleased with Sarah's answer and assuming mine, then stood, her long body painted in orange and shadowy firelight. "*We* trust. None of us are going to rat out the others to our parents. We know that what we do stays here. We keep each other's secrets. We keep each other safe."

Sarah nodded, and so did I, although I couldn't help but

think that Juliet didn't really have to worry about anyone getting upset with her. Was anyone even checking in on her? There was no indication of it. But all Juliet asked for was for us to ask no questions, and that wasn't so much. I closed my eyes and swayed. Juliet's voice was incantatory, like she was whispering in my ears alone.

"But what if the people you thought were your friends, the ones you trusted—what if they betrayed you?"

A sick feeling rose in the base of my stomach, as if Juliet was speaking about one of us. I couldn't think of anything I'd done wrong, but I still found myself trying to find a fault. Beside me, Sarah looked like she was doing the same math.

Juliet pulled one of the Polaroids from her bag's front pocket. "Sarah, you trusted. And this is what they did."

She handed the photograph to Sarah, and Sarah looked at it once more. She was less hesitant than she'd been before, really studying the image this time. With just a little more concentration, it would probably start to singe and smoke.

Like a sadistic magician, Juliet pulled the photograph of me out of the air and put it into my hands. Once again, I saw the limp girl suspended between the two boys. It was hard to believe she was me, but she was.

How had I gotten there?

"You trusted them," said Juliet. "All these girls trusted them in one way or another."

She took the pictures back from our hands, carefully, like they were relics, and returned them to the bag. She stood up and began to pace, walking between us and the fire, her voice rising as she spoke. "This happens again and again. You trust someone, and then you stumble home with your shirt on backward, missing a sock. You trust someone, but then you have to shower and shower to get them off you. You trust someone, and then your supposed friend calls, the one who left you there, *left you there*, to kindly inform you you're a whore. So you tell anyone who will listen, because you *trust* they'll do the right thing. But they don't listen, not really, and nothing happens. Nothing changes. And here we are. Again."

By the end of this, her voice was shaking, and her eyes were focused on something beyond us. I couldn't look away from her agitation, or the sense that for the first time I was seeing the real Juliet. But did that mean the rest was fake?

She stopped pacing and took a deep breath, gathering herself. Once more, she was calm. "Tell me, do you think it's right that there are no consequences for these fine young men?"

"No," said Sarah beside me, softly.

"Trust has to *mean* something. We have to trust each other, no one else. We can fix this. We can humiliate them—we can punish them—because no one else will," she said.

She sat down again, the fire behind her like a flaming crown around her curls. "Do we trust each other," she said, her voice breathless, "that we can right this wrong? With our hands?"

Later, I would say I didn't know what she meant by this. Haven't I said that all along? That I didn't understand. I couldn't know.

I knew. We knew.

"Yes," we said in one voice. Sarah took my hand and squeezed it.

"Louder," Juliet said. "I can't hear you."

"Yes," we yelled. Our voices in the cabin were fierce. The hair on my arms rose.

Sarah and I had to laugh then and try to undo the magic we'd conjured. We weren't comfortable with power. But Juliet never joined in, and our laughter died out as quickly as it had begun.

"I've brought a present," she said to us.

Sarah's face lit up like a kid's. I smiled back at Juliet, but more warily.

Juliet brought out from her bag a small green leather box, bound with a braided cord.

I did a double take. I'd seen this box before.

Juliet, watching my face, nodded.

"It's real," she said.

In the role that convinced everyone that Jesse Bergman could Actually Act and was More Than Just Pretty, he played a young private in World War I. We see him grow up in the trenches from a scared, idealistic kid to a man at peace with his own death. I don't have to tell you it's a noble, self-sacrificing death, do I?

It's very good. He got an Oscar for it, but more impressively, Criterion released a special edition of it. Blah blah blah chaos of war, blah blah blah cinematography—I would tell you a lot of intellectual-sounding stuff but what I really remember was this was the first movie where I understood why people thought Jesse Bergman was sexy.

Remembering that now, sitting across from Juliet, deeply weirded me out.

This box was from the tattoo scene. The private visited a provincial French town, not yet touched by the front. It's very charming, lavender in every cottage's window box. He loses his virginity to the improbably gorgeous town prostitute and gets a tattoo from a wizened man in a bar, drinking through the pain while being good-naturedly mocked by his comrades. Rite-of-passage stuff.

Sarah looked at the box with curiosity, not recognizing it. Sarah didn't watch a lot of secular movies unless she was at my house. Her mother was far too strict. She could watch *The Ten Commandments* and *VeggieTales* to her heart's content, though.

Her eyes widened when Juliet opened the box and she saw the jar of ink, the needles.

"Obviously, these aren't the same needles from the movie. I picked up some sterilized packs and new ink. Plus, alcohol swabs. One hundred percent less tetanus. Nothing but the best for my besties."

I swallowed.

"Soldiers going to war got tattoos of their country's flag, of their loved ones' names. You need armor when you are going into battle. You need talismans, protection," she said.

Sarah stood up, finally realizing what was going on, wavering on her feet.

"I'm sorry," Sarah said. "I just can't. My mother would kill me. This is—this is too much."

Juliet shook her head. Gentle. In the firelight, she looked beatific, like a saint.

"You don't have to," she said. "This is something *I'm* doing, to show you both my dedication. Will you sit by me, while I do it?"

Sarah hesitated, then nodded, and sat back down by Juliet. Juliet smoothed Sarah's hair like she was a child, or a skittish dog.

"I would never make you do anything you didn't want to do," said Juliet. Her words were kind, wise, an adult voice she could trot out whenever she needed it.

And it was true. Or at least, I told myself it was.

"I'm sorry," Sarah whispered again. The shame in her was visible, surrounding her like oily smoke. I took an unpleasant enjoyment in it.

"Don't be," said Juliet very seriously. "It's good to know your limits. Okay? I never expected it."

Sarah nodded.

Juliet looked to me.

Another test.

I moved closer. I said the right words.

"How can I help?" I was the good friend, loyal and true. I could be trusted.

Juliet slid the shoulder of her shirt down, exposing the top of her breast. I was grateful for the shifting firelight, hiding any blushing on my part.

As the fire popped and hissed, I swabbed the top swell of her breast with the alcohol wipe and popped open the first needle container. She instructed me to pour the ink into a small metal bowl that she'd heated by the fire's edge. She demonstrated on her arm with an ink pen how to make small pokes into a line.

"I want you to make a moon. A crescent moon," she said. "Like a fingernail."

"I'm not an artist," I said, horrified. I wanted to assist; I didn't want to be the one marking her immaculate skin.

"I trust you," she said. And just like that, there was no saying no.

She drew the outline of a crescent moon with a fine-tipped felt pen. She had a steady hand. Moon for female, she told us, for Artemis, the virgin huntress, who needed no man and who ran with her women in the woods. Whose dogs tore trespassing men to shreds.

It took forever. Dipping, pricking the skin, dipping again. The whole time Juliet just watched me. Under her eye, and with her faith, my hand followed her lines perfectly.

When it was done, we smeared it with Aquaphor and covered it with a bandage.

Juliet didn't ask me in words. She just looked at me.

She wanted consent. Or she wanted obedience. Did it matter which?

I nodded yes. Mark me. Mark my outside like you've already marked me inside.

Sarah squeezed my hand. Encouragement? Worry? I didn't

look at her. I could only look at Juliet as she neared me, unbuttoned her borrowed jumpsuit to reveal my bra. She slipped one strap down and I shivered.

She inked mine freehand, dipping a new needle into the ink over and over, the first prick making me wince, and every stab after that. It felt like a cat scratch at first, if the cat's paw was dipped in cayenne and was stabbing from hell's heart. Sarah squeezed my shoulder while Juliet worked on my chest, pulling the skin of my upper breast taut, her brow furrowed. Her hand moved quickly, assuredly. She'd done this before. Was there another moon on her body somewhere? A star? A constellation of girls following her into battle?

I wasn't surprised when Sarah changed her mind. Those wide, believing eyes were back.

Juliet asked if she was sure. Was it really what she wanted?

Sarah said it was.

Her eyes welled with tears as Juliet worked, but she smiled at me. She could feel the way these marks pulled us tightly together, like a needle drawing fabric tight. I was ashamed of my jealousy over Juliet's attention. I vowed to be a better friend to Sarah, and at least in that moment, I meant it.

When Juliet wiped away the ink and blood, there was a little moon on Sarah's breast, just like mine.

Sarah giggled to see it. She was riding the weird rush of euphoria that hit each of us after the initial pain. I joined her in laughing.

We were sisters again. My mother would have been happy.

She'd loved Sarah and had tried to give her things she wasn't getting at home: warmth, understanding, rationality. Whenever Sarah had suffered under her mother's regime, my mother had been there to suggest alternative strategies, ways to circumvent her restrictions without rousing her mother's ire. If my mother hadn't been so sick, she would've yelled at me for pushing Sarah away like I did. I couldn't go back and undo what I'd done, but I could at least try to fix it.

Juliet wouldn't have fit into the warm, rational world my mother tried to create for us. Its atmosphere would poison her.

Juliet brought out a bottle of wine and she and Sarah took long drinks straight from the bottle. She handed me a bottled lemonade and I felt stupidly pleased at the thoughtfulness of it.

Juliet stood up and pulled us to our feet. She started to dance, and woozy with endorphins, I did, too. Sarah joined in and let out a long howl like a wolf. We followed suit. We crowed and howled and danced before the fire, our bodies golden, our skin smeared with the excess ink that didn't take, glistening with the Aquaphor we worked in after. We danced and sang and kissed each other's cheeks. We tumbled to the ground, and we pulled each other back up. We chanted from a past where women were feared, their lips purple with wine, their eyes mad and lovely. If you looked closely, you would have seen our hands were full of blood and flesh.

NOT LIKE THAT

There's this bird—the killdeer—that has a great trick. Say a fox draws too close to its nest. The killdeer pops out of the brush and starts peeping her head off. She drags her wings and to all the world looks like she is struggling to get off the ground and can't. That's pretty appealing to a fox—nice, easy catch. The killdeer draws the fox off the nest, and just when the fox thinks it's in the bag, yummy killdeer lunch, the killdeer flies off, chirping whatever the bird equivalent is of "See ya, sucker."

That was basically our plan for Caleb, but instead of flying off, a whole flock of the killdeer's buddies fly in to peck the fox's eyes out.

Metaphorically, of course.

Sarah was the lure. Sarah, whose rich curves concealed new muscles, whose hair was thick and loose and hiding her face. We left her sprawled on the ground in the parking lot next to Brohmer's feed store, a spilled book bag by her side. She hunched over and began to sniffle. We watched from behind the dumpster.

I wanted to throw up. We were doing it. We were really going to confront Caleb about the pictures. This was insane. Juliet smiled at me. I could only see her eyes over the bandanna, but they were crinkled with delight. Juliet was incandescent, a kid fidgeting in line for the roller coaster.

She'd told us we were ready. So we were.

Soon, we heard his steps. Caleb Winters—the dancing crotch grinder from the party—was the kicker on the football team, and a bit smaller than the others. One likes to ease into jumping people, after all.

We'd watched him for days. Sarah and I had taken turns and reported back to Juliet.

"He's almost always with people," Sarah said. "He's not a long-walks-in-the-woods type."

But there were times he was alone. He was often the last one picked up at football practice, because his mother was usually getting his sister first from soccer. He didn't have a car because he'd totaled it a few months prior. He'd sit outside the school, throwing rocks into the parking lot. But that was an open space, easily seen from multiple directions. Not ideal.

Caleb's parents had a Friday date night, and his younger sister usually stayed over at a friend's. But what if someone came home early, or Caleb had invited friends over? Plus, we'd have to find a way into the house.

The best option was his walk to his summer job, so here

we were. Every weekday, Caleb walked to Zoe's Cantina, our town's attempt at a Mexican restaurant. On his way, he took a shortcut through the parking lot between the feed store and its warehouse. Brohmer's Feed and Supply was only open on weekends. Walking between the buildings effectively blocked you from the street's view.

Bonus: he listened to music as he walked.

Hiding made me feel ridiculous, like a child playing a game she was a little too old for. But I could barely think straight—what was the plan again? Hit him, push him down, humiliate him. What was I doing here at all?

There he was. I could just see him. He was listening to music, as expected. He carried a backpack and one of his shoelaces was untied, which I found myself staring at senselessly. He was smaller than the others, but I had no doubt he was much stronger than I was. This was insane.

He spotted Sarah, who was the very picture of distress. Even I, knowing what I knew, felt myself wanting to go to her, to comfort her and see if she was okay. Her legs were awkwardly splayed, and her hair covered her face like a veil. She shook with tears.

A damsel, no question about it. Pretty little bird.

"Hey," he said, removing an earbud from one ear. "Hey, girl, you okay?" He was wearing a baseball cap that covered his short red hair and shaded his eyes.

Sarah began to cry a little harder, as if his attention had hurt her further.

He was surprisingly cautious approaching her. Maybe it was the way she didn't respond to his question but just kept crying, like she was a looped GIF.

But still he crouched down next to her and put his hand on her shoulder.

I know that looks like kindness, like he must be a good person, that we'd made a mistake somewhere, that the same guy who'd show concern for a stranger wouldn't possibly have taken pictures like that.

But each of us has in us so many different selves. We're not all good or all bad. That's not how people work.

When she turned to him and he saw the lower half of her face was covered by a bandanna, did he imagine it was some odd kind of joke?

Whatever he thought, he had very little time to think it before Juliet slammed into him. She was gone from my side before I knew what was happening. She kicked him hard, and he balled up. She kicked him again.

"Get in here, goddamnit," Juliet barked at us.

Sarah and I had frozen. This wasn't the plan. We were going to hit him, knock him down, but not like this. We were going to show him the pictures. We were going to shame him.

I suppose in that moment we both realized how stupid that sounded, how that was never the plan at all.

Then we were on him immediately, our own handkerchiefs turning our breath steamy against our faces. He was clutching his head and trying to rise but hampered by his heavy backpack and his disorientation. One of his earbuds had dislodged from his ear and landed on the gravel. His phone had skittered away.

For all the practice we'd done, it was mostly a lot of kicking. The sounds of our feet striking him were surprisingly muted; football players come with natural soundproofing, I guess. Caleb curled up into a ball, his arms over his head, trying and failing to protect himself.

I'd like to say that it's a hard thing to attack a man when he's down, that you must overcome some sense of decency to do so. But decency is an idea that only works if everyone buys in, and Caleb Winters had shown he wasn't a believer.

I'd like to say I hesitated.

But I can't.

Once you start ruining a thing, it's all you want to do. There's a pleasure in destruction, in seeing how a body reacts to its damage.

I didn't want to stop.

"That's enough!" said Juliet. We stopped, even though it pained us, even though our legs and hands longed to do more.

This was the last time Juliet would show such forbearance.

Caleb sobbed on the ground. He looked so small at that moment. We watched him like he was a member of a foreign species. It was hard to believe that minutes before I'd been worried about how his speed and strength might be our undoing. His face was smeared with blood and snot, and one of his eyes was swelling shut in a purplish mass. I'd read somewhere that redheads feel more pain than others. Good.

Then I suddenly thought of his family, how I'd seen them shopping just the day before at the Piggly Wiggly, affectionately disagreeing over Little Debbies.

Crying, he looked like a little boy.

But everyone was somebody's kid. Sarah was somebody's kid. So was I. That's what Juliet would say. So, I said it to myself until I believed it, which didn't take long.

"Tell us about those pictures," said Juliet.

Caleb cried harder.

She crouched down next to him. "The Polaroids you and your shitty friends took of passed-out girls." She reached over and smoothed his shirt, like his disarray was not of her doing.

His swollen eyes widened. Had he thought this was random? That a band of roaming girls just attacked him out of the blue?

He tried to sit up and failed. When he spoke, his voice was tremulous.

"I didn't—I didn't *do* anything."

"You were there," said Juliet. "We saw you."

He nodded weakly, then started crying again. Sarah and I shifted nervously, worried that someone might hear his mewling. The longer we were here, the more likely someone might notice something. How many others used the parking lot as a cut-through?

"They're just pictures. It's not— I told them we shouldn't! I told them we should stop."

He'd meant to do something. He'd thought about doing something, he really did. He wasn't to blame.

"Do I need to kick you again?" said Juliet. Her eyes over the handkerchief were cold.

He took a deep, shuddering breath.

He only snapped the pictures, he swore. Except for all the ones he was in. He only watched what they did. He never did anything, not that anyone did anything, but if they did, it wasn't anything serious. Dumb stuff. Messing around. But nothing really *bad*. None of it was great, he admitted that. But they weren't, like, *rapists*.

"I mean, we're not like *that*," he said.

There was more, but I couldn't hear through the rushing blood in my ears. I couldn't take in any more.

Out of nowhere, I gave him another kick in the ribs, and he groaned and curled up tighter.

Juliet looked at me. She'd told us to stop, and I'd disobeyed. But she wasn't mad. Instead, she seemed to finally like what she saw in my face. *There's my girl*, I could hear her say in my mind.

Juliet leaned closer to him.

"I don't care," said Juliet, "if you kept your dick in your pants. I don't care if you keep your dick in your pants for the rest of your life, and for the record, you should. You were there, you're one of them, and you all are fucking monsters."

She stood up and coldly looked down. He was struggling to stop crying; every time he seemed to get a handle on it, he started up again.

"I want you to remember this every time you see someone helpless. If you don't do something, the universe will trade your places."

Then she took out the mint-green Polaroid camera we'd stolen from Richard's. His eyes widened as much as they could through the swelling. He recognized it. There was no doubt. She stepped back and took two pictures of him: small, balled-up, and sobbing.

"One for you," she said, "and one to frame." The camera ejected the photo with a cheerful whir, and Juliet spun the small white square like a playing card through the air to land on Caleb's thigh. He flinched at the light contact. The picture was cloudy when it landed, but it would develop soon enough into a record of his weakness, an image to haunt him as we'd been haunted. Already the colors were blooming to the surface.

She tucked the second picture inside her shirt.

We left him there and ran, quick as mercury and just as poisonous.

As soon as we were no longer hidden by buildings, we stuffed our handkerchiefs into our pockets and slowed to a walk.

Just like that, we were ordinary girls again. No one looked at us twice.

But inside we were warriors. We were our own weapons, and we needed only each other.

HANGOVER

We were counting on a certain kind of shame. After we left, we knew Caleb would move like an old man, sore all over, hacking bloody spittle onto the ground. He'd pick himself up, then find his phone, which wouldn't work so well after Sarah stomped it. He'd try to brush the dirt off his pants, but it would be ground in.

He'd realize just how much he'd told us, that he'd cracked open whatever pact of secrecy he'd had with the other boys through his fear and weakness.

He'd also realize he'd just had his ass handed to him by a bunch of girls. And so, he'd lie to his parents, his friends.

"That's how they get away with it," Juliet said, "and that's how we'll get away with it, too. They know you'll feel stupid and ashamed. That you'll run the scenario over and over in your head trying to get it to come out not your fault. But you always decide it is. So, you con yourself and pretend it didn't happen because you can't trust that telling anyone will help. I mean, look what happened the last time you trusted somebody?" She laughed.

Right or wrong, his shame was our cover.

There was no shame in Galaxy House. We returned as victors. We donned laurel crowns that Juliet pulled out of Galaxy's movie souvenirs, and we preened and strutted through the house. We held Sarah up on our shoulders, the queen of the hour, the best pretender. Juliet shook up bottles of prosecco and sprayed it at us, and we collapsed into a sticky, laughing muddle in the middle of the foyer. I laughed on my back until my sides hurt, my eyes closed against the brilliant shards of the chandelier above us, spinning like a glittering top.

I couldn't imagine being happier than at that moment.

But as the night came to a close, the doubts crept in, and with them, a sense of unreality that left me feeling like I'd kicked myself off the earth and was floating far above it. I walked from room to room, lost in a far-off, melancholy feeling. Sarah and Juliet were laughing in the kitchen when I exited the house through the front door and sat down on the steps. Outside, the windows cast an amber light onto the lawn, and the sounds of gaiety at my back felt like another world I couldn't reach.

What was I doing here? And what had we done? Unbidden, the image of Caleb came to mind. I saw his face, clenched in pain against the gravel.

Why was I feeling bad for him? Richard's bloody face had brought me nothing but delight.

But I wasn't the one who hit Richard with a tray. I very much kicked Caleb.

"Thought I'd find you here," said Juliet. "You had that Sensitive Girl look on your face."

She closed the front door behind her and joined me on the stairs.

"You look like you've got a case of the regrets," she said. "Tell me about them."

This was a little like I was back at the grief group, only no one at the grief group sat this close, or leaned their body against mine.

"I just . . . I—I keep thinking about what he looked like, on the ground like that. He didn't even have a chance to fight back."

"Most people feel empathy for helpless, injured things. But remember what he really is."

"I know, I just—"

"We should have—what, challenged him to a duel? One-to-one fisticuffs?"

I smiled ruefully. "Yeah, something like that. I thought we were going to . . ." I trailed off. It felt ridiculous to say what I'd thought. That we were going to talk to him? Hurt his feelings? Threaten him with words?

"It's sweet that you feel pity," she said. "I admire that, even if I think you're wasting it on the wrong person."

I nodded.

"It's a valuable thing, pity. You just can't let it get in the way of what we're doing."

"What is it we're doing?" I asked. "I mean, what is this?" I gestured at her, the house.

"A little late in the game to get existential."

"I know . . ."

"Do you trust me?" There it was again. She gave me a hard look, and suddenly I felt like the wrong answer would really cost me something.

"I do, I do," I stammered. "I just— I've been thinking. We've *got* the photographs, you know? If we took them to the police—"

"The photographs don't change anything. It's not like anyone would say it didn't happen. They just wouldn't think it mattered."

Whenever I talked with Juliet, it felt like she had an answer for anything I said. I didn't disagree, not exactly, but there didn't seem to be any room for me.

"Is this really about poor Caleb Winters, going home to cry?" said Juliet.

"What do you mean?"

"Isn't it more about what this says about you? That you thought you didn't have it in you, and now you know you can kick a man when he's on the ground, crying."

"Something like that," I said. "Can we change the subject?"

Juliet shrugged, and then put down her drink and stretched. She was wearing a denim jacket and a cropped white T-shirt, and when she raised her arms, her belly flashed for a minute. She pointed her toes and her legs looked impossibly long on the stairs.

I averted my eyes. Sometimes I really wanted to forget I had a body, and I wished it would stop making its demands known. I couldn't think when she was next to me. I knew there were answers to her questions, but I couldn't access them because my heart was beating too fast. The smell of dried prosecco wafted off both of us, making me feel queasy.

"Here you are," said Sarah, opening the door.

Thank god. Also, goddamnit.

She sat down beside us on the porch steps.

"Rabbit here is feeling regret," said Juliet.

Sarah looked at me, then took a sip of bubbly from a comically long flute.

"'Trust in the Lord with all your heart, and do not lean on your own understanding. In all your ways acknowledge him, and he will make straight your paths,'" she said solemnly.

Juliet spat out her drink in a spray.

FAMILY DINNER

My father was a problem.

Maybe it was because I wasn't tucking him in every night since I'd been sleeping over at Juliet's as much as I could, or maybe he finally took a look at the piles of bills I'd started putting into a cardboard box under the key hook by the door. Maybe it was Sheila, who he had officially started dating. How adorable.

Whatever the reason, more and more, he started to wake up.

It wasn't all at once, and it wasn't consistent. But some days he'd look like total hell, and I'd know he hadn't had anything to drink the previous night. Anything. That was hard to wrap my mind around. There were fewer bottles in the garbage. Fewer lemons and limes seeping sticky juice on the counter. Fewer ants. More surprise dinners. More effort.

I should have been happy. That's what you're supposed to be when your dad starts being less of a drunk. But it made me mad. Mad that he was starting to ask me questions about where I was going, when I'd be home. Mad when he said I should come home for dinner, telling me he was making my favorite mac and cheese. All these gestures were normal before my mother died, and his wanting to return to them like nothing had happened made me furious. I wanted to tell him that you can't skip out on being a dad for months and then just start up again like nothing happened. How could he think I'd tell him about my day like we were in a sitcom, like my mother was only running late and would be home any minute? He'd gone to pieces and left me to deal with everything alone. And when he finally started to get it together, it wasn't because he noticed I needed him. It's because frowsy Sheila looked at him twice and didn't notice the alcohol fumes.

But I didn't say any of that. I knew without Juliet telling me that if I started mouthing off at my dad he'd only get in my way. He'd start paying more attention to who I was seeing, what I was doing.

And he already had questions about where I was spending my time instead of being at home.

"Every night it's 'Where are you going? To do what? When are you coming home?'" I complained to Juliet one day. Sarah's mother had taken her to a tent revival, so it was just the two of us in the car. We'd told Sarah to come back healed, and she'd scowled at us. Juliet and I had spent the day driving aimlessly like gas was free and the planet wasn't on fire.

"Hmm," said Juliet. "Well, there's only one thing for it. We've got to convince him I'm a good influence so he doesn't mind you spending time with me."

"But you're not a good influence," I said, laughing.

"It depends on your values," she said. "Ugh, I should have just introduced myself when I started picking you up. That was a mistake."

"Nothing to be done about it now," I said. "You're just the rich kid tempting me into a life of shallow pleasures." I should never have said Juliet's last name. My dad had a chip on his shoulder about rich people because he liked nice things and couldn't have them. He'd immediately soured on her once he realized who she was.

"My pleasures aren't shallow," she said in an offended tone. Then, more seriously, "This won't do. I need to fix this." She nodded her head resolutely, and her brown curls shook in response.

I liked driving with her when it was just the two of us. When her eyes were on the road, I could look at her as much as I wanted.

"I don't think you can," I said. "His good opinion once lost is lost forever."

"Everything is fixable," she said, pulling up in front of my house. "Now, go inside and ask him if I can come in for dinner."

"What?"

"You heard me. You already told me he was making spaghetti—"

"That is literally all he makes."

"Well, it turns out I love spaghetti, and also, I have to eat alone in that big empty house every night. I'm a neglected child."

I stared at her.

"That's what you say to him, you dummy. Now go in. I'll wait here for the verdict, looking sad."

Juliet was charming.

I'd known she would be. Everyone found her so.

Then why was I disappointed that my father was charmed? That his reserve toward her, so evident the moment she stepped through the door, melted away within a few minutes? He laughed at her jokes and smiled like they were old friends. When Juliet asked for a second helping of spaghetti, my father preened under the compliment. By the end of the dinner, she was holding her stomach, moaning that she'd overeaten but couldn't help herself. He beamed.

Couldn't he see he was being played?

The conversation wasn't anything special. My father asked goofy, intrusive questions about her home life, as I knew he would. He was always very interested in the lives of people who weren't us.

"I don't mind the empty house," said Juliet. "To be honest, it's a relief. When I'm with my dad, I'm not really with him, you know? I'm with a tutor or his personal assistant. It'll be better attending a real school and having classmates, if that ends up happening. I'm also getting really good at cooking frozen pizza."

It was just the right amount of indifferent bravery to evoke sympathy. The frozen pizza thing really touched him, too, though I'd been subsisting on that for months while he was checked out.

My father bought it. Once she assured him that she did have a guardian checking in on her (who? when?), he was content to think her safe if pitiable.

Poor little rich girl. Juliet could don that costume whenever she wanted.

We three sat around the dining room table, a stubby candle burning among us to make the occasion festive. The ghost of our last attempt at family dinner flitted about the room. But that ghost vanished as Juliet's enjoyment filled the little, dark crannies of the house with light and warmth. The candle painted our faces softer, kinder, and my father's glass only had water in it, a new kind of miracle.

I knew none of it was real. Juliet was insincere; my father was a sucker. It made both of them smaller in my eyes. But I wanted it anyway. I wanted to believe. I didn't want the evening to end, this little candlelit moment. It was the closest to a family feeling I'd had in so long.

At the end of the evening, Juliet helped my father clear the table and I could hear them laughing in the kitchen. It was more animation than I'd seen from my father in weeks. He was bringing out the full repertoire of dad jokes and Juliet was giggling with what seemed like real amusement.

I couldn't help but smile, listening.

Juliet stepped out to the bathroom, and my father joined me in the dining room.

"She's a nice girl," he said. He looked pleased.

I laughed. Of all the words to describe Juliet, I'd never have come up with *nice*.

"I worry about her in that house all alone," he said. "But I guess she's got someone watching out for her."

I nodded. That fictional caretaker was doing a great job. Really instilling in her a moral compass.

"You should invite her over again," he said. "Good to have some laughter in the house."

I could have been offended by this but I wasn't. He was right. It was good to have someone laughing in the house.

I guess my father didn't want the night to end, either, because he suggested dessert. We happily said yes, although I couldn't imagine what he had in mind. He came back from the kitchen with a petite boxed cake from my favorite bakery downtown. A surprise treat, just for me, and now for Juliet, too. This was the kind of surprise my mother liked to give. Cake for no reason. A small celebration on no particularly special day.

The cake was dense, flourless chocolate, thin and intense. My father sliced us each a piece and Juliet gave a moan as she ate her first bite. I blushed, and then blushed again because my father had heard it, too.

"Ugh, oh my god. This is amazing. You know the only thing that would make this better?" said Juliet. "A nice glass of merlot."

My father looked startled.

Juliet laughed. "I mean, I know, it's America, we aren't allowed. But it's so silly. When my father and I traveled in Europe, there was wine with every meal. You'd see kids having sips of beer. It's just not a big deal there."

Juliet Bergman, cosmopolitan jetsetter, everyone.

My father was looking at his remaining cake, as if suddenly it wasn't as delicious as it had been moments before.

My smile was still on my face, but it was a mask I couldn't remove. Suddenly, my stomach hurt from the rich cake, from watching my father's mood darken and shift.

"Oh well," said Juliet, turning back to him. "Just a few more years anyway," she said lightly, lifting another bite to her mouth.

Juliet grinned at me. I couldn't tell you what that grin meant.

Do I have to tell you what happened next? That my father laughed and said, "Why not now?" Do I have to explain that he walked over to the wine rack and pulled out a bottle?

He poured us each a shallow serving, and himself a heftier one.

"Cheers!" said Juliet. "May your beautiful lips never blister!"

My father laughed and clinked his glass to hers.

"Rabbit?" said Juliet. She held my gaze, her glass aloft and waiting, daring me not to join in.

I grimaced and met their glasses with mine.

My father drained half his glass in one gulp, and Juliet took a speculative swallow. I put mine back down, untouched.

"Rabbit, it's bad luck not to drink," she said, chiding me.

My father looked at me, as if suddenly realizing something was wrong with the picture.

"Rabbit doesn't drink," he said. He flushed, remembering he'd poured me one without thinking.

"Oh, I didn't know," said Juliet lightly, then smiled. No big deal.

I glared at her. She knew. And she knew why.

My father put down his wineglass, just for a beat. As if he'd had a thought to stop, out of deference to me.

Wouldn't that have been something?

But then he picked it up again, and by the time Juliet left, he'd polished off the bottle. He'd start in on the gin when I went to bed.

At the end of the night, I saw her to the door.

"Why did you do that?" I hissed.

"Do what?" she said innocently. Big eyes.

"You're not funny."

"Look, things needed smoothing. I smoothed them. You won't have any trouble coming out to play now." She said it like it was a solved problem on a chalkboard—obvious and apparent. "Hell, you should come with me now. He won't mind. I'm a goddamn delight." She stepped out onto the porch and beckoned. "Come on."

"No," I said. "Just go."

She looked hurt and disbelieving. Juliet looking hurt made me collapse inside.

"Oh, c'mon, Rabbit, don't be like this."

I steeled myself and closed the door.

THE WINDOW SCENE

Around midnight, I sat bolt upright in my bed, my heart racing. Something had awakened me.

I listened. Nothing. Not even the wind.

Stupid brain. It was trying to put me in a straight-to-cable thriller.

Just as I was settling back down into my pillow, there was a knock at my bedroom window, right next to my head. I clapped my hands over my mouth to cover my yell.

I could just make out a dark shape behind the glass.

It rapped again.

I recognized Juliet's silhouette, crouching on the front porch. She made a cranking motion, like she was asking me to roll down the window in an old car. I stared at her. I was still mad. But nonetheless, I raised the window but left the screen down. I needed some kind of barrier between us, flimsy as it was.

She shook her head at my token resistance, then jiggled the screen up from her side. She leaned into my bedroom like a friendly neighbor in a sitcom with her arms crossed on the window ledge.

"Hiya," she said, like one does when it's midnight and you're half in and half out a window.

"It's— Hi," I said flatly. She thought she was cute.

"Let's go for a drive," she said.

"I was pretty clear with you earlier," I said. "You can't just— you just can't do these kinds of things."

Her smile fell. "Oh, you're still mad."

"Yes, I'm still mad. Also, it's the middle of the night, Juliet. My dad's asleep, you know."

"No, he's not," she said. "He's passed out. Totally different. There's no waking him."

With that, she shimmied her way through the window onto my bed. I drew back and pulled the covers up like an idiot, even though I was wearing a tank top and underwear.

I put my head in my hands. Why was there never any stopping her? Why did every interaction feel like a foregone conclusion?

It was easier if I just didn't fight.

"So, this is where the magic happens," she said. She patted my pink coverlet. It looked childish under her hand.

"No magic happens here," I said tersely.

"That's a goddamn tragedy, Rabbit."

"I'll let the Office of Teenage Celibacy know," I said. "What do you want?"

"I thought we could go for a drive," she repeated gently, like I was a sweet moron.

"Oh. Oh, yeah. It's a great night for it," I said. "Moon's out."

She grinned, and then the smile fell. "Oh, you're messing with me."

"Yes, I'm actually not enthusiastic about you right now."

"Please come," she said.

Maybe it was the *please*. How often do you get a *please* from Juliet Bergman?

More likely it was the pouting face she made.

"Fine," I said grudgingly, giving in to the foregone conclusion. I was already reaching over for my jeans beside the bed, pulling them on as well as I could under the covers. I turned away from her to tug on a raggedy bra with a dangling bow. God. "Where to?"

"Can I tell you when we get there?" she said.

I paused with my arm halfway in a hoodie. "Why?"

"Oh, I just wanted to see if you'd come without knowing."

"Fuck you."

"Okay, okay," she said, laughing and raising her hands in surrender. "I really do want to drive around, real American-like. Come on."

I rolled my eyes, but there was never any doubt about what I was going to do. I followed her through the window like Alice through the looking glass.

DRIVING BLIND

She'd parked her car several houses down from mine. Walking with her through my silent neighborhood felt surreal. All those houses held dreamers inside, and we were the only two in the world awake.

"You're driving," she said.

I looked at her quizzically.

"I'm a danger to myself and others," she said. "I'm a menace."

The car keys felt foreign in my hand, but the Camaro started with a roar. It didn't look like much, but it was responsive.

Under her direction, we headed away from town into farmland, the houses few and far between, set off the road at a distance. I left the radio off, and all I could hear was the sound of the engine and the occasional pops and pings when I hit a rock on the road.

We didn't say anything to each other for a long time. I wasn't exactly holding out hope she'd apologize for what she did—I didn't even have words for it myself—but I thought she'd at least acknowledge it. But that wasn't Juliet's style. The longer I waited, the more I realized I was being foolish to expect an apology. It was like planning a sunny-day picnic when the forecast was flash floods.

I let it go. It was easier, and it made me feel better in that moment. I just wanted to be with her and enjoy myself.

I never said I was a long-term thinker.

"Turn down that road on the right," she said. I nodded and complied.

This road was narrow and twisty. There were no streetlights, just the illumination from the headlights. I frowned. If I kept the headlights low, I couldn't see as far. If I put on the high beams, I was more likely to have a deer freeze in front of me.

Before I could decide, Juliet unbuckled her seat belt and leaned over, close to me.

"Hey, safety," I said, jokingly but not joking. But she didn't put her seat belt back on, and she didn't move away.

"Do you trust me, Rabbit?" she said. Her hand was on my thigh, and I could smell her shampoo, some kind of aggressive apple.

"I trust you, weirdo," I said, laughing, glancing at her sidelong. "We've done crime together." But even as I said this, I thought of her bringing up wine in front of my father and frowned.

I flicked my eyes back to the road, and her lips brushed my ear. I shivered.

"I'm serious," she said softly. "I want you to trust me. I want you to know that everything I do, I'm doing for you."

She sidled even closer, despite the bucket seats, practically sitting on the center console. Then her left arm draped around my shoulders and all the hairs on my body rose at once. I'd wanted her this close since she'd straddled me at her house, but I felt invaded.

"What are you do—" I said.

She put her hands over my eyes.

"Juliet, cut it out, I'm driving!" I yelled, and batted her away. The car veered a little, but I corrected.

I was furious, scared, and I wanted her to touch me again. I couldn't separate any of it.

"Shh. Just show. Show me you trust me," she said, like she was soothing a skittish horse. She slid her hands up my shoulders, my neck, her fingers as soft as a kiss. Then to my temples, waiting for permission this time.

"You're crazy," I said. "I can't drive if I can't see."

She leaned in and I could feel her breath against my cheek. "Trust me," she said.

I can't explain myself.

I closed my eyes. It felt like a relief, like giving in was the natural thing to do.

She placed her hands over my eyes, and my lashes fluttered against her palms.

She whispered directions in my ear, her voice all I could hear. I knew the car was a metric ton of steel and glass, I knew that deer with suicidal ideation were waiting to leap in front of us, but I couldn't think about anything other than her words, how close she was, how if I only did what she said I'd somehow please her, and pleasing her was all I wanted to do.

I was driving a car blind, and all I could think about was her mouth.

"Now, you're going to make a gentle curve to the left. Little more, little more, good, now straighten . . . nice. Straight for a while. Just listen to me. Now decelerate, and we're curving right, a little sharper—sharper, okay, yes. Now speed back up. Faster."

With her voice in my ear, she guided me for what felt like a half hour. I was sweating under my arms, down my back, scared we'd crash, scared she'd stop touching me.

I was also turned on, which scared me almost as much as what we were doing.

"Now, to the right, turn harder, yes, and slow, slow, slow . . ." she said. "There."

I gasped as I felt the car dip off the road onto gravel, then another dip as we rolled onto softer dirt, on and on.

"Now stop. Turn off the car."

I did, then sat there with my eyes still closed, my blood roaring in my ears.

"Open your eyes," she said, removing her hands.

She'd driven us off the road into a fallow field. We were parked beneath a tree. There were a few shadowy silhouettes of pecan trees, but otherwise nothing. The road was far behind us. I could barely see anything, just dark blue shapes.

I closed my eyes once more. The night gathered around us. I was watching myself from a distance, sitting beside her, her body still arching across the shifter, still touching mine. From a distance, the scene looked like a movie about a life I was scared to lead. I was as still as possible, listening to her breathing beside me.

She smiled—I couldn't see it, but somehow, I could feel it—and I felt her withdraw, heard her lean back in her own seat while the car's still engine pinged to sleep. When I finally looked at her, she was the one with her eyes closed, and the upward lilt of her mouth made her look like she was listening to an amusing story.

At the same time, I could see myself, like in a dream or a nightmare, starting to move.

Please don't, I told myself. Don't do this. This will change everything.

I didn't listen. I shifted my body to face her.

I'll tell you now what I couldn't tell you then, what I couldn't tell anyone, much less myself.

That I wanted Juliet Bergman more than I'd ever wanted anyone or anything, that I'd thought about what it would be like to feel her hands on me, first gently, then less so.

I'd wanted her with a low deep ache that kept me awake at night.

The only thing that scared me more than trying to kiss her was that she might let me.

I looked at her across from me but her expressionless face

gave me nothing. I could read her closed eyes as sleeping, or I could read them as waiting.

What did I want to see?

Stop thinking. Stop thinking. Just do something.

THE FIELD

There's always a scene in a romantic movie where some-one declares love in the rain, usually against their will. *I have tried to deny my feelings, but I cannot any longer. I have been with others, but it was always you, you, you. I am dramatic, but I am sincere, and the weather is in accordance with my feelings.*

It's always so brave. They speak so eloquently, even when they're saying they can't be eloquent.

I am not brave.

When I try to talk about love, I stick like a stubborn zipper. I fall off track, I stutter and stall. I don't have the words.

And what was I going to say to her? Was there anything to say?

Juliet, I have a problem, and it's your mouth.

Not very eloquent.

I kept quiet. We breathed in the dark. A simmering antic-ipation pressed in on the car, as if all the nighttime insects thrumming in the field were waiting to see what we would do. What I would do.

I turned in my seat to face her, and she didn't move. I reached out, tentatively, but pulled back. This was crazy. Touching her was crazy, and her sitting there with her eyes closed as if asleep was crazy. I felt like it was one more strange test. *Here I am*, her body was saying, *vulnerable and unaware. What are you going to do about it?*

I couldn't tell how to pass. Was I supposed to respect her fictional sleep? Was I supposed to touch her?

It wasn't bravery that made me reach out once more to softly touch her cheek with my fingertips. It was pure fear. I was afraid that if I didn't touch her now, I'd never have the opportunity again. And touching her just briefly felt like it was worth the risk.

She breathed in and leaned against my hand. Her mouth parted and I could see the tips of her teeth.

Oh.

I leaned closer. Her eyelashes fluttered, like she was dreaming, and then I brushed my lips against hers, soft, so soft she'd barely feel me.

The Juliet I knew, or tried to know, was imperious and mocking. But this was a new Juliet, soft, pliant.

I pulled away, suddenly scared. I touched my fingers to my lips like they'd betrayed me, my breathing shallow.

"What are you doing?" she said. Her eyes still closed.

It's a trap, said a voice inside me. I was trembling all over.

From fear or desire? I couldn't tell the difference.

"I'm . . . I'm sorry, I—" I said, panicking.

She opened her eyes. "I mean, why are you stopping?"

With that, she turned toward me, pulled me closer, her arms and hands strong. I felt small in her arms, insubstantial. She could snuff me out like a candle.

She took my hand and returned it to her cheek. Her eyes held mine. Then she moved my hand from her cheek to her neck. Her pulse throbbed beneath my palm.

"Pull me closer," she said.

I did as I was told.

For the span of a heartbeat, we were still, our foreheads touching, breathing in each other's breaths.

There are moments in your life when you feel time stop ticking forward and instead it holds for one shimmering beat, the choice you could make laid before you like an embroidered coat, waiting to be put on. Potential hummed in my ears and a fire caught light in my blood.

Then I kissed her, and she kissed me back, my hands were in her hair, and time rushed forward once again, around us and over our bodies, but there wasn't enough of it. I couldn't pull her to me tightly enough even though she pressed me against the driver's-side window, even though I wrapped my legs around her waist. I couldn't pull her under my skin.

She drew back, her teeth gently tugging my lower lip as she did, leaving me aching.

"I knew you could do something wonderful if you just stopped thinking," she said, smiling slyly.

"Oh god," I said, laughing. "I love you. You're terrible."

She laughed in response, and I pressed the small of her back and she lowered herself to kiss me again, her hair spilling around us.

It was only later I realized she never said "I love you" back, but what did I care? I was the filament in an incandescent bulb, and someone had finally turned on the current.

After Juliet dropped me off at the foot of my drive, I waited until her taillights blazed red and disappeared before I walked up the gravel to the dark house. It remained quiet and still. My window was still open, waiting.

For a while I stretched out on my bed, still in my clothes, the ones she'd had her hands on, under, the ones that now smelled like her.

But after a while, I went into the bathroom off my bedroom, and turned on the light. I stood there, my hands on the bathroom counter, looking in the mirror and trying to see who stood there looking back.

Did I look different? Was I the same girl I'd been earlier in the day, before I kissed her? I'd started wearing eyeliner ever since the party with Juliet, and it was smudged beneath my lashes. My lips were swollen from kisses, and I raised my hand to touch them, to feel her again. I looked tired and mussed and more beautiful than I'd ever felt in my life.

I didn't know if this kiss with Juliet meant I was gay or bi or what. I didn't have the language for it. I didn't know a word for loving Juliet Bergman.

STORYTIME

In the morning, I woke up with my heart singing for Juliet. I put out cereal and a bowl and spoon for my father, still sleeping off the wine and gin. I left a note telling him I'd be out for the day and signed off with *X*s and *O*s, and then sent him a text in case he missed the note. I felt generous to him and to the world. I'd kissed Juliet. I could be kind. The world was full of good things, and I was one of them.

It was a gorgeous day in late July and the bike ride to Juliet's was nothing but green lights and soft breezes. When I reached her yard, I jumped off the bike and let it roll on without me. I rang the doorbell and the chimes sounded, a song that couldn't compete with the one in my heart.

No answer.

I waited. Good things come to those who wait.

The birds were singing lilting songs about territory and sex. There were no sounds inside the house.

I shrugged, as if someone was watching, and then walked around to the back. No one on the deck. But there, out on the dock, was a figure silhouetted against the sky.

Juliet. I called out but she didn't turn.

I cautiously picked my way down through the greenery and washed-up sticks to the dock, which swayed a little as I stepped on. Still no response from Juliet.

Even when I stood beside her, she remained a silent statue, watching the water. There was a soft gray fleece around her shoulders against the breezy morning air, and she was wearing a gauzy nightgown that looked straight out of a 1960s Hammer vampire film. If she had been carrying a candle and looking for secret passages, the picture would have been complete.

Standing this close to her made me feel as though the air between us was vibrating in response to our bodies, like the air shimmered with my desire.

I took a deep breath, wanting to share everything in my heart.

But how do you tell someone all that?

You can't.

You don't.

I didn't. I just stood beside her and watched the lake.

"The others will be harder," she said.

I shook my head, like I was in a dream that wasn't going the way I wanted. The last thing on my mind was Richard or Duncan. I wanted to talk about that kiss. Or rather, I wanted to kiss again and not talk at all.

"Sarah's going to waver," she said, like a general surveying a battle plan. "She knows we're doing the right thing, but she's afraid."

"But I'm not?" *Tell me I'm tough. Tell me why you like that about me.*

She glanced at me. "You," she said. She looked at me coldly and I felt the orchestra that had been playing in my chest peter out. "The trouble with you is you're in for the wrong reasons."

Where was the girl who'd kissed me last night? Who was this, telling me I wasn't up to snuff? Just like that, my temper flared. "Excuse me? How could I have kicked Caleb any more enthusiastically?"

She shook her head. "You should believe in what we're doing. But you don't, not really, so you're scared."

"You're unhappy I'm not one hundred percent excited that we're planning to beat up a bunch of guys whose biceps are bigger than my head? That's not fear. That's just understanding the situation."

What was happening? This wasn't how I wanted this conversation to go.

"That shouldn't matter. You should care about the principle of things. You should have ideals."

"Ideals? You want to talk to me about ideals? You nearly drowned us," I blurted.

She stared me down, and I went quiet, still. The water lapped against the dock.

"Then why are you here?" she asked.

I opened my mouth to speak, then looked down, embarrassed. Dark shapes circled under the waters. Catfish, invasive carp, fish that lived in mud and muck.

"You need to think about the bigger picture. About people

other than yourself," she said.

"You said I should stop thinking," I said weakly. She was telling me I was selfish. It felt unfair, but I also couldn't argue with her. I didn't really care about revenge for girls I didn't know or hadn't known for years. I just wanted to be near Juliet.

She turned back to the lake. A million years passed. Then she finally spoke.

"When I was little, I had a dog named Bad Dog. Found her on set in Marseilles and my tutor let me keep her. She was all ribs and patchy fur, but even when she fattened up, she was always ugly. You could see her pink skin through the white fur, like she was a pig in disguise. But she was a nice dog. Not bright. But nice. I adored her."

I smiled warily. I imagined Juliet as a child, loving an ugly, stupid animal and naming it Bad Dog.

"Problem was, she loved to chase. If it ran, she ran after it. One day she got out of the trailer and started chasing a car on the lot. She came up alongside it, barking her head off, so the car sped up, and Bad Dog, she knew it was going to escape. So she ran so hard you couldn't see her legs, and she caught the tire, and the force of it drove her nose through her brain."

I didn't know what to say, so I started to reach my hand out for hers. I wanted to comfort her. I wanted to touch her.

She looked down at my outstretched hand, then away. I pulled my hand back.

"Sometimes you get your dream, Rabbit, but it's not what you were expecting," she said.

THE PLAN

"**O**h my god, I am made of bugs," said Sarah. She put down the bucket of water she'd lugged from one end of the cabin to the other to brush herself off frantically. "This only confirms what I always suspected," I said. "You're not a girl, you're just a pile of spiders in cutoffs."

Sarah stuck her tongue out at me and, having confirmed that she was free of tiny passengers, dipped her mop into the bucket and began to clean the floor.

It was nearing midnight, and Sarah and I had each snuck out of our houses to join Juliet in cleaning the cabin once more. This time with real water, although it was water we had to carry in buckets from the bed of a pickup truck. Jesse Bergman had a lot of vehicles. Juliet had flicked on the lights of Galaxy House's downstairs garage like a magician performing a flashy trick, revealing Juliet's old Camaro, two motorcycles, a steel-gray BMW, an electric-yellow sports car that seemed to be from the future, a car that looked like a cream-colored tank, and this incredibly beefy silver pickup. The keys were ready for the taking on a pegboard by the door. The three of us lined the truck bed with a huge plastic tarp, secured it with duct tape, and then filled it with water from a hose. We drove this makeshift pool until we were as near to the cabin as you could get from the road, losing half the water in the process. Bucket by bucket, we'd emptied the truck bed and used the water to remove the layers of grime. Our first attempt at cleaning had been mostly symbolic. This time, the cabin really was becoming habitable.

Maybe we could stop being avenging angels and just become homesteaders. We'd wear calico and gingham and learn how to sew. Sarah could read to us from the Bible every night and I'd pop Juliet's suspenders playfully, because of course in this scenario she was wearing button-fly pants and a rustic white shirt and good god, what was wrong with me? Juliet hadn't touched me since her little speech about overly ambitious dogs. It had been three days.

I scrubbed the floor harder.

Juliet stopped wiping down the wooden furniture and, instead, kept rearranging the small table, and the chair beside it. Then she'd stand in the doorway of the cabin and look at it. Then she'd move it again. It was like watching an exceptionally precise child play house.

"You achieve your vision yet?" I said. I dropped my mop and sat down on the damp ground. If the floors had ever been waxed, that wax was long gone. The wood drank up the water and held it.

"Setting matters," said Juliet, frowning again at the table and chair. She moved the chair an inch over. "Set designers are the unsung heroes of filmmaking."

Sarah followed my lead and sat down, too. We were exhausted. Juliet fussed a bit more, then stood again in the doorway, surveying our work.

"It's good," she said. "This will do."

"For what? Restarting the church of McCracken? Worshiping lake scum?" I asked.

Juliet grinned. "Please, I'd run such a better cult than him."

"So what, then? Are we going to lure the guys here with beer?" said Sarah.

Juliet snorted. "Like those guys could follow directions through the woods to this cabin. We'd have to line a path with flares."

I briefly enjoyed the thought of Richard and Duncan crashing around in the woods, maybe falling face-first on a sharp stick or surprising a bobcat. We'd heard the big cats screaming at each other in the woods that night, sounding like women possessed.

"This isn't for Duncan. He doesn't deserve our effort," said Juliet, "but we will definitely lure him."

"To where?" I asked. "And with what?"

"I haven't decided on that yet. And blowjobs."

"Excuse me?" I said.

"We're not going to actually blow him," said Juliet scornfully. "And it won't be us. A Kelly will call."

"The Kellys are many things," I said, "but they are not helpful."

Juliet rolled her eyes, took a deep breath, and proceeded to give a dead-on impression of Kelly Proud.

"Duncan, I know this is so *bad*, but I have this *fan*tasy—oh god, I can't say it—I just, I really want to be with you and Kelly Number Two at the same time. Like, all three of us. I just get so—so *hot* thinking about it," said Juliet as Kelly. Then she dropped the voice and the affect and was Juliet once more.

"Juliet Bergman," I said, laughing. I don't know what was funnier. Watching Juliet channel a Kelly or the idea of Kelly Proud saying those things. Kelly Proud showed her purity ring to anyone who would look at it. It's not that I minded the celibacy—it was the idea that she was somehow better than everyone else because of her virginity. An intact hymen seemed like flimsy criteria for salvation.

"Whoa," said Sarah. "You've got her voice down cold." She looked in awe.

"I have an ear for idiocy," said Juliet.

"Wait," I said, "that's the plan?"

"That's the fantasy," said Juliet, deadpan.

"That's— I don't think that's a good idea," I said.

"We handled Caleb just fine," said Sarah. I frowned at her.

"Exactly," said Juliet. "It went off without a hitch."

"But that's my point. Everything went right with that. This sounds messier. He could realize you're a fake Kelly, or he could follow up with another Kelly, or—"

"Twice the danger, twice the fun!" Sarah said, grinning.

I widened my eyes at her like a disapproving owl. I did not need her chiming in like a cheerleader for chaos.

"Where are we sending him? How do we keep him from telling someone about his upcoming big night with Kelly? What about—cell phone records? I just think we need to slow down and think about what's the best way to do this. I don't think this is it," I said. I used my best, most reasonable voice.

"You mean you think we shouldn't do it at all," said Sarah. Her voice was tremulous. God, what was wrong with her?

"No one's saying that," said Juliet. "Are they?"

I shook my head. I was not saying that.

"Then let's talk about it later. We all need sleep. We'll hammer out the details and come up with something everyone is on board with," said Juliet.

We packed our cleaning supplies into the empty buckets, and Sarah and I each took a mop. Juliet paused once more in the doorway and grinned.

"It's perfect," she said.

We were exhausted by the time we'd unloaded the truck back at Galaxy House, and by unspoken agreement, the night ended. Or, the day, I should say, as it was nearing two in the morning.

"You coming?" said Sarah. She was straddling her bike on the lawn, waiting for me. We'd biked over together.

"You go on," I said. "I'll catch up."

She nodded and glided off.

"Well?" said Juliet.

"I wanted to talk to you," I said.

"Clearly." She folded her arms and raised an eyebrow.

I swallowed. I'd told myself I would ask her about the kiss. I would ask her why she'd told me to back off with a weird dead dog story. It had been kicking around in the back of my head all night. What better time to ask someone about their feelings than when you are covered in grime and cleaning solution? I understood romantic timing.

The words died inside me. I couldn't. This was a huge mistake.

"You know, never mind," I said. "I was going to talk to you more about the plan but you're right, we should wait until we're rested, so I'll get out of your hair."

Perfect. Super cool. She'll never suspect anything.

She stepped a little closer to me.

"Did you want to talk to me about the kiss?"

Fuck.

Fuck fuck fuck.

I bit my lip. Yes, I nodded.

She looked down, and gently, so gently, took my hand.

"You're confused," she said.

My confusion at this point reached heretofore-unrecorded levels, so I nodded again. Indeed. I was acing this conversation.

"The most important thing to me in the world right now is keeping you and Sarah safe through this. I need to have a clear head."

"Okay," I said. "I understand." I didn't, of course, but I knew she was telling me nothing else was going to happen. It was all I could do to stop myself from crying.

"But whenever I get close to you, I forget all that. You set me spinning, Rabbit," she said. She touched my cheek and moved my hair away from my face. My eyelashes fluttered.

Then she kissed me. Her tongue was warm and soft, and when it touched mine, I felt nervous, and pulled back.

"No?" she said.

I closed my eyes.

I don't know why you're kissing me now, I thought, and I can't bear it if you stop. I opened my eyes and said, "No, no. I mean, yes. Yes, kiss me. I'm just—I feel like I don't know what I'm doing," I said. "From a—from a technical standpoint."

She grinned. "Ah, from a technical standpoint."

"Yeah."

"You're doing fine," she said. "Technically."

"Fine sounds . . . adequate."

"More than adequate," she said, kissing me again.

"Fine," I said.

"Fine," she said.

THE MOST BORING THING

Many kisses later, I walked my bike down the dark driveway, sporting a grin for no one but myself. Behind me, Galaxy House was a gilded box of light, and the music drifting down from inside the house cut off with the closing of the door.

I was exhausted, filthy, my lips were sore from kissing, and if I thought about her hands on me, then I didn't have to think anything else, which was all I wanted. For a weird moment, I felt like a very normal teenager, albeit one who was in love with a leader of a vigilante girl gang.

I laughed out loud at the idea of being in a gang, the sound abrupt in the quiet night.

"You and Juliet, huh?" said a voice.

I froze. I could just make out a dark shape ahead of me. Looking back at the house had ruined my night vision, and I was almost blind.

But I knew Sarah's voice.

"Yeah, kinda," I said. I realized in a mortified flash how on display Juliet and I had been, standing in the light on the steps of the house, like two figurines in an illuminated case.

I'd thought Sarah was long gone. Apparently not.

She didn't reply. I was starting to make her out now. The moon above us was fat and full, and Sarah's face silvered in its light. With her dark crown of braids, she looked like a moon princess.

"You didn't tell me," said Sarah.

"It literally just happened!"

"That wasn't the first time," said Sarah. "No way. I *knew* there was something weird going on, I knew it."

"I—I couldn't talk about it," I said.

"Juliet told you not to?" she asked. A little hesitation. As if that would make it okay.

"No, no, not at all. I mean, I just . . . I don't know. I wasn't expecting it."

"I'm your friend," said Sarah. "Why didn't you tell me?" She sounded hurt.

"Sarah, we're friends, but—"

"I don't need you," said Sarah tightly, "to be my *best* friend like we used to be. I only wanted you to— Can't you try? Can't you two act like I'm here?"

I opened my mouth, closed it. Every time I'd resented Sarah's presence, she'd been resenting mine. It shouldn't have surprised me but it did. I'd been wrong to think our friendship could be fixed, that we could go back to how we were. Juliet had brought us together, but without her, we'd fall apart once more. It wasn't real.

"I'm sorry," I said. "I'm sorry I— I'm sorry. I didn't mean to . . . to hurt your feelings."

"Couldn't you let me have one thing? Couldn't you let me have this?" She gestured back at the house. Her voice was thick with held-back tears. The last time I could remember seeing Sarah struggle to keep it together like this was when she learned my mom was sick. My mom told her and then held her. I'd stood awkwardly apart, watching the two of them hug in our kitchen. Even then, I couldn't figure out the right thing to feel.

"I don't understand," I said, helplessly, stupidly.

"Listen," she said, "you're getting out of this town. I know you think you won't, but you will. You've got the grades, you'll write a sad essay about your mom, and then you'll get into a good school on scholarship and never look back. I know that. But I can't— My mother— I'm just stuck. I'm either here or somewhere exactly like it, and Juliet—these nights—this is the thing that makes it so I can stand it. You're going to mess it up for me and you don't even *need* it."

I shook my head. The essay comment was a cheap shot, but it whizzed by me without making a hit. I was too overwhelmed by the idea that Sarah had *seen* us. "I'm stuck, too."

"You are not. You don't even fucking believe in any of this! You don't get it. You're only along for the ride because you fucked Richard."

"Wow, first of all, I should get hazard pay for that, and—"

"You don't care what happens to the next girl. You don't believe in what Juliet says. *I* do. *I* found that picture. *I* wanted to do something about it. *I'm* all in. You just go along with things and it's the most fucking boring thing about you."

I was still reeling at the improbability of Sarah cursing when she hopped on her bike, pedaling away, leaving me alone in the dark with my thoughts.

DISCOVERED

I took my time biking back, thinking about Sarah's unexpected craziness, about Juliet's lips on mine, and was halfway through my window when my dad turned on the bedroom lights. I yelped and proceeded to fall on my bed gracelessly, headfirst, my face smooshed into the coverlet for one interminable, undignified moment.

"Where have you been, Sadie?" my father demanded, his voice a taut rope.

"I— What?" I sat up and pushed my hair out of my face. I'd never really been in trouble. Apparently, my instinctual response was to pretend to be deeply stupid.

"I said, where have you been?" My father was sitting in a chair he'd pulled into my room to wait for me to show up. The chair suggested forethought and dedication; it meant he hadn't simply happened to open the door and find me gone.

"I was— I took a walk."

"A walk," he repeated. "Where were you walking at two thirty in the morning?"

"Just . . . just up and down our road," I said. "Just nearby."

"You were not on our road, because I drove the car up and down it, looking for you."

"Oh."

"Oh," he repeated sardonically. "I thought to myself, there's no way my daughter is so stupid as to leave our house in the middle of the night. That's not possible."

My father was clenching and unclenching his fists in his lap, like he wouldn't mind committing a mild strangling.

"You know the only reason I didn't call the cops?"

I shook my head. It did not seem like the time to tell him I'd have to be missing for twenty-four hours before the cops did anything. That was true, right? Maybe not if you were technically a child.

"Because Sheila convinced me that you would come back, that this was normal teenage behavior. But I think—"

Just then we both heard a car park in the driveway.

"There she is now. You stay here, young lady."

"You invited her over?!" I asked, incredulous.

"Stay here," he said warningly, and left the room.

I seriously considered going right back out the window, but the idea of Sheila seeing me exit the house ass-first discouraged me.

On the bed, I put my head in my hands. I'd known there was the possibility that my father could catch me, but he was such a sound sleeper. I'd been sneaking out for weeks and nothing had happened. Why now?

Sheila came in, and I could hear them talking, my father's voice rising and falling on waves of anger until it stopped suddenly. I heard a kitchen drawer slam, followed by his bedroom door.

There was a soft knock at the door.

"Knock knock," said a feminine voice.

Oh god.

"Come in," I said grudgingly.

Sheila poked her head in. I was used to seeing her in Group, sitting primly on the folding chair with a binder full of *Psychology Now* articles open on her lap. She made an outline before every meeting and referred to it whenever she lost the thread, which was often. Sometimes I could see that she'd drawn hearts next to the really moving parts. Now here she was in my bedroom. Seeing her in the same room as my stuffed animals made me want to throw them at her until she suffocated.

"Your dad needs a little time to cool off," she said.

"Yeah," I said. "I picked up on that."

She stood there, uncertain of what to do next. You and me both, I thought, feeling an unwelcome stab of sympathy for her. I gave a little nod of my head to indicate she should come in, so she stepped into the room. She gravitated toward joining me on the bed, then clearly decided that was too bold a move. She moved the chair my father had recently occupied to sit near to me.

Sheila was wearing a bathrobe over her pajamas, and I was fairly confident this was not how she envisioned meeting me in her new role. Her hair was smooshed on one side. She'd clearly been sleeping, and I felt some amount of chagrin for this woman being pulled out of her bed by my father in the middle of the night, due to my actions.

But not a lot.

"I know I'm the last person you want here right now, but your dad called me, completely freaking out, and he said he needed me, so . . ." She put out her hands in a classic "What are you gonna do?" gesture.

I hugged my knees to my chin. Maybe if I was still enough, she'd decide I was a rock and go away.

"Your dad . . . he, uh . . . he was worried maybe you were off doing something stupid."

I looked at her blankly. I had done a lot of stupid things lately. I needed her to narrow it down.

"You know, he was scared; that's why he's so angry. Because a while back you tried to . . ."

My eyes widened. Of all the conclusions for my dad to leap to, this one hadn't occurred to me.

"It wasn't—it wasn't that."

"I know, that's what I said. I told him you were out being a normal teenager. Off seeing some guy, I'm guessing." She gave me a conspiratorial smile.

Oh god, this was hell. I was in hell.

"Are you . . . are you being safe?" she asked, leaning forward, her forehead furrowed.

I resisted the urge to laugh in her face. My life had not felt anything like safe lately.

"I'm not going to get pregnant, if that's what you're asking," I said.

"Just know you can call me, if you want to talk," she said, then lowered her voice to a whisper. "I'm also happy to take you to a doctor," she said. She tilted her head in the general direction of my father. "Men can be kinda clueless about this stuff."

I realized my only hope to escape from this conversation was to join in.

"Yeah," I said. "Clueless."

She smiled, beaming. She'd broken through. We'd made a connection.

Hoo-fucking-ray.

I contemplated flaking away into a pile of ash. It didn't matter that Sheila was actually being pretty decent to me. I was mortified.

"I'm glad we got to talk, even under these circumstances," she said. She leaned over and gave my knee a squeeze and I barely managed not to squirm away.

Too much, Sheila.

Then she left, shutting the door behind her.

Almost immediately, my father opened it without knocking, and stuck his head in to say one thing before closing it, hard.

"You're grounded. Two weeks."

UNDER LOCKDOWN

Thus began my imprisonment.

In the morning, my father poured coffee for himself, for me, and for Sheila, who it seemed had spent the night. Gross. We sat around the kitchen island without speaking, despite Sheila's attempts to make friendly eye contact with both of us.

Once he finished his coffee, Dad left us in the kitchen to rummage around in the garage. It wasn't long before he returned with a yellow toolbox. The sight filled me with alarm. If my father was picking up manly tools, things had truly gone sideways.

"Where are you going with that?" I said sharply. He was heading to my bedroom.

"Arthur?" said Sheila, sounding a little worried. Clearly this was new behavior to her, also. I wondered what her perception of him was. Grieving widower? Fixer-upper? Potential murderer? Maybe all three. Can this murderous bachelor be saved?

I followed. Wordlessly, my father slammed the toolbox down on my bedroom rug, opened it up, and pulled out a hammer and a box of nails.

With his shoes still on, he stepped on my bed and began to hammer my window to the sill.

"Arthur, that's—"

"What the fuck are you doing?!" I screamed. The sight of my father standing on my bed with a hammer in hand was so surreal I couldn't quite process it, but I knew I felt violated.

"What if there's a fire?" said Sheila, still trying to be the voice of reason.

Oh, Sheila, we are way past reason.

He paused. "We're just going to have to hope that doesn't happen," he said, then gave the sill another whack. My father was not skilled, and my window looked like a drunk handyman had attempted surgery on it.

"No sneaking out and no setting fires, got it," I said tersely. I was vibrating with anger. "Anything else?"

"You're going back to Group," he said. "I know you've been skipping. I know you've been lying to me about it, and that's changing right now. I'm taking you there every night it meets."

Sheila broke in. "You know I resigned from Group, sweetie, so there's no problem there. Trisha took over."

I ignored her.

"Are you serious?!" I said to my father, horrified. "Dad, come on, let me bike at least."

"I want you in the company of an adult at all times. You've

shown me you can't be trusted. You have to earn that trust back."

"Group is stupid. It's not helping."

"I don't care," he said, his voice rising. "If it isn't helping, maybe you aren't trying."

"I'm not trying? Trying to do what, exactly? Forget Mom is dead? Should I drink till I pass out every night? Seems to work for you. You're moving along just fine," I yelled.

Sheila, who'd followed us into my bedroom, widened her eyes even farther and slowly backed out of the room. Good choice, Sheila. Back right on out of the house.

He clenched his fists, then looked down and realized he was still holding the hammer. Then he closed his eyes, took a shaky breath, and opened them again. The anger left his body and he looked smaller, weaker. He put the hammer back in the toolbox. He shakily closed the lid and snapped it shut.

"Treating me like a prisoner doesn't make Mom less dead," I snarled. I didn't want the fight to end. "You should have boarded up the window a long time ago. You should have dug a moat around the house and protected me—you're so blind. I was sleeping with a monster for fun, and you didn't even notice."

He didn't look at me, though he flinched a little at the monster bit. I wondered how oblivious he'd been, really, and if it was better or worse if he'd known. His eyes flicked to the window and its fresh line of crooked nails. There was a new crack in the glass. He looked ashamed.

Good.

But he didn't pull the nails out.

When he closed the door behind him, I threw a book at it.

My father worked remotely so he could stay home with me, like I was an actual child. This meant he was on video conferences all day with people who were passionate about internet speed, and that if I turned my music up in my room, he'd beat on the door until I turned it down. He drove me to Group on Friday, where Trisha greeted me like a lost lamb, and I remained silent through the whole tedious hour.

My days became very regular. The best strategy, I felt, was to lie low and wait the two weeks out. It wasn't that hard. My anger with my father was so intense I couldn't even look at him, so I interacted as little as possible and didn't talk with him. He couldn't stay home forever. If I played the part of Dutiful Daughter long enough, he'd go back to ignoring me like he had for so long. He had Sheila to distract him, after all, and gin. The levels in the bottles still lowered, if not as fast.

Juliet didn't call. She didn't answer my texts.

Neither did Sarah, not that I expected her to. I clearly wasn't her favorite person.

Neither one of them, not even once, checked on me to see why I wasn't coming around.

We'd spent over half the summer together. Wasn't either one of them going to break me out? When I undressed for bed, I'd catch a glimpse of my crescent tattoo and feel a flash of fury, of bitterness. None of it had been real, had it? And now I had a mark to carry around with me for the rest of my life, a nice reminder that sisterhood was a sham, and a kiss wasn't worth much at all.

So, I waited, and tried to keep myself alive through movies. I watched *Blue Valentine*, and *Gone Girl*, *500 Days of Summer*, and *A Simple Favor*. Happy stuff. When I wasn't watching movies, I read the *New Yorker*'s descriptions of indie film festivals and I tried to picture myself in the audience, like my mom would have wanted. I read the music reviews and imagined swaying in a hazy neon-lit club, smoking, dancing—everything I was too chicken to do in my own life. If I pretended hard enough, I was riding a Greyhound all the way to NYC, with only a change of clothes in my backpack and whatever novel I was in love with that day. My mother would have wanted that for me. Most of the time, Juliet was by my side. But sometimes, I just looked out the window at the imaginary countryside, and watched my reflection, feeling her loss. Even in my fantasies, she left me.

I'd thought for sure that Juliet would show up outside my window again. I'd do a dumb show about how it was nailed shut, and then I'd try to sneak out the front door, if I could. My father was sleeping on the couch every night like a crazy person, so that he could see the front and back doors. If she had only appeared on the porch, wanting me to join her—that would have made me feel like my imprisonment was a solvable problem.

Night after night, Juliet didn't come.

It turned out that they'd been busy without me.

Halfway through my two-week grounding, my father was

watching the news and I was pointedly ignoring him. When my mother was alive, she'd banned all TV during dinner. Now we regularly watched the news or a sitcom while we ate, if we ate together at all. I rarely paid attention, but I did that night.

"Reportedly, a group of masked young women lured the teenage boy with promises of sexual acts to a bathroom in Hart's Run State Park's lakefront, long after hours," said the anchor. His voice became increasingly incredulous. "They then proceeded to beat the boy savagely, leaving him unconscious. A passing ranger saw flashlights and investigated."

The camera cut to footage of a man wearing the brown uniform of a park employee, shaking his head in consternation.

"I never seen anything like it. I was expecting—well, I was expecting something kinda—you know what people get up to in these buildings. But a pack of girls attacking that poor boy? Unbelievable. Just unbelievable."

Not a pack. Just two.

Back at the news desk, the announcer said, "No motive for the attack is known, but authorities speculate it might be gang related. There's no word yet as to suspects. The injuries do not appear to be life-threatening, and the teenager is expected to recover fully."

"Crazy," said my dad. "That's not something you hear every day."

"Yeah," I whispered, forgetting in my shock that we weren't speaking. My fists were clenched so tightly that I could feel my nails cut into my palms, a searing line on each hand. My head was roaring with anger and hurt and disbelief. All that time, all that training, all her words. *Kissing* her. None of it was enough to slow her down, to just *wait* one more week until I could join them. They'd carried on without me like I'd never been one of them. "Who does something like that?"

A SURPRISE GIFT

N ear the end of the second week of my incarceration, my father had to stay overnight in Atlanta for work, and still didn't trust me to go to Group on my own. But Sheila agreed to see that I got there, and to spend the night in our house. A "girls' night," she had called it. When I got in her car to go to Group, I saw that Sheila had a plastic tag hanging from her rearview mirror that said, Blessed Be Your Heart.

Wow. Really.

We drove quietly for a while, which suited me fine. It wasn't far to town. If I could extend this silence until we got to the church, we'd both get out of this situation relatively unscathed.

"Your dad's got his dander up about all this," she said.

No such luck.

"Yeah, when he gets mad, he commits," I said. His anger with me had lasted over the length of my two-week grounding, seemingly with no abatement. Probably the last time I'd seen him this mad was when I woke up in the hospital. And then, he'd been alternating yelling at me with hugging me. It had been disorienting, to say the least.

"We'll get there early," she said. "Is that okay?" She deftly passed a slower vehicle, then settled back into the lane. Sheila drove like someone from out of town, impatient with slow-moving horse trailers and tractors.

"Yeah," I said. "I'll just see my friends."

Sheila knew I didn't have any friends there, but acknowledging that would be admitting she'd failed to create a "warm and welcoming community."

We drove for a few moments in blissful silence, but Sheila's constant need to hear her own voice meant this was short-lived.

"You know, when I was your age, I went through the same thing."

I sincerely doubted that.

"I fell in love with this guy, and I dropped all my friends. I was so wrapped up in him!"

I looked at her quizzically.

"Mind you, nobody called my dad and ratted me out! But I'm sure they thought about it," she said, laughing. She pulled up behind the church. The door leading down to the basement was ajar. "He wasn't a bad guy, though, and I learned moderation, eventually. Sometimes you have to work it out of your system. Here we are!"

"Someone called my dad?"

The smile froze on her face.

"Oh," she said.

"Who called my dad?" I said.

"Well, I—I don't know exactly," she said. "He just said your friend called and woke him up and told him you weren't home."

Sarah. It had to be Sarah.

"Unbelievable."

I stared straight ahead out the car's windshield. I could see some of the Group members milling around outside by the door, even though the sky was threatening rain. No one wanted to be the first in the room.

"Rabbit," she said, "you okay?"

I bundled up my anger and tied it into a small package. It would keep.

"Yeah," I said. "Just dumb stuff."

"Listen, your dad means well, but he's been kind of over the top," she said. "I was thinking that maybe instead of Group you'd like a few hours out on your own. Maybe you could meet up with your special someone? Actually introduce him to your friends? Sometimes it makes all the difference with people if you show you're making an effort." She smiled tentatively. She was offering me a gift. All I had to do was be okay with her speculating erroneously about my love life, and oh, dating my widower dad, and she'd cut me a break.

"So, what, do I call you in a few hours?"

"How about he drops you off?" she said lightly. "I'll be back at your house. But you can come home whenever."

Sheila would like very much to be cool, I thought, even at the risk of teen pregnancy.

"Yeah," I said. "Yeah, that would be great."

She grinned. I matched it as best I could. In her Sheila way, she was trying. I appreciated it, and it touched me a little. But not so much that I wouldn't take advantage of it.

Outside the car, I milled around with the other grieving losers and mimed calling my imaginary boyfriend. I gave Sheila a thumbs-up and she waved and drove away. Then I was out of there. Tootles, Sheila.

A FLOOD

I didn't have a lot of time. I wanted to find Sarah, but I didn't know how. Sarah's house was back toward mine, but I somehow doubted her parents would let her come out so I could kick her ass.

But you miss all the shots you don't take, I told myself, and I walked to the front of the church. There were usually a few bikes in the stand out front, and if I could find an unlocked one I could "borrow" it for the night.

I identified a mustard-yellow bike with a bent handlebar as my likely candidate, and sure enough, it wasn't locked. Bless you, trusting small town. Based off the rust on the spokes, there was probably good reason for it, but I couldn't be choosy. If it would get me to Sarah's, that was good enough.

I'd just pulled it out and swung my leg over when I looked up and saw Sarah, staring right at me. She was standing between two other girls at the front of the church, each of them wearing pajamas and carrying overnight bags.

Sarah's pajamas had little cats festooned on them. Because of course they did.

It was as if I'd somehow manifested her through sheer will.

Later, I'd remember that Sarah had mentioned her mother had changed churches. She was there for a lock-in, hence the pajamas.

The two girls with Sarah gave me a confused look. I wasn't wearing pajamas, for one thing. I also was staring at Sarah with what I assume was a murderous glare. I put the bike back in the rack.

"Sarah, do you want . . ." said one girl, looking from me to Sarah and back again, like I was a snake in their path. A few drops of rain hit the sidewalk between us, then a few more.

"It's fine. We know each other," said Sarah. "I'll meet you in there."

They looked dubious, but also clearly wanted to get inside the church and find a good place to set up their sleeping bags so they could dream about their boyfriend Jesus all night. They were gone and we were alone, at least until the next group of pajama-clad acolytes arrived.

She had the nerve to look surprised when I landed a punch to her face that nearly broke my hand.

But she had it coming.

Sarah was back up before I could recover from the shock of landing the punch, slamming into me with all her weight. I collapsed beneath her as she grabbed my hair and yelled, "What the fuck?" into my face.

It was not my best performance.

"You told him!" I yelled back.

She grunted, and pushed herself off me, kneeing me in the stomach as she did so. I curled up around the pain, unable to curse with the breath knocked out of me. Still, I managed to get back to my feet, and rushed at her with a yell, forgetting everything I'd been taught about not signaling my intent. But it didn't matter that she saw me coming; I still managed to get another blow in. Her head snapped back, and she staggered, putting her hand to her mouth.

When we'd first started to train, I'd hated my clumsy feet and their hesitation. I hated how my body was heavy with everything I'd ever been told. Cross your legs. Don't take up space. Speak when spoken to. Don't hit. Don't talk back. Be quiet. Be quiet. Be quiet. All those words had made me pull my punches, made me kind when I needed to be cruel.

I wasn't pulling my punches anymore.

Sarah wavered and sat hard on the ground. It began to rain in earnest.

"Fuck," she said.

I was still breathing heavily, my hands up, ready for whatever she did next.

"I'm sorry," Sarah spat out.

"What?" I wasn't prepared for that.

"I'm sorry. It was—it was awful of me to call your dad."

"It was beyond awful," I said. I grimaced. I wanted to accept the apology, but I couldn't stop talking back.

Her mouth drew tight, and she pushed herself off the ground to standing. It looked painful.

"Why did you?" I said. By now, the rain was heavy, and Sarah's hair was plastered to her head. I could feel water running down my neck onto my back. Three pajama-clad girls ran screaming through the rain into the church, none of them sparing us a second glance. This town lacked civic feeling.

"You . . . you just don't get it," she said. "You don't get it—how good you've got it."

I laughed. "Yeah, my life is a dream. I watched my mom turn into a toothpick and blow away. My drunk dad's dating a motivational poster. And my so-called friend thinks it's fine to rat me out."

She let out a sound somewhere between a laugh and a sob. Her face twisted up.

"You're so— You're ridiculous. Your dad cares enough to ground you," she said.

"What, you're jealous of my dad!? He's being psycho."

"Yes! That! Everything! Maybe right now you're grounded, but normally you do whatever you want. No one makes you go to tent revivals and church lock-ins or wear purity rings. My mom wants me to live at home while I go to a Christian college. She's already got it all picked out. It's the kind of place where they report on you to your parents. You can get kicked out if you go to a bar. It's going to be worse than high school. I thought the divorce meant I'd have a chance. I thought my dad would take me with him, but he's going to move out of state and leave me with her," she said, her voice ragged. "He gets to escape, and I'm trapped with her. I'm trapped."

"Oh, oh, Sarah," I said. My heart felt like it was flooding with all the rainwater. I hadn't known. Or, more accurately, I hadn't paid attention.

"There, there it is. Your pity. You know what's even worse than the way you don't notice anything about my life? When you do, and then you *pity* me. I just wanted *one thing*, one thing to be mine."

"You wanted Juliet," I said. It clicked into place. She'd seen us kissing, and then she'd called my dad. "You like her."

She shook her head violently. "No, no, no. You're still not listening. I didn't want her, not like that. I just wanted— I wanted one thing in my life that my parents didn't know about, didn't have a say in. One thing that profoundly had no Jesus in it. That used to be you. Hanging out, watching those stupid movies—I *loved* that. Your mom made popcorn and curled up on the couch with us, and it felt like home, like a real home. And then she died, and you *left* me, and it was all gone. This thing with Juliet—it wasn't the same, but it was something. But you had to have more than me. You couldn't be part of something *with* me, you had to make it only for you."

"I didn't set out to— You want me to apologize for—for having feelings for her?" I said.

She gave a shrill laugh. "Oh, what, you're in love with her or something?"

"Yeah," I spat. "I'm in love with Juliet."

She went very still. The mockery left her face. "Oh, wow," she said.

"Yeah," I whispered. "But it doesn't—it doesn't feel as good as I thought it would, being in love."

Sarah's eyes softened.

And just like that, just from that look of kindness, I started to cry. It could not have been more ridiculous, crying in the rain, but we don't get to pick our moments. All the frustration I'd felt about Juliet, all the ways in which she'd put me second or treated me like an afterthought or acted like my desire was amusing—all of it shook out of me in fat, hiccupping tears. I felt stupid and ugly.

Sarah put her arms around me, and I sobbed harder.

"This is me," she said, "pitying you, by the way."

"I know," I said. "Thank you."

She let me go, and I rubbed my face clean of tears and snot.

We looked like hell. Sarah's cat pajamas were covered in mud, and I was covered in my own snot. I couldn't help but laugh a little at the two of us.

"Rabbit, I'm sorry I asked you to go to church with me. It was dumb. I missed her so much, and you were hurting, and I didn't know what to say."

"Well, you've got me at church now," I said.

Sarah looked at me with a straight face. "I'm waiting for you to burst into flames."

I laughed. "So, I guess you got to have some quality time with Juliet, though. Beating up boys." I tried not to let my jealousy rear its head again, but it was hard. It hurt that they'd done it without me, even if I hadn't liked the plan. *Why didn't you call?* I wanted to say. *Why didn't* she *call?* But I couldn't bear to say out loud how much this had wounded me.

At my words, Sarah shook her head. She looked frightened. "Who was it?"

"Duncan," she said. "She wants to save Richard for last. Juliet, she's— It was vicious," she whispered. "I thought the first time was bad, but that was nothing. She really—she enjoys it."

I thought about how I'd kicked and kicked Caleb Winters, and the look of approval Juliet had given me. *There's my girl.* How excited I'd felt for her to see me. How sick I'd felt later.

But I'd enjoyed it, too.

"She's not worried about getting caught, but I am," she said. "That's why I'm here. I'd rather deal with the Holy Spirit than her. I'm not going back to that house—she'll just convince me to do it again. I can't seem to say no when I'm around her."

I knew what that was like. But I didn't want to say no, not really. And I couldn't understand Sarah giving up. This was what Juliet had seen so clearly. Sarah had believed but couldn't follow through. She lacked courage.

She looked at me, and started to speak, then closed her mouth.

"What?" I said.

She squeezed her eyes shut, and then opened them. "Rabbit, I know right now you think I'm a coward. I'm okay with that. I probably am. But it's not bravery she's asking for. I just— I know you love her. I do, too. Not the same way, but I do. But don't go back to her. She doesn't care what happens to us in all this."

I nodded, the way you do when you want to show you've listened, but you'll never do what they're asking.

She gave me a sad smile. She knew.

Everyone has to make their own mistakes, I guess.

But I was already saying goodbye. I had to find Juliet.

WONDERWALL

B y the time I arrived on my stolen bike, Galaxy House was a black cutout against the flaring sunset. The front door opened as I pulled up, and light poured out like honey over Juliet silhouetted in the frame. I stopped in the drive, and stared at her without waving, without moving. I was standing on the edge of something, a pool of deep water with no bottom.

"You in or you out?" she called.

I was in. Who was I kidding? I was in.

In the two weeks I'd been away, the interior of the house had taken on a nested quality, like when mice settle into a pantry and start pulling out all the goods. The spartan lines of the house's interior were destroyed by clothes strewn everywhere, by piles of dirty laundry. A bronze statue of a boxer in the foyer had gained a feathered hat and a smear of lipstick across his mouth. There was a lingering scent of burned oatmeal in the kitchen, and there were multiple pans soaking in the sink. For the first time, Galaxy House looked like a real human being lived in it. A really messy one.

I didn't care that the place didn't look like a magazine spread anymore. I was vibrating with excitement to be inside it again. To stand next to her. All I wanted to do was touch her, to kiss her again.

"We should go," she said as I stepped toward her. She grabbed a backpack from the kitchen counter and cinched it shut.

"Go where?" I asked stupidly. My hand was still outstretched to take her by the waist. I wanted her to ask me where I'd been, and why. Had she tried to visit me? Had she been turned away? Was the radio silence because I'd done something wrong, or precautionary now that the police were involved?

But I had forgotten the mission, and the mission was everything. I put my hand in my pocket. Smooth.

"Richard's," she said as if I wasn't keeping up. "He's alone tonight. His parents are in Atlanta for a fundraiser and won't be back all weekend. I was going to do it alone but I'm so glad you're here. Sarah hasn't answered her phone all day."

"Sarah told me— Sarah's out," I said. "She said—she said things were crazy. That you— She said *you* were crazy."

Juliet rolled her eyes. "She *would* think that. It was nothing. It was like fraternity hazing, at worst. Duncan exaggerated because he couldn't stand the idea that two girls got the best of him. Whatever," she said dismissively. "She was never serious." Sarah was out.

Weirdly, I almost defended Sarah. Sarah had been the serious one, not me. Sarah had been ride-or-die, until whatever happened with Duncan. But I didn't. Sarah wasn't here anymore, I was, and that was what mattered.

I was made of different stuff than Sarah. Juliet had made me into what she needed. I was stronger now; I could fight.

"Let's do it," I said. Like I was in an action movie. *Let's do this. Lock and load. We're not so different, you and I.*

For once, we didn't take the Camaro, but instead, the boxy, tanklike vehicle from Galaxy's massive garage. It was incongruously cream colored and looked like it could roll over a small village and all its inhabitants, no problem. The interior was far too luxurious for what otherwise looked like army surplus. Probably that's what it was—an expensive artifact from a recent war, retrofitted with the finest Corinthian leather and chrome dials.

Despite the size of this metal beast, Juliet backed it out of the garage with verve, smiling at me as she did. I smiled back. We were going to show Richard a thing or two. And then this whole mission of Juliet's would be over, and I would have her full attention.

As we drove toward Richard's, Juliet turned on the radio and the cab filled with Oasis's "Wonderwall." Juliet began to sing along. Her voice was surprisingly pretty.

I laughed in surprise.

"What?" she said. "I can like Britpop."

"I pegged you more for Angel Olsen."

"Please," she said, "like you've got my number."

We exited the town limits quickly, which was good because the vehicle drew interested attention from every car we pulled up alongside. A group of guys leered and whooped at us at a stoplight, and I feared for their safety. Once we were on country roads, she slowed her driving. The night was foggy, and the headlights could only just pick out the next curve in the road. A sheet of low-hanging fog rolled over the car and fell behind us in a wall. It made me feel like we were traveling through a tunnel to some magical realm; two girls, singing together, badly. If I didn't think about our destination, I felt full of joy, my skin effervescent. Juliet turned the radio up, and I opened my mouth to belt the chorus.

Then we hit the deer.

In a collision between a luxury tank and a deer, the deer loses spectacularly. The doe's body was illuminated for one moment in the headlights, but too quick, too close to veer, and before I knew what had happened, we'd struck it and sent it flying.

I was dimly aware that Juliet hooked the tank onto the side of the road, halfway into a ditch. The air was misty and smelled like chemicals, and I distantly realized that the airbags had deployed. Did airbags come standard in tanks? Or were they after-market additions? Either way, they both spilled over the dashboard like deflated marshmallows. The seat belt had sliced my collarbone, and I had abrasions on my chest and cheek from the bag.

The deer was about twenty feet from the car, twitching in the light from the headlights. I'd seen deer walk through our backyard many times, and once watched one strip a rosebush down to nothing but the canes. They'd always looked like long-legged rabbits with oversize eyes, stupid and beautiful. I loved to see them pick their way slowly through a field like gangly ballerinas.

This deer had none of that alien grace. This one was a short-circuiting animatronic replica of a deer. Its legs circled continuously, and its eyes fixed straight ahead on an unseen point. It seemed determined to ignore us, or maybe it thought it was still running across the road and had successfully made it to the other side. There was a terrible whirring moan emitting from its open mouth.

"Oh god," I said. "What do we do?" My voice was high and panicked. I'd exited the car to stand near it but didn't remember doing so.

"Just a second," said Juliet at my side. She had a bruise swelling on her forehead. She turned away, back to the car.

I waited for her to rejoin me, relieved she was taking charge. Juliet would know what to do to help this creature. She always did. She could make fancy coffee, transform a plain girl into a French minx, and render a boy senseless with her fists. She could save a deer. We somehow had to get it to a vet or get a vet to it. We had to keep it from suffering.

"Still alive?" she said, again by my side. She was watching it in a very clinical way. I could barely stand looking at it, but also I couldn't look away. It felt like I had to keep watching it so that I was fully punished for what we'd done.

"Yeah, can we get it into the car or—"

She laughed. "That's insane. We can't move that thing. If one of those hooves hits you, you're a goner. Kindest thing we can do is kill it."

"Kill it? Like, euthanasia? So, we call a vet and—"

Then I saw the gun.

There were a few prop guns in Galaxy House in display cases, with labels designating which film they'd been featured in. I hadn't given them much notice. I liked Galaxy's war pictures well enough, but I didn't find weapons very interesting (except for the katana from his weird samurai movie—that thing was gorgeous). This pistol was not a prop gun, however. Something about it was weightier, realer. Suddenly I understood the color "gunmetal" as I hadn't before. It looked strangely appropriate in Juliet's strong hands.

Because I am nothing if not astute, I said, "What the fuck is that?"

Juliet grinned at me.

"A knife, dummy," she said.

At a safe distance she circled the deer that continued to run sideways across an invisible field. I imagined it flicking its tail to signify danger. Because here was danger, all five feet ten inches of her.

"You have to aim down from the top of the head," she said. "That's how people mess up, killing animals. Or themselves, for that matter. You can put a gun to the side of your skull, but bullets do crazy things. They ricochet and spin. So you want to aim down, so you get the spine in the mix. Do as much damage as possible."

I decided this was another bit of knowledge she'd gained from movie sets. I did not want to consider how else she might know.

Her eyes flicked from the deer to mine.

"You want to do it?" She said it like it was a real treat she was offering me. A favor.

"I absolutely do not want to do it," I said.

She shrugged.

She cocked the gun. The sound was loud and mechanical, distinct from the rhythmic swishing of the deer's cycling legs against the grass.

She squatted beside the deer's head. It still didn't seem to register us, which was a good thing. Juliet was right that it was dangerous, I realized. It weighed as much as I did, maybe more. All it had to do was to thrash and one of us would easily go down. She pressed the gun against the top of the deer's skull, pointing down the length of its long, lovely neck. It didn't register the touch.

"I'm sorry about this," she said to the deer.

She did sound sorry, a little. The way you apologize when you've accidentally jostled someone walking by them. No bad intent, and no real harm done.

But before she could fire, the deer's legs abruptly stopped. The deer's eyes, focused on some ideal meadow we couldn't see, lost their light and became glass.

The hairs on my arms rose. I thought about my mother, who'd died in her sleep at the hospice. The nurses were sure she'd have a few more days and had told us to go home and get some rest. But she slipped away in the night while my father and I slept, not knowing the person who'd kept us together was gone. It was just like her not to make a fuss. She'd always told me that the best exit from a party was a French one; just leave without saying goodbye to anyone. Goodbyes, she'd said, are inconvenient to everyone involved.

Had I wanted to see her go? To say goodbye? I didn't know.

How weird that this was the first living thing I'd seen die.

"Well, problem solved," said Juliet, standing up. She turned away from me and performed some kind of maneuver on the gun with it pointing toward the ground.

"Where'd you get that gun?" I asked.

"The gun show." She laughed, making a muscle with one arm.

"Seriously," I said. It's not that I never saw guns. I lived in the sticks. But mostly I didn't see handguns. I saw Glocks on park rangers, or hunters with rifles. I had seen more compound bows from white dudes claiming they were a quarter Cherokee than I had ever seen handguns.

She rolled her eyes. My questions were annoying her. "I picked it up somewhere. Come on, let's get going. Richard's not going to shoot himself!"

I froze in my tracks. The deer's head in Richard's carriage house flashed before my eyes.

"You never said anything about shooting anybody," I said.

"I'm kidding, I'm kidding," she said. "My god, can't you take a joke?" She shook her head at me.

And just like that, I was sheepish. At times like these, she made it all seem so normal. The dead deer. The gun. All of it was a weird story we'd laugh about later. We'd laugh that I could have ever thought she was serious about shooting Richard.

How could I question otherwise?

I followed her back to the car, leaving the deer where we'd found it. Of course I followed her. I always did.

HOW TO SURVIVE UNTIL THE END

Richard Cummings didn't watch horror movies.

That was the only explanation for why he came outside into the dark, alone, to investigate a weird noise.

Or maybe he thought he was one of the ones who wouldn't die. Golden boys never think anything bad will happen to them.

But there are so many things you aren't supposed to do in a horror movie if you want to stay safe and make it to the sequel. You don't have sex or do drugs or have an ounce of fun.

Richard was all about the fun. Fun was calling a girl over and over. Fun was pushing her down to the ground. Fun was taking photos with your friends. Such fun pictures. Richard wasn't going to make it until the end.

We'd watched him in his house for a while from the backyard. The lights were on in the kitchen and an enormous TV was playing a basketball game. The back of his head was lit up by the house lights, angel-curled golden boy.

I must have thrown five pebbles against the sliding glass doors before he finally registered the noise. He turned away from the screen, but with the lights on inside all he could see was the reflection of his own classically symmetrical face.

When he stepped out into the night, my heart raced. This was really happening. This was a thousand times worse than Caleb. He could see my dark shape on the other side of the pool, partially illuminated by the lights shimmering beneath the blue chlorinated water. I was wearing a scarf wrapped around my face. I wasn't big, and there was nothing imposing about me. But no one was supposed to be there, and the wrongness of it registered in his body. He hesitated, and I could see him debating whether to confront me or to step back into the house to find his phone.

The phone was the reasonable option.

But golden boys never take the reasonable option. I was small, and he was certain in his body's mastery of the world. He stepped forward, his bearing suddenly aggressive, looming. All my fear evaporated. I walked toward him swiftly. My heart was singing a song of retribution. I was Artemis. I was her arrow.

He didn't even have time to say anything. That's how quick Juliet was on him.

Only, she didn't do what she was supposed to do.

She'd told me she'd hit his knees to knock him down, and then I'd help. That was the plan. We were going to make sure he didn't play football anytime soon. We'd hurt him, possibly badly, we'd scare him, and he'd never hurt another girl. And then we'd make our escape.

Instead, she hit him upside the head with a ceramic plant pot. He collapsed to the ground.

Before what she'd done really registered, I had a brief moment of surprise. One, I was surprised that the pot didn't break. A lot of Bugs Bunny cartoons had suggested it would. Two, I was surprised that we were now committing murder.

But his chest was rising and falling as he breathed on the ground. He wasn't dead, thankfully. He was, however, most decidedly unconscious.

Juliet stood over him, looking satisfied, with the air of someone who has just completed a challenging crossword puzzle.

I joined her and looked down at Richard. There was blood in his curls. Head wounds, I'd read once, look far worse than they are. They just bleed and bleed.

"Better off than that deer," she said.

"That's not saying much," I said. The deer had been an accident. This was not an accident. Juliet took my hand and squeezed it.

"C'mon, softie. Help me get him to the car."

I nodded, as if in a dream. I couldn't see any other options. Things are simple in a horror movie. There are the monsters and the killers, and there are the victims and the survivors. Everything was so clear. Richard was a monster, of that I was sure. And I'd been a victim. All the girls in that stack of photos were.

Was this how I survived? Or was I just another monster in a different shape?

MONEY ISN'T MONEY

Did you know that two young women can, if motivated, successfully drag a high school quarterback from his home into the trunk of a suburban tank, bind him, drive him off the main roads to a lake, and pull him through the mud and bracken to a small cabin?

It can be done!

But it's not easy. Richard was mostly muscle, heavy, and his body was unruly and floppy. Carrying him between us was nothing like the picture of me, swung loosely like a rag doll between Caleb and Duncan, but I thought of it anyway. Mostly we dragged him.

The cabin was almost invisible in the dark. I couldn't make out the path to the door, but Juliet seemed to know it by heart. Maybe she'd practiced lugging a sack of potatoes in the dark, night after night. That seemed like something she'd do. Once we'd pulled him inside, she switched on an electric camping lantern on the table. It cast a cold light over the cabin and its spartan contents. The bare shelves looked even emptier, and the table more rickety.

The chair was waiting for him, just where she'd left it. Setting is everything, she'd said. The hardest part was getting him into it. Every time one of us got him to sit up and the other tried to reach for additional ropes, some other part of his body would slide or slip away. It was like trying to secure a fleshy beanbag. Meanwhile, my body ached all over from the work of pulling him around, and I was starting to realize that I felt like one big bruise after hitting the deer. I was sweating and my fingers were clumsy and stupid.

But finally, we got him in place, and stepped back to admire our handiwork.

Richard slept on. Can I call it sleeping when someone has a head injury? Probably not. I was thankful he'd stayed unconscious. I suppose that's one benefit of living in a small town. Everything is close by. No long waits in traffic with a kidnapped boy in your trunk. So convenient.

Juliet placed a sack over his head. It looked like it was a period piece from the cabin. Maybe it had once held flour used to make tasteless crackers that cured absolutely nothing. Now it held small bugs and the head of one unconscious quarterback.

Not being able to see his face made the scene even more unsettling. He didn't look like a person anymore.

The back of the flour sack slowly bloomed with Richard's blood. The creeping red made me think about that gun of Juliet's, about terrible interrogation scenes in terrible movies.

About executions. Was the gun still in the tank? I didn't know where it had gone after her near deer euthanasia.

In a distant way, I registered that the fact that I'd lost sight of the gun suggested I was not operating at full capacity. Guns seemed like things one should keep an eye on.

"So, can we go?" I whispered, because I was still a girl who believed what she'd been told. Because that was what she had promised me. We'd beat him up. We'd humiliate him. We'd leave him to cry alone like a mewling baby until someone finally found him.

Of course, that was before I'd seen the gun and her willingness to execute Bambi's mom. Before she hit Richard in the head with a blunt object. Before we moved him from his house, where neighbors might hear him, where his parents would eventually find him when they returned from Atlanta, to this cabin in the woods, out of sight and out of mind.

But we were still in the same solar system of the original plan, weren't we? We hadn't spun off course entirely. And I wasn't thinking yet about the plan's flaws, such as how committing crimes on your own property wasn't the smartest. I'd realize all that later.

Juliet laughed.

I smiled reflexively, the way you do when you're not sure of the joke. But of course, I knew the joke. The joke was that I'd ever thought we wouldn't end up here.

The universe is always spinning outward, farther than you can imagine.

She grabbed Richard by the shoulder and shook him. He didn't move. She rolled her eyes and pulled a cylindrical packet from her jeans pocket and held it under his nose.

"Wakey-wakey, Richie baby," she said.

"Hey . . . Hey! What's going on? Who's there?" he said, jolting awake. His voice was clear and strong through the flour sack. He turned his head to try to see us through the loose weave.

"It's Kelly, Richard," said Juliet. She winked at me.

Richard paused before responding. "You're not Kelly. You sound nothing like Kelly. Any of them," he said.

"No, I'm not a Kelly. But you know she's why I'm here, right? Her and all the others. You know why your buddies have come down with broken faces. Were you wondering when we'd get to you?"

"I don't know what you're talking about," he said. He struggled with the ropes. I must admit, I was impressed with Juliet's knot-tying skills. He was a strong guy, but they held, no problem.

"I've got a picture that says you do. A few of them, actually. I talked with Kelly Xu, you know. Every day she's remembering a little more."

That gave him pause. "We didn't do anything. And if we did, we were all fucked up anyway. Not just her. Us, too."

"But you were conscious! That's the big difference. How did you like being unconscious, by the way? Do you like what we did to you? We used a bottle. You'll feel it tomorrow."

Another wink my way.

"What the— That's not funny. Let me go right now or—"

"Or you'll do what? Get me so drunk I can't move? Roofie me? Leave me to pick up the pieces? You know, a girl's first time is so special. It's special to wake up and not be able to walk," she said. Her voice was rising, and for the first time, Juliet looked really angry. Not amused or sarcastic. So angry that her voice was as tight as her clenched fists. "How many girls have to go through this before you get it through your heads? How many girls have to wake up with bruises they can't explain? Why do I have to be the one taking a pack of birth control pills at once, and just hoping for the best?"

I held her shoulder as she stepped toward him, and I shook my head. I didn't know what was happening, but I knew that if she touched Richard right now things would go more than south. We'd fall into the center of the earth.

Juliet took a deep breath and composed herself. Richard, sensibly, stayed quiet. Clearly, he sensed that there was no answer to these questions that could possibly get him out of this situation, and many that could make it worse.

"We're going to ask your parents how much it's worth to have their darling boy back. Then we'll see what we do with you."

I gave Juliet a quizzical look, which she ignored.

He was silent, thinking.

"You didn't ask anybody else for money," he said. His voice was pitched gentler, kinder. Eminently reasonable. Just asking for information.

"Not exactly. I took Caleb's wallet. Duncan donated as well. But you, don't you deserve special treatment, Richie?"

I took in her words, confused. I remembered she'd crouched down next to Caleb. She'd straightened his shirt. I hadn't seen her pick up anything, but maybe she hadn't wanted me to. The news report on Duncan's beating hadn't mentioned money. Maybe a robbery wasn't as interesting as "gang violence" by a bunch of girls.

Richard didn't reply.

"Your parents are the only hicks in this town who have money. Not good money, but enough. We beat up your delightful friends so your parents would know you really are in danger. See, the problem with ransoming someone is that there's always the element of doubt. But now they won't doubt. We laid a foundation."

I blinked at this. That was not what I'd thought we were doing.

"So, all this is just about money," said Richard. This sounded like something he understood.

"Money is *never* just money. When a spoiled monster like you gets into trouble, it's money that gets you out. Cops look the other way because you come from a 'good' family and it's only the dirty poors who do crimes. And even if they didn't, that money pays for the fancy lawyers your victim can't afford, lets them delay and delay until that poor girl will do anything for it to be *over*, even if it means giving up on justice. Not that she'd get it. Because the jury looks at you in your nice suit and hears your educated voice and just *knows* you couldn't have done it, and the judge can't imagine a boy like you behind bars, because he's a boy like you, too. So after all that unpleasantness dies down, your parents will donate a building to their alma mater and that school finds a place for you. There's always a place for you. Money means you get to keep your future even while you crush someone else's. So yes, I'm asking for money because if I drain your parents' coffers, I'm hitting them where it hurts, and I'm hitting you, too. That's the cake. If I happen to humiliate you while I do it, that's just icing. Money isn't all I care about. But it's the only thing people like you understand."

Richard didn't say much else after that.

MONEY IS MONEY

"**J**uliet," I said. We were standing about fifty yards from the cabin. We'd left Richard to, as Juliet put it, "think about what he'd done."

"Can we skip this conversation?" she said. "I think we both know how it ends."

"You mean, it ends with me agreeing with you?"

She grinned. "Something like that."

"Look, we never talked about this. We weren't going to knock him out or move him. We were never going to ask for ransom. This—this is kidnapping. Extortion. This is serious."

She laughed. "Oh, is this serious? You just noticed, and now you're pulling out your big words? Sarah caught on faster than you."

Sarah was probably singing about Jesus right now. Sarah was a genius, and I was an idiot.

"What is the money for?" I asked.

"Was I not clear when I explained this to Richard? This

is what we said we'd do. Punish them. You can't punish them unless you take away the money. They'll just do it again."

"But what are we going to *do* with the money once we get it?"

She took a deep breath, then let it out. When she spoke, there was the slightest tremble in her voice, so faint I almost thought I'd imagined it. "I meant everything I said to him. Every word. But I also need money to get out of here. I need cash to do that," she said.

I shook my head, confused. "What do you mean? You're rich."

"No, *Galaxy's* rich. He's rich and he doesn't even acknowledge me in public. He shuttles me from place to place and puts me in rich-girl day camps and stupid schools. Every now and then, I visited him on set, and I was always so *happy* to be there that I didn't even care that no one knew who I was. He didn't send me to this crap town because I got kicked out of school; I came here because I knew the house was empty. He had just kicked me out and cut me off. It's a real inconvenience, you see, when Daddy's producer gets you fucked up, then fucks you. Because the producer needs to be happy, or the movie doesn't happen."

"Jesus, Juliet," I whispered.

"It's not like Jesse Fucking Galaxy couldn't get another movie. He could have done anything. Exposed the guy. Quit the film. But all that makes news; it's scandal, it's breach of contract and endangers the bottom line. Can't have that."

"I'm so sorry," I said. I didn't know what else to say.

She shrugged my sympathy away like a dog shaking off water.

"It's fine. But I used up most of my money getting here and no more is coming. If I can get to Paris, I can crash with some people there."

"Can't they send you money?" I suspected that anyone in Juliet's circle had more to offer than the Cummingses did. Whatever lifestyle Juliet was used to, it couldn't last long on Hart's Run's version of big money.

"They're not friends, not really. You cannot comprehend how quickly you become nobody with these people. Out of sight, out of mind. Plus, they're goddamn cowards. They don't want to piss off Galaxy, because they want to be models and actresses and other useless drains on society because their parents are in the industry and that's all they know. But someone will let me crash so they can tell me how sorry they were not to help sooner, because one day I might be worth knowing again, and I'd owe them."

"They sound awful," I said.

"It's not personal. So Richard's parents are my best shot. They're probably the only people in this town with decent money."

I nodded. But I didn't really understand.

"Couldn't you just . . . get a job?" I asked. Even as I said it, it was impossible to imagine Juliet behind a register, scanning bar codes. It would be like seeing a unicorn pulling a plow. I also didn't think Juliet had any idea how to save money, no matter how badly she wanted out of this town. It wouldn't occur to her. It was beneath her. Poor little rich girl.

She smiled, watching me answer my own questions.

"Or maybe I could help?" I had some money I'd saved up for college. Some of it was from summer jobs, and some of it was birthday gifts from my grandparents. It wasn't a lot, but I could give it to Juliet. It hurt me, though, to think that she'd run off to Paris, to her lousy friends who wouldn't even send money, and leave me behind.

"That's sweet, Rabbit," she said, and gave me a fond look. It was not unlike the look you'd give an eager-to-please dog, one that follows you even when you told it to stay home.

Maybe one that chases cars.

DEGREES OF AWFUL

"**H**ow much did she ask my parents for?"

Juliet had left to drop off a letter detailing her demand for Richard's weight in gold, or however you phrase a ransom note. It requested cash, with a veiled threat that if they contacted the police, the kidnappers would release material damning Richard's future. Or kill him, I guess. She included one of the Polaroids, one that mercifully didn't show a girl's face, but Richard's presence in it was clear. She offered to let me read it but I didn't. The less I took an active role, the more I could convince myself I wasn't really part of this.

I didn't know the answer, and wouldn't like it if I did, so I said nothing.

"She's going to kill me, you know," Richard said.

"She's not going to kill you," I said. My voice sounded surer than I felt.

Accessory to murder was better than murderer, right?

No. We were definitely not doing murder.

"She is," said Richard. "Because I know who you are. Who both of you are. I'm not an idiot. I can recognize your stupid voices."

I felt cold all over. Somehow, I'd convinced myself that a thin cloth sack over his eyes was enough to hide our identities. Juliet had acted like it was. So, I believed. That was foolish.

But he hadn't said my name, so he might be bluffing. He hadn't even looked twice at me at his party, and that was just after a haircut.

"If you're really not an idiot, you wouldn't tell me that," I said.

He was quiet for a blessed moment, and then blurted, "And you. She'll kill you, too. She's crazy."

"Shut up, Richard."

He did, finally.

The night was a symphony of frogs and crickets, of the breeze blowing in the trees and rippling the surface of the lake. If I just listened to those sounds, and not the sound of Richard's noisy breathing, I could pretend I was alone. I could close my eyes to the cabin and imagine myself floating in the lake again, the stars above me.

"I don't want to die," he wailed abruptly, really crying now. I flinched with surprise at the sudden sound. I could hear the way his voice thickened first, and then the sobbing started.

It might say something unflattering about me that his hiccupping gasps immediately made me want to leave the room. Or kick him.

"Please let me go," he said through his snot-stuffed nose. "Please don't let me die."

Jesus Christ.

He'd tried to guilt me into staying with him, then he'd hounded me for weeks. He'd tried to force himself on me; I could admit that now. And those pictures—

"I want you to explain my picture."

"What?"

"The picture of me. Where I'm passed out. You took it. Caleb and Duncan are carrying me."

There was a long pause. If he hadn't known for sure who I was, he did now.

"What do you want me to explain?"

"I tried to kill myself that night. I was at home, but I ended up in the ER. No one knows how."

Another long pause.

"You called me," he said.

"Bullshit," I said.

"Okay, you didn't call me. I called you."

"Because you're a gross stalker who doesn't know when to quit."

"I loved you, Rabbit. I wasn't— That's not who I am. I *loved* you."

I clenched my teeth and said nothing.

"You were weird on the phone, kind of loopy. You were friendly—you hadn't been friendly to me in so long."

"Because we *broke up*."

"I know, I know."

"Go on."

"You said we could pick you up, so we did. We all hung out. It was fun."

"Super fun. So fun my shirt came off, apparently."

"That—that shouldn't have happened. But nothing else bad happened," he said hurriedly. "I promise."

"Can you say the same to the other girls?"

He went quiet.

"How did I get to the hospital?"

"We were sitting on the couch together. You were leaning your head on my shoulder. It was really sweet."

"This is grossing me out," I said.

"Okay, okay—you leaned over, and you said something. I could barely understand you. You told me you'd taken pills, and then you laughed."

No doubt thrilled that I was going to die in his house and cause him embarrassing problems. I smiled a little at that. Nice work, past me.

"Then you threw up on me and passed out," he said flatly. "That's when we got you in the car. I drove you to the ER and put you in a chair. Then I walked out."

Of course. When you're Richard Cummings, you just deposit girls anywhere and walk off. No one thinks anything of it.

"They found me on the floor," I said.

"Well, you're lousy at sitting up, I guess," he snapped.

I glared at him, hunched over in the chair, his golden curls covered by the flour sack. It was possible I was alive because of the worst person I knew. Sure, mostly he didn't want a dead girl in his house, and maybe I'd thrown up enough to survive on my own, but he did take me to the hospital.

Did I owe him?

I'd hated him, and now I pitied him, which only made me hate him more, and myself a little as well. He was a gross speck I wanted to wipe from the earth, so that he was gone and done with, and Juliet and I could walk off together—

To go where?

My stomach dropped. I wasn't any part of her Paris plan. In fact, she hadn't mentioned me at all.

I remembered kissing her in that field, her skin hot under my hands. I'd told her I loved her. It's easy to say true things. They just fall out of your mouth, even though after you say them, all you want to do is grab them with both hands and stuff them right back in.

She'd never said it back.

Then I thought back to that hot day on the docks with her and Sarah, talking about football and how the world is made by and for boys and their teams, their clubs, their brotherhoods. How girls like us were divided and set against one another. How it made us easy prey. Juliet was right about all of that. Even if I hadn't wanted to see it then, I couldn't see it any other way now.

But she'd lost me when she said we had to *be* like the boys to beat them, that the only way to win their game was to play it. Playing to win a rigged game warped you and made you ugly inside. That was the thing I hadn't been able to put into words then.

I wanted a world where people like Richard were held accountable for their terrible deeds, and where I didn't have to become the thing I hated for that to happen.

For that world to exist, I'd have to make a different choice than what Juliet offered. I knew that now.

Richard sniffled under his hood.

A deer cycling its legs in the grass.

A dumb dog catching a tire.

Goddamnit.

The knots were nowhere near untied when Juliet came back.

SNUFF OUT THE STARS

I ran.

I shoved past Juliet before she could do much more than yell in surprise. Her hand grabbed my hair, and I left a wad of it clutched in her fingers. In the commotion, Richard shouted to know what was happening, to beg me not to leave, to finish untying him, but I was past hearing him or anyone. Every part of my body was telling me *get out, get out, get out*, and I listened.

The dim lights from the cabin were quickly behind me, and if there was a path under my feet when I started, it was gone almost instantly. My legs were on fire from scratches from thorns and stray branches, but I barreled blindly ahead with my hands outstretched to try to protect my face. I could hear her charging behind me, crashing through the underbrush.

"Goddamn, Rabbit, just stop, slow up!" she yelled behind me. I ran harder. I wasn't the best fighter out of all of us, but, thanks to Juliet, my conditioning was no joke. I could swim and I could run. She had taught me to endure. I could hear her breath and it was shorter than mine. I didn't have the keys, but if I could make my way back to the car, I could make my way back to the main road. Then flag someone down, tell them to drive far and fast away. I could be the girl who survived.

"Rabbit, stop already! Why are you running?" She almost sounded like she was laughing, like I was pulling a funny prank. It had to be a joke; why else would I turn tail so late in the game? Why else would I have tried to untie Richard?

I was a deer, running. I was fast and fleet and I could escape.

But deer see well in the dark. Humans don't. A fallen log grabbed my foot like a hand, and down I went, barely able to protect my face with my arms before I planted into the dirt. Something hit the side of my head—a log, a rock. For a long second, I felt all my momentum transfer into the earth, then shock me backward. I couldn't move. My breath was knocked out of me. I gasped on the ground helplessly.

Juliet turned me over. She straddled me but kept her weight off my chest when she heard me struggling to breathe. Thoughtful of her. This was love.

"Rabbit, Rabbit, why are you running?" she said. Kind. Questioning. Like a mother confused by her darling child's actions.

I started to cry. I could barely see her in the night. She was a field of darkness blocking out the stars above, crowned by the arching tree branches. She was impossibly big.

"Rabbit, I would never hurt you. Did he tell you that I would? He's a liar. You know he's a liar. I'm doing this for us, for all the girls he'd do this to if we don't stop him. We have to make him an example. We have to help everyone see what guys like him do," she said, "and then what happens to them."

I closed my eyes against her. My breathing was returning to me. She pressed her hips on mine, gently.

She cupped my face in her hands, and I opened my eyes. She bent closer, brought her face to mine, her lips against my ear.

"The violence is necessary. No one listens otherwise. The money is necessary. We can leave this town. We can go together. Come with me."

She rested the gun on my chest. Then she kissed me, and all the stars went out.

EVERYONE DESERVES
WHAT THEY DESERVE

"We should go to Barcelona instead. Do you know that somehow, I've never been to Barcelona? How is that even possible? I have a friend who winters there, and we can take his house for a while. He won't mind. We can do postcard things together. I'd adore that. I'll take you to museums and we'll play tourist. Do you like octopus?"

"What?" I said. My head hurt so much I could barely think, and I weaved as I followed her back to the cabin. The right side of my leg felt like someone had slashed it with a knife. Thorns, I guessed. It would heal. All that mattered was that gun. At first, she'd pressed it against the small of my back after helping me to my feet, but as we walked, she'd relaxed. Now she waved it periodically to make her point.

"Octopus. The grilled octopus in Barcelona is supposed to be delicious. I don't like smoked paprika, though. That makes me a bit of a philistine."

I nodded. Yes, smoked paprika was the one thing really bringing down Juliet's cultural standing right now. Except for that, she was quite the lady.

"And I was thinking, once we're in Europe, we can look up my dad's old director. I feel like he could use a little talking-to. Can you imagine if we got to him at Cannes? I'd leave him in a shirt that says, 'I rape little girls.' That would do it. It's not like anyone would be surprised. He hasn't been in America for a decade, because he knows they'd throw him in jail. My father *knew* that, you know. He knew that and he still signed up to work with him."

One foot, then the other. My head was clearing, even as I felt a trickle of blood wend down my cheek. Her words washed over me, taking up residence in my brain. She wanted to do this again. Richard and his friends weren't a one-off. They were a warm-up. She wanted to do this again.

The director sounded like he deserved it.

Probably a lot of people deserved it.

Probably Richard deserved it.

Director. Hadn't she said he was her father's producer, not his director?

All those photographs—why hadn't we taken them to the police? If Chief Powell wouldn't listen, Kelly Costa's mother would have used her PTA energy to pitch a fit the likes of which our town had never seen. Kelly Xu's sister would come back from college and stage a revolution. The Kellys were terrifying, and they came from terrifying families.

But Juliet had been so sure we were the only ones who could handle it.

That she was the one for the job.

Where were the pictures now?

I didn't know.

"Once we get the money, we will need to lay low for a little while. You should start school, just like normal. Give it a few months. And then we can go. You'll need a passport."

"Right," I said. "Let's make our criminal enterprise international."

"It's not crime," she said, laughing. "It's retribution. It's balance."

"How am I supposed to start school when Richard knows we did this? When he tells his parents? The police?"

My father would do more than nail my window shut. He'd nail me to the ground. If I lived.

"Richard won't be a problem. Here, watch out," she said, and held a thorny vine for me. Chivalrous. I walked under and she kept going, the vine swaying behind us.

"If you don't like Barcelona, we can go somewhere else. It's just an idea. Austria is super pretty, and I love it in autumn. You should pick the place, really. Let's fill your passport."

This was a gift to me, letting me choose.

A present, provided I didn't ask any more questions. Sensible questions like: Why wouldn't Richard be a problem, exactly? How hard is it to leave the country after committing various crimes? If we got to Europe, what was going to happen when we ran out of money? Because we were going to run out of money, of that I had no doubt.

For Juliet, this was the best she could offer. This was love. A choice of travel destinations and a gun at my back.

After all, who was Richard to me?

Nobody I cared about. No one I loved. He'd already hurt me. He'd hurt others.

A vicious little princeling.

Just like Juliet.

I looked down and a fallen branch was in my hand. It had appeared there like magic. But surely I had plucked it up as we walked, like picking a flower. I squeezed it experimentally. It would do.

I swung it like a hammer and down she went.

A CONVERSATION
ABOUT RESPECT

I kept the tiny light of the electric lantern from the cabin in my sights and shot myself toward it. I didn't know how long she'd stay down. What if I'd really hurt her? I thought of Juliet bleeding on the ground and stumbled. Or maybe it was my swelling brain that made me clumsy. Head injuries bleed a lot—Richard had taught me that—but the skull isn't as tough as we think. I'd dropped the branch after I hit her, but my hands still felt the rough bark as I'd squeezed and swung.

Faster. If I was going to escape, I needed to be faster. If I was going to escape with Richard, I needed to be faster than I'd ever been. I tripped, caught myself, crashed through fallen branches like a drunk woman.

Oh god, what was I doing? For a moment, I thought of my mother, trying to explain this to her. *Well, you see, Mom, I was very sad and thought I'd hit boys until I felt better. Well, Mom, I really liked a girl and so I did everything she said.*

Well, Mom, you had to up and die, so really, who's at fault here?

Sheila would say I had unresolved anger. Sheila would say I was wrestling with my shadow self. I should embrace the negative parts of me.

Well, I'd left my shadow self in the woods with head trauma, so self-acceptance would have to wait.

The door to the cabin was still open. I had a wild moment where I thought that maybe Richard had freed himself and I was shed of him, could just find the keys to the tank and escape. But he wasn't that ambitious. He was still there, though he'd managed to fall over onto his side in the chair. Good job, Richard.

I crashed to a stop beside him. He flinched when I touched him, but then whispered, "Thank you, thank you" as he felt my hands on the ropes.

"Shut up, Richard," I said. I hated his gratitude more than I hated him, and that was saying something. The slight progress I'd made on the knots before Juliet had found me had been spoiled by his struggles—he'd tightened the knots again by pulling against them. But I could get them loose if I just kept at it.

"Where is she?" he said.

"On her way," I said. "Or bleeding to death." I cast my eyes around the cabin. What I wouldn't give for a rusty turn-of-the-century knife.

I heard a gunshot, and a furious yell.

Well, I hadn't killed her.

Juliet wasn't thinking straight. That sound would carry for miles across the water. It wasn't hunting season. Someone would call the cops.

Finally, the knots at his wrists released. He pulled the flour sack off his head and gave me a savage look. I can safely say neither one of us liked the other very much. But there were bigger concerns. We worked on his ankles and every time our hands touched, I gritted my teeth.

"Come on," I said as he shook his feet loose of the rope.

The keys to the tank were still on the table where she'd left them. I snatched them up. I didn't know if we could find our way back to the tank—I wasn't even sure I'd headed in the right direction earlier—but we could at least keep her from it. Juliet on foot was better than Juliet with three hundred horsepower.

Richard was wobbly on his feet. I didn't expect that. Maybe Juliet had done some real neurological damage to him. Maybe we were going to be murderers, after all. But he steadied, shook off my hand, and then we were out the door. I started running in the general direction of the road and I heard him behind me, awkward at first but then steadying, his football training serving him well. Does your brain hurt? Just keep running!

I heard another shot, and the air beside my body shuddered and displaced. I almost fell to the ground in surprise and fear but caught myself. We were far enough away from the cabin's light to be obscured, but our sound wasn't subtle.

It sounds stupid, but I was really hurt that she'd shot at me. Also, terrified.

"Rabbit!" Juliet called out. "I won't miss next time. Come back."

This did not motivate me to come back. I cast a glance backward to see her standing by the cabin, legs akimbo, the gun braced in both hands, her stance steady as a rock. She looked like an action hero, the stalwart, hard-as-nails cop who always gets their guy. Barista classes and shooting ranges. Of course. That's the girl I love. Jesse Bergman's Jane-of-all-trades monster of a daughter.

"I want to talk, to have a little conversation about respect," she yelled out. She was running again.

Richard pulled ahead of me. There was a stitch in my side that felt like a red-hot poker, but at least it kept me from saying yes to her anymore. Because even now, there was a part of me that wanted to. The producer—her father's abandonment—all of that was real, no matter the details, and it made me want to turn back to her. I still wanted to help her set fire to the wicked until everything was in flames, until there were no cities left to burn. I still wanted to hold her.

"Come here, Rabbit!" she called. "Where are the keys, you bitch?"

Another shot. A thud in a tree beside me.

I yelled out in fear, and tried to run faster, which was physically impossible. My lungs were burning, my legs felt like fire, and I still wasn't sure we were going the right way.

Then, up ahead, I saw lights.

Red and blue, flashing.

Richard and I crashed through the bracken to the road and collapsed in front of the police car. Two deputies pulled their guns in surprise, and I passed right out.

GONE

ere we are at the end. Evil has been vanquished, and order restored. Because that's how movies end, and stories, and how we feel good about the closing of a door. Everything didn't just happen, but happened for a reason; a neat narrative circle that contains just enough satisfaction and surprise to justify its existence.

But we still want to know what happened to everyone, right? Let's roll end credits and do a little bit of peeking into the future.

So, imagine a shot of Richard Cummings. He'd probably prefer you show him at the beach with his boys, laughing in the sun, a shot where he still looks like the world makes sense and turns on his whim. But instead, I'll choose a shot with the flour sack on his head, when he was sobbing for me to help him. That's the one I prefer.

Now let's read the text at the bottom of the screen and learn what happened to Richard, and by extension, to me. Because oddly, Richard saved me as much as I saved him. Only, I happened to deserve it.

Richard's parents didn't press charges against me, and Richard wouldn't testify against me. Was it because, in the end, I saved their beautiful boy? Did Richard tell them to go easy on me because I'd ultimately recognized the sanctity of human life (or at least his)? I don't know. More likely his parents were too busy with Richard's new legal problems since the police recovered the photos of all those girls from the Bergman house. I'd told them to look for the envelope, praying Juliet hadn't taken it with her, and they found them in a junk drawer in the kitchen. That's where you put a pretext, I guess.

It wasn't clear what was going to happen to Richard and the other boys legally, but in the meantime, they were dropped from the team, their college acceptances were withdrawn, etc. The usual too-little-too-late. It was the least the town could do, and I do mean the least. They went from promising young men to pariahs. There was some satisfaction in that, even as the Kellys claimed they'd always known what horrible monsters they were, and never liked them.

But the boys will recover. They always do.

So let's put a note under Richard saying his parents donated his way into a second-tier Ivy. Maybe one day he'll run for office. Cummings for president. Sounds about right.

Here's a shot of Sarah. She's reading a book under a tree, but it isn't the Bible. Some kind of spicy fantasy novel. Good for her. She still looks like Snow White and always will. She deserves a hopeful note under her shot. She manages to go to a regular college, not a church one. And let's say she eventually uses her sweet choir-trained singing voice to front a rock band. Because why not? She likes sequins and being secretly sultry. I'd love that for her. Sarah and I never really talked again. There was too much to say, and neither of us wanted to say any of it. She'd been right—I hadn't listened—and she just wanted to forget all of it. I couldn't blame her. If I could do the same, I would.

The Kellys share their shot, crowding in and making their most model-y faces at the camera. I never found out what they thought about the Polaroids. I do wonder if Juliet had been right—that sometimes it's better not to know. Kelly Costa goes into marketing, because of course, and Kelly Proud is the bane of the school board. Kelly Xu, the best Kelly, became a costume designer. You've seen her work. I really spent a lot of energy hating them. That seems dumb now. They were never the villains in my story. They didn't really think about me all that much.

My dad and Sheila get a shot together, but you guessed that. He's holding her hand at the justice of the peace as they get married, and her hair is exuberant. But a shot like this doesn't show the harder stuff behind the scenes, like how they came with me to the meetings with the lawyer they hired and the cops. It doesn't show how Sheila acted like a sane buffer between my dad and me, payback for me not telling my dad she'd let me off his leash. Or how my dad got sober for real, and the AA chips multiplied in a bowl by the door. The way they struggled together to get their finances in order after my dad's dereliction of duty, after all my lawyer bills. All that matters, but I don't know how to show it really.

What shot do I choose for Juliet? The moment I saw her leaning against her car, her thumb hooked in her belt loop and her face so sure I'd follow? Or when she took my hand outside her house and told me she couldn't stay away? I often think about her eyes closed in her car, willing me to kiss her, daring me. Her face on the dock, closed and cold. Then the darkness of the woods, and the flash of a bullet firing.

It doesn't matter which shot I'd pick. Juliet was nowhere. Her belongings were already cleaned out of Galaxy House like she'd never existed, leaving only dirty dishes and the Polaroids behind. She must have done it days before we set foot on Richard's pool patio, leaving the proof of the boys' crimes behind in case she couldn't come back. The Camaro was gone, and the entire supply of prosecco. So, maybe just an empty landscape for her. Maybe a black screen.

It turned out the Bergman place had been quietly listed with a real estate agent in France, months prior to Juliet's arrival. Just like Jesse Bergman not to use someone local, but then, no one local could afford the place. It never sold, of course. No one wanted to come to Hart's Run, Georgia. Particularly not the French. I assume Bergman is still sending his extra awards to that empty house.

After she was gone, there were a lot of people saying that Juliet wasn't really Jesse Bergman's daughter. That it was all a con. After all, Jesse Bergman's people never commented on the story, which didn't ever get any traction in the media anyway. Possibly the story was squelched. The going theory in town was that she was hired by Bergman's people as a caretaker of the house, or a cleaner, getting it ready to sell, and then just put on airs.

I don't know if any of it was real.

But it was real to me.

She was real to me. Her pain, her anger. It was real, the way she made me feel like the only girl in the world, and how a cloud passed over the sun whenever her attention wandered. Her mouth on mine was real, and her teasing me because I wanted more.

The way it felt when I kicked a boy in the ribs was real.

Anyway, I don't know what I'd write under her picture. And maybe trying to wrap this up like an '80s comedy isn't going to work anyway. After all, I'm supposed to tell you how I learned some valuable lessons about love, and trust, and my dad and I had a heart-to-heart, and it was all better, and I realized that violence wasn't the answer, that Juliet wasn't perfect, that blindly following someone you love leads to heartache and jail.

And obviously, I'm supposed to tell you I'm at peace with my mother's death, and how I understand that my grief was why I went along with things like I did.

That I've really grown as a person.

But none of that is true. I didn't learn any of that, not really.

What I learned was that I had a real and serious need to blow up my life. I wanted it ruined because I no longer liked the look of it, and if I couldn't step out of my life, I could at least make it into something radically different. I'd tried and failed to do so with Richard. So I went bigger. If it hadn't been Juliet, it would have been somebody else. Or something else. Ultimately, I was responsible for what I did.

She was just there to help.

I took the money that was supposed to be for my first semester of college, and I bought a ticket to Barcelona and a rail pass. My dad and Sheila didn't like it, but as my dad admitted, they didn't have much of a say anymore. I told them I'd be careful. They didn't look convinced. To be fair, I lack credibility.

When I hand over my passport to the immigration agent, I see him look at me, and look at the photo, and back again. In my new passport photo, I still look like the girl Juliet pulled out of me. Short hair, dark-lined eyes, a little dangerous. It's a look I'm holding on to, for now, until I feel inside what I look like on the outside.

I want to figure out who that girl is, what her future holds.

And maybe, just maybe, I'm going to find Juliet. Then we'll have a little conversation about respect.

ACKNOWLEDGMENTS

So many people helped me while I wrote *Rabbit & Juliet* that I'm terrified I'm going to forget someone! This is my best attempt to share my thanks.

First, thank you to my agent, Marcy Posner, and her literary assistant, Jess Macy. I'm so grateful that you saw what my book could be and believed in it. You helped me find my way to fully understanding my characters and their world, and I am lucky to have you as my champions. Thank you for pushing me and keeping me on track.

My amazing editor, Alyssa Miele, for her hard questions and her smart suggestions. You shared my vision and helped me see ways to accomplish it that I couldn't have found on my own. Also, your notes are very funny and that's important to me.

Huge thanks to the entire team at Quill Tree. No one can appreciate how much work goes into a book until they get a glimpse behind the scenes, and my book has had the support of rock stars. Many thanks to my publisher, Rosemary Brosnan; the designers, Kathy Lam and David Curtis; Audrey Diestelkamp in marketing and Samantha Brown in publicity; the production managers, Meghan Pettit and Allison Brown;

the production editor, Alexandra Rakaczki; and the copyeditor, Christina MacDonald. I could not ask for a better group to usher this book into the world.

Many of my friends read this book in earlier drafts and gave me invaluable feedback. I'm forever grateful to Marshall and Amber Bellsdale, Claire Kohda Hazelton, Laura Lippman, David Lott, Reid McCall, Janet McNally, Barrington and Paul Seetachitt, and Désirée Zamorano for giving me the gift of their time and their thoughts.

Judith Mitchell, Jessie Lee Kercheval, Kit Frick, and Christy Clancy encouraged me to take my work seriously and talked me through the scary prospect of seeking representation. You demystified a daunting process and pushed me to try!

Ages ago, Brittany Cavallaro encouraged me to write a novel. It took me a long time to take her advice, but I'm glad I did.

My thanks to the incredible women of the Grotto. I cannot tell you what being a part of this group has meant to me. We were drawn together by writing, and now I count you among my true friends. We share our griefs and celebrate our triumphs.

Thank you to the Yellow House Alumna. That weekend was magical and generative, and I return to it in my mind again and again.

Thank you to my parents, who brought me up in a house filled with books.

Rabbit & Juliet draws inspiration from many sources. As a teenager, the book *Foxfire* by Joyce Carol Oates and the movie adaptation of the same name rewired my brain, as did the movie

Beautiful Creatures. Girl, Interrupted and *Heathers* are in the mix as well. The real seed of the idea, however, came from a YouTube video of a short film called *Jane Austen's Fight Club*, directed by Emily Janice Card and Keith Paugh. Once I saw it, I couldn't stop thinking about how different the movie *Fight Club* would have been had it centered around a group of women instead of men.

Thanks to North Central College for awarding me a summer grant to draft a novel. This book isn't the one I said I was going to write. Thank you also to the Virginia Center for the Creative Arts, who awarded me a residency for writing poems. I'm sorry, but I worked on this instead.

My thanks to librarians, who more than ever deserve our support for their defense of intellectual freedoms. They also tend to have fantastic style, as evidenced by Michelle Boule Smith, who met me for writing sessions.

My thanks to booksellers, who advocate for the books they love. You are better than algorithms.

And above all else, thank you to Mark Stafford. Mark, you are always my first, best, and hardest reader. I dread your feedback in the best way. I could not have written this book without your support and belief.